A Cruel Deception

CATHRYN HUNTINGTON CHADWICK

D1479124

ZEBRA BOOKS
KENSINGTON PUBLISHING CORP.

ZEBRA BOOKS

are published by

Kensington Publishing Corp.
475 Park Avenue South
New York, NY 10016

First printing: December, 1990

Printed in the United States of America

To Bob,
my hero

Prologue

Charles Verelst, Lord Shallcross, and his son and heir, the Hon. Jeremy Verelst, had enjoyed a capital day of sport on that lovely April day in Hampshire that was destined to be their last.

They had gone shooting in the morning and bagged several game birds which, at the conclusion of an exhilarating day in the fresh air and sunshine, tasted like ambrosia after being basted with wine and turned on the spit by the female half of the couple from the village that came to the hunting box each day to take care of the gentlemen.

"Nothing like this, eh, boy," Lord Shallcross said for the third time as he took another helping of the crispy-skinned fowl and washed it down with a gulp of claret.

"No, sir," said Jeremy, grinning. He wondered what dainty Margaret Willoughby, the heiress his mother was determined that he should marry, would think if she could see him with his elbows on the table like a country gawk and grease dripping down his chin from the roasted bird carcass.

"Now, this is the life for a man," said Charles expansively. "At one with Nature. When I am here, I wonder why man ever invented balls and routs and

7

picnics al fresco."

"He didn't," said Jeremy dryly. "Woman invented them. That's why man takes every opportunity he can to escape to hunting boxes."

"If that isn't the truth," said Lord Shallcross, his face clouding. "Your mother wants you to marry the heiress. Nice gal. I wouldn't mind. Your affair, though. Don't want any of my children forced to live under the cat's paw."

"I'm very much obliged to you, sir," said Jeremy, "but damned if I won't oblige Mother and marry the heiress, anyway."

Lord Shallcross laughed aloud.

"Well, *I'd* be obliged to you," he said. "I don't mind telling you my life would be a great deal more peaceful if you'd marry the girl and save me your mother's tantrums at not getting her way."

"Father, did you and Mother ever love each other?" asked Jeremy. He had never before asked such a question of his parents. He usually pretended he didn't notice their discord.

"Oh, yes. You wouldn't think it now," said Lord Shallcross, "but there was a time—but that doesn't bear thinking of. She was a beautiful woman. Still is. Marriage would be well enough if all I had to do is *look* at her. But *living* with her—" He finished his sentence with an eloquent shudder.

"I don't think Miss Willoughby is like Mother," said Jeremy, a bit defensively.

"My boy, *no one* is like your mother," said Lord Shallcross, "thank God."

He wiped his face with a napkin and rose a bit stiffly to his feet. His body had received much unaccustomed exercise that day in the saddle and he was feeling sore, though satisfied with his day's entertainment. He was glad he and his son had taken this hol-

8

iday together to get to know one another better. In recent years he had regarded his tall, handsome, blond son as something of a fribble. In London, Jeremy wore the fashionable clothes of the dandy set, and he had rather a bad reputation as a rake. But Charles learned something interesting about his son these past few days in Hampshire. He was a bruising rider and, he was damned good company. He might shape up well, after all, no thanks to his mother's influence.

"I'm for bed," Charles told Jeremy, stifling a yawn. "Nice thing about being in the country is you don't have to keep town hours. Jeckle and his wife have already left. Are you coming up to bed?"

"No, not yet, sir," said Jeremy, rising as his father got up. "I think I'll go outside, maybe take a ride by moonlight."

"Well, be careful. Mrs. Jeckle thought you were a ghost one night riding that black horse with your cloak flapping in the wind, and I almost was bereft of a housekeeper."

"I'll be good," said Jeremy, smiling in contentment. He lingered over a glass of claret after he watched his father's retreating back stumble slightly on the dark stairs to his room, his candle flickering. Then Jeremy rose, went out to the stables and saddled his horse.

To one who was accustomed to being waited on hand and foot, it was an unaccountable luxury to be in Hampshire and not have servants under his feet every moment.

On that thought he heard a rustling sound from one of the darkened corners of the barn and took his lantern toward the noise to have a look.

"Uh, Mr. Jeremy? Is that you, sir?" asked a hesitant male voice.

Jeremy shone his lantern on the two figures standing against one of the supports of the barn and burst into laughter.

"Good evening, Frank," he said, peering into a face very similar to his own.

Frank Watson and Jeremy Verelst had become acquainted in Yorkshire, where Frank had been born to an unwed chambermaid at Crossley, the viscount's principal seat, within two years of Jeremy's own birth. This was before the present Lord Shallcross's tenure. If what local gossip said was true, Frank's father was Jeremy's grandfather, which would make Frank Jeremy's uncle, in a manner of speaking.

When he was a youth and his resemblance to the Verelst heir became too often remarked, young Frank had been spirited away to serve an apprenticeship with a craftsman. Since then he had received a fairly good education because the present Lord Shallcross felt somewhat responsible for this tangible result of his father's senile indiscretion, much as he deplored its existence. Frank had been an appealing though not particularly industrious youth, following much in the tradition of legitimate Verelst males.

Frank and Jeremy had met occasionally over the past ten years or so. Frank's apprenticeship in London had been rather a failure, and so was his short tenure as a clerk in a counting house. He had been living off and on without leave at the hunting box in Hampshire, having nowhere else to go. He justified his uninvited visits at the hunting box with the conviction that, in a way, he was a Verelst and he wasn't hurting anyone by keeping an eye on things when the viscount wasn't in residence. When Lord Shallcross and Jeremy rather unexpectedly decided to take a jaunt to Hampshire, Frank hurriedly made arrangements to stay with a friend in the village.

10

His mother still lived in Yorkshire, an invalid of sorts to whom Frank dutifully sent money when he was in a position to earn some. The present Lord Shallcross, who was very nice in his notions of propriety, had made it clear that the illegitimate child of his father's former servant who so resembled the present heir was not to be encouraged to linger at Crossley.

Frank was most embarrassed to be surprised by Jeremy in his present occupation. His companion was just 15, a buxom, flaxen-haired country lass whose smoky blue eyes held more than a hint of sensuality.

Since her brother was the friend with whom Frank was staying in the village, the choice of a place for their tryst became a problem. Frank had chosen the stable because he assumed none of the family would be lurking about there. Also, his fair companion was impressed by his connection, be it ever so dubious, with the Verelsts. In a peculiar way, she appeared to think being tumbled in their stable by one of their number, even if he was born on the wrong side of the blanket to be real Quality, would be a novel distinction.

Young Molly had been leaning with her back to the stable support, and Frank had been towering over her, about to make short work of the lacing at her bodice. Both trespassers were considerably disheveled, and Frank's breathing was not quite steady.

"Uh, Mr. Jeremy," began Frank.

"Don't mind me," said Jeremy, running an expert eye over the young person. He winked at her impudently. She returned the wink.

"I didn't know you were still hereabouts, Frank," Jeremy added, eyeing his unofficial relative with curiosity. They were of much the same height, and

11

their hair was the same guinea gold color.

"Not for long," said Frank, making an attempt at a nonchalant tone. "I'm just visiting in the neighborhood before I go to sea."

"To sea?" asked Jeremy, surprised and somewhat envious. He had always thought it would be a grand adventure to go to sea.

"It's all arranged," said Frank. "I leave soon. I have already been to Yorkshire to bid my mother farewell, and there were a few people I wanted to see in Hampshire."

"So I see," said Jeremy with a bark of laughter. "Well, don't let me disturb you. I was just fetching my horse."

Leaving the amorous couple behind, Jeremy rode along the primitive road that served the hunting box, enjoying the feeling of the cold, brisk wind ruffling his short, fair locks and the cadence of his stallion's powerful hooves against the pounded earth.

When he started back toward the stables, he thought he smelled smoke on the air and wondered if some poacher had dared light a campfire.

He returned just before ten o'clock to see the hunting box in flames and a hushed crowd of countrymen roused by Frank. Jeckle and his wife had come up from the village when they smelled the smoke on the wind.

"Father!" Jeremy breathed.

Jeckle materialized from the darkness with Frank close behind him.

"Mr. Jeremy. Thank God you wasn't inside," said Jeckle.

"But my father!" Jeremy shouted. "Where is he?"

"Dunno. We hope he got out in time, but there's been no sign of him."

Wordlessly, Jeremy began running for the house,

Jeckle and Frank in pursuit.

"Mr. Jeremy! Come back! You can't do him no good!" Jeckle screamed.

"Mr. Jeremy!" Frank shouted at the same time. "This is madness! Perhaps he got out by a window and you will have risked yourself for nothing."

"Father!" shouted Jeremy, breaking into the house by a window. "Where are you?"

"Up here," came a voice choked with smoke.

"I'm coming," shouted Jeremy, his voice breaking off in a cough.

"No! Save yourself," Charles shouted back. "There are flames between me and the door. Please—"

Jeremy pulled his cloak around himself, hoping it would be some protection from the flames and tried to make his way to the stairs.

"Mr. Jeremy," came Frank's voice from behind him. "Come back!"

"Father!" rasped Jeremy. "I'm coming!"

He was on the stairway when it collapsed and became engulfed in flames.

Chapter One

It was just after noon when the merchant vessel *Sultan's Prize* was sighted on the horizon. She had been at sea, traveling throughout the Orient and the West Indies for four years, and her arrival had been awaited with much anxiety by a young woman who came every day to the London docks to ask about her. The sister of a seaman, she knew much about the departures and arrivals of the various merchant vessels. But it was not her brother she sought today.

As the ship's crew began unloading her wares, Molly Harnish watched anxiously, a lump forming in her throat. What if he were dead? How would she have known? And she would have left her family in Hampshire for nothing while she eked out a living as a barmaid in a hotel and kept her vigil at the docks.

But she was rewarded at last with a glimpse of the man she sought, his shoulders straight and broad, his figure tall and sinewy. Sunlight glinted on his guinea gold hair. Strangely, despite an impression of athletic grace, his stride on dry land was slightly awkward in the manner of men who had spent many years traversing floors that move upon the sea. But he was whole and safe, and that's all that mattered to Molly.

The man who his mates knew as Frank Watson was shaking the hand of his commanding officer when Molly hesitantly approached. He didn't see her.

"You're a good man, Watson," said the captain cordially. "You won't change your mind about staying with us?"

"No, sir. I thank you, but I have personal business that requires my attention."

"Well, I won't press you," said the older man regretfully. "I have only myself to blame. I should never have put you in the way of making all that brass, as you would say in Yorkshire."

"And I am exceedingly grateful, sir," said Frank.

"Aye, you've got a good head for business, the imagination for canny trading, and a stomach strong enough for the sea. I'm sorry to see you leave us," said the captain with a final wave of his hand. "If you get tired of dry land or your funds run out, you'll know how to be in touch with me. The lads on the decks and the wenches in the ports will miss you, Watson."

Frank turned, arrested by the sight of Molly, whose comeliness had already attracted the unwelcome attentions of some of his mates. Her hair was flaxen and made a charming if untidy frame for a lively, pixy face and large blue eyes with smoky depths. Her figure, revealed by the much-washed and patched blue dress, was voluptuous without being plump.

"An old friend, Frank?" taunted one of his acquaintances good-naturedly. "If you won't kiss her, I will."

"You'll keep your paws off her if you value your worthless hide," said Frank genially.

"Ooooh, that be the way of it, eh? Well, I'll take

my unwelcome hide out of the way, then."

"Do that," said Frank, almost absently. He took Molly's arm and led her out of his mates' earshot.

"What are you doing here, Molly? This is no place for a girl like you. You should know better than to—"

"I'm not a girl anymore," she said. "I'm nineteen. And I've come to warn you. Some man's been asking about you. I don't like his looks. He's been asking me a lot of questions about your people in Yorkshire, and he's been offering money for information about you."

"His name?"

"He calls himself Martin. Says he was a valet or something, but all I got to say is, he don't look like no valet to me," she said contemptuously. "He looks more like a—"

"Never mind that," said Frank, cutting her short. "What did you tell him?"

"Nothing. But he already knew an awful lot."

"Such as?"

"About me. That I knew you, I mean." Molly's face flushed delicately. "He knew about the fire in Hampshire, and that I'm the one who took care of you. He knew what ship you were on and when it was due to come back. If you ask me, he's been buying a lot of drink for certain people, sometimes right under my nose at the place where I work, and I don't like *their* looks, neither."

"I see," said Frank thoughtfully, swinging his bag of belongings to the ground. "Molly, if he comes again, you haven't seen me."

"Do you think you need to tell me that?" she asked indignantly.

"Of course not," he said, looking at her with more interest than he had shown previously. "You're even

17

prettier than you were all those years ago. Why aren't you married? What are you doing in London?"

"I'm in London because my brother chucked me out, and I had a fancy to see the city," she said, defiance in every line of her slender frame. "There aren't too many men as would want to marry the likes of me on account of the baby. No one I'd have, leastways."

His eyes, which had strayed to the dock, fastened on hers abruptly.

"What baby? Yours?"

"Yes," said Molly steadily. "Only she's not a baby, exactly. She's three and a half. You can count, I reckon."

"Molly, I didn't know—"

"I know you didn't," she said a trifle bitterly. "Don't think I'm sorry. She's a good child, and smart as a whip."

"Where is she?"

"In the country with my mother. My brother could chuck me out because I wouldn't marry the man he'd found for me, but Ma wouldn't let him chuck Becky out with me. I get to see her sometimes. At Christmas Ma sent enough money for me to visit 'cause Tom was at sea. The trouble is, Tom don't go to sea much anymore. Tom told Ma I could come back, but only if I marry Mickey. He's old as hell, and he stinks and paws me—"

A tear coursed down her cheek and Frank touched it with his forefinger.

"You're a brave girl, Molly. Don't worry. I'll take care of you now."

She made as if to flee. "I have to go now. I'll be late for work."

"Molly, I have to leave London soon. I can't tell

18

you why. But I'll come to see you before I go. Where are you staying? It will probably be tomorrow."

She gave him her direction and melted into the crowd.

He continued on down the congested streets and became aware of someone following him. He turned abruptly into a shadowed doorway and grabbed a small man by the scruff of his collar as the little man, whose weasel face was half-hidden in a wool scarf, looked around frantically for his prey.

"Were you looking for me?" Frank asked his startled captive.

Martin's clothes had been respectable at one time, and they still were to the casual glance. The dark coat was good wool, but grown shabby. A Malacca cane clattered to the street, loosened from his grasp when Frank accosted him.

Frank tightened his grip when no answer seemed to be forthcoming.

"Watch yourself, Watson," said Martin sharply. "I can make you a rich man."

"Indeed? I hear you've been annoying a friend of mine. You will never approach her again."

The menace in his voice was unmistakable, but Martin still ventured a retort.

"A 'friend,' is she?" he said with a sneer. "This is the first I've known her kind to be called anything so grand."

Frank shoved him so hard that he sprawled heavily on the cobblestones.

"You've found me," Frank said coldly. "What do you want?"

"No need to take offense," said Martin ingratiatingly, rising and brushing himself off, but still keeping himself at a safe distance from Frank's powerful hands. "Let's go where we can talk privately. I have a

19

proposition to make which I think you'll find interesting."

"I doubt it, but I may as well listen," said Frank with a shrug. "I suppose you'll just keep following me if I don't."

The two repaired to Martin's lodgings, which were in the Bird In Hand, a less-than-reputable establishment in a less-than-savory neighborhood. Martin's rooms were, like Martin's appearance, respectable after a fashion, but sinking fast. Martin removed the stopper from a bottle of gin and poured some into a glass. Frank, seeing that none of the glasses were overly clean, declined with an infinitesimal shake of the head Martin's invitation to join him. The gesture annoyed Martin.

"So you're too good to drink my blue ruin, are you? Don't think you can put on airs with me, Frank Watson," he said angrily. His hand shook, spilling a few drops of the precious beverage.

"Was I? I didn't know it," Frank said mildly. "State your business. I believe you were going to make me a rich man."

"Yes, if you've got the wit to be guided by me, which I doubt," said Martin. "You're the spit of him all right, looking down your nose at me as if I was a clod of dung in the road."

"The spit of whom?" asked Frank sardonically.

"And talking like you were one of *them,* too. Don't think I don't know what you are, for all your fine education above your station."

"And what is it to you, Martin?" Frank asked coldly. "State your business. You're wasting my time."

"What does a bastard have to do with his time?"

"More than sit in a hole like this and listen to your insults."

"Damned if I don't think you'd pull the thing off," said Martin speculatively. "You've the manner of it all right. With the right clothes and some information about the family I could put you in the way of—How would you like to be Lord Shallcross with an estate in Yorkshire and a handsome fortune?"

"Lord Shallcross!" Frank exclaimed. "Now, what the devil—"

"Jeremy Verelst, Lord Shallcross, to be exact. He died four years ago in a fire in Hampshire, and you're the spit—"

"You've already said that," said Frank, his eyes narrowed. "Since you know so much about me, you also know I am his grandfather's bastard. I'm well aware that I have the family looks. What about it?"

"Well, after he died, the title passed to his cousin, Mark Verelst. All you have to do is convince the family that you are Jeremy Verelst and you survived the fire—"

"You are demented," said Frank, annoyed. "Do you mean you brought me to this sty for this—"

"Yes, and with my help you can do the thing. I was valet to Jeremy Verelst, and I know more about him than—"

"I might have known it was something like this. Forget it," said Frank. "If I were interested in a scheme like this, which I'm not saying I am, I wouldn't be enough of a flat to get involved with the likes of you."

"Oh, not so fast, my fine fellow. I happen to know that four years ago, just after he died, there was a certain young fellow in Hampshire claiming to be the heir—"

"Oh, for heaven's sake," said Frank in an annoyed tone. "That was merely the ramblings of a brain fevered by burns. It was thanks to the gossip that I was

21

spilled aboard the *Sultan's Prize* before my injuries had healed, presumably by the hirelings of the new Lord Shallcross. I'll thank you not to remind me of that folly."

"No. It was damned clever. It could work," said Martin earnestly. "I could make it work. What you need is someone who was intimate with Jeremy Verelst to vouch for you and put you in the way of a few things. And who was more intimate with him than his own valet?"

For the next hour, the dark head and the golden one were bent over the guttering candles as they plotted Frank Watson's return to Yorkshire, the place of his somewhat ignominious birth.

Margaret Willoughby's manor house had a drawing room that accommodated fifty persons comfortably, a dining room that served twice again as many, a ballroom that easily contained the gentry of three adjoining neighborhoods with room to spare, an assortment of handsome salons, eight bedrooms aside from the one she used herself ready for occupation at a moment's notice and rather more available at several moments' notice.

So it was somewhat ironic that the rich, the independent, the much fawned-upon Miss Willoughby was effectively held captive within two feet of space surrounding a fragile Louis XIV chair in her own parlor with no hope whatever of escape thanks to the unwanted attentions of two of her least favorite suitors.

Margaret, a young lady aged two-and-twenty who still would be judged excessively pretty even if she were not a considerable heiress, eyed the two claimants for her affections with decided disfavor. Both lounged with rather self-conscious informality, if not precisely, at her slender, expensively shod feet, at what she considered rather too close a distance.

Both were moderately handsome. In defiance of their mannered upbringings, they spurned the morning dress that was correct visiting attire for gentlemen in favor of black cloaks, skintight pantaloons, white linen shirts and black neckerchiefs knotted carelessly around their throats. A lock of hair slightly camouflaged the brow of one. The fact that the hair of the other did not affect the same art was through no fault of his. A receding hairline made the romantically windswept look impossible for him to adopt, much to his regret, and in later life he would blame this circumstance for the fact that Miss Willoughby, her dowry of twenty thousand pounds, and the considerable revenue derived from her father's fecund acres and equally fecund horses, cows, and poultry had eluded his grasp.

The heiress, whose fine eyes had been rapturously compared to those of a turtledove ("How sweetly insipid," she had crowed), a calm at sea and a silver moon ("Pretty words for plain gray," she'd laughed good-naturedly) were now glacially cool. Looking at her swains, she realized each was prepared to waste her whole afternoon in an attempt to outlast the other, and it really wasn't very flattering to her that they apparently had forgotten their lodestone entirely in their reluctance to leave the field to a rival.

Margaret, who, sick of the Byronic counterfeits that had sprung up all over the neighborhood since she was rash enough during a visit to a nearby manor to bestow some tepid praise upon some poem or other of Lord Byron's, made a mental note never to say a kind word about Sir Walter Scott. It would be the outside of enough to be forced to contend with an army of hopeful young men dressed in full armor and swinging battle-axes in her drawing room.

If Margaret were not at heart a sensible young lady who considered her physical attractions of a profusion of light brown curls, a dainty, elegant figure, expressive eyes, and delicate facial features well enough without deeming them particularly ravishing, she might justifiably have had her head quite turned by all this slavish devotion. For in addition to her two visitors she could boast, if she were so inclined, at least ten others like them just in the immediate neighborhood.

But the heiress knew that without her considerable dowry and the income from her inheritance she would be pronounced merely a good-looking gel and, while worthy of perhaps a passing glance or two, would hardly be thought deserving of all the homage which she had enjoyed since her come-out at the tender age of sixteen.

Both of her suitors, while determined not to budge an inch, were beginning to feel somewhat foolish. Both had come with invitations for the heiress. Mr. Giles Stanhope was the bearer of an invitation for Miss Willoughby to take tea the following day with his mother, who could be relied upon as his most fervent ambassadress to impress Margaret with all his sterling qualities as a prospective husband. The Hon. Phillip Wychwood had been sent to beg the honor of Miss Willoughby's presence at a ball in London several weeks hence which would mark the engagement of his younger sister.

Although such errands would seem, on the surface, to be of a trifling nature, easily discharged, neither of the gentlemen wished to enlarge his invitation to include his rival, which mere civility would demand if the invitation were made within his hearing.

Neither intended to leave until his business was discharged. Nor could either discharge his business without giving his adversary an advantage. Therefore, they were deadlocked, and Margaret, trapped by the dictates of her own excellent manners, was deadlocked right along with them.

So, when her butler intruded upon this rather dismal gathering to announce that Margaret's cousin, Mr. Edward, was come to beg a word with her, and Edward rather rudely put the old man aside to demand private speech with the heiress, Margaret permitted him to stare her visitors so out of countenance that they rather hurriedly took their leave.

He turned on her impetuously, his black cloak swinging magnificently. A slight curl of her lip and the mischief in her eyes distracted him from the cold, dignified speech he had rehearsed in the privacy of his carriage on the short distance from his parents' modest estate to her door.

"Blast you, Margaret, it's your own fault," he said in exasperation, reading her mind so effortlessly that Margaret wondered for about the hundredth time why she had so far failed to fall in love with him despite his best efforts to attract her.

He was romantically handsome with dark, glossy hair that arranged itself more by inclination than design in the all-too-familiar windswept manner. The cloak, she had the justice to acknowledge, was not donned in any imitation of the poet but was, in fact, a favorite style of garment for her active cousin who quite by accident had learned to exploit the devastating power it had over susceptible maidens long before he knew George Gordon, Lord Byron, existed.

Not a bookish sort, Edward had never heard of

the fellow before all of Margaret's admirers started tricking themselves out in imitation of him for her gratification. He found it a source of much irritation that one couldn't go ten feet within distance of his cousin without falling over some besotted figure of fun twirling his cape at one and attempting to look melancholy under the weight of Old Sins.

Privately, Edward, who was no more unconscious of his handsome good looks than he was bookish, was secure in the knowledge that at least some of his contemporaries in the neighborhood sought to imitate, not the poet, but himself. While he was happy to have his own good opinion of his virile male beauty reaffirmed, he knew that Margaret was beginning to find the poet and all his faithful imitators extremely tiresome.

So, instead of being reduced to self-conscious blushes by the sight of Edward's tall, graceful figure and brooding, long-lashed dark eyes looming over her, his odiously indulged cousin was rather too inclined to giggle whenever he struck one of the heroic attitudes that served him so well with lesser women, and he resented it.

"I'm actually glad to see you, Edward," Margaret said cordially, "even though I know why you are come. You have my gratitude for ridding me of that pair of foolish boys."

"Gratitude? That's an odd word coming from you," said Edward forbiddingly, relieved that she had given him the perfect cue for his carefully conned speech after almost managing to distract him from it. "I wonder your treacherous lips can form the words after the way you've treated a man who has stood as a father to you for so many years. And one, moreover, who is closely related to you by blood."

"I have done nothing," said Margaret patiently,

"except relieve him of his duties as my steward and ask him to move back into his own house. He should have done so of his own accord last year when I came of legal age to conduct my own affairs."

"My poor mother has the vapors."

"Yes, I know," said Margaret, repressing the desire to point out that her aunt was almost continually in the vapors and had been so for most of the twenty years of Margaret's acquaintance with the lady. "I regret that. But what I have done is for the best. You have pointed out yourself that your father is getting on in years. The care of the estate is getting to be too much for him."

"He has lived only for you and for your welfare since you were two years old," Edward continued, warming to his theme. He was anxious to deliver the whole speech before he forgot the rest of it. "Why else would he have neglected his own property to administer yours?"

Because he could not resist the temptation to put all of his servants at half wages and house his family at my expense all these years, she thought shrewdly, abandoning an unworthy impulse to give voice to her thoughts. In justice to Edward, she acknowledged that he did not join his parents in imposing upon her hospitality. As soon as he was of age he took lodgings in London, which he could well afford to do because of a legacy from a childless uncle on his mother's side.

"I will not be bullied by you or by your father," said Margaret calmly. "Please remember that this is my home and my estate. I have the right to manage my own household if I choose."

"Even now he would forgive you," said Edward, his voice husky with emotion.

Margaret was not impressed. She had no intention

of inviting her uncle, Sir Robert Willoughby, and his overbearing wife, Samantha, to renew their residence in her home now that she finally had gotten rid of them. The heiress hardened her heart and drew herself up to her full five feet, two inches of height.

"That will do, Edward. I shall not explain myself to you."

"What about Anne?" he asked, naming his younger sister, who, as a child, used to follow Margaret around like an affectionate but awkward puppy.

"What about her? This has nothing to do with Anne," said Margaret, rather cynically reflecting that Edward's parents in their supposed grief at being so callously dismissed by their ungrateful niece were not too proud to send their most presentable child to make sure the heiress would not renege on her commitment to make her London town house available for Anne's debut ball some weeks hence.

That Edward was her aunt and uncle's emissary she had no doubt. They needn't have worried. Margaret was quite willing to bear the chief expense for the come-out of her 16-year-old cousin, although it was hardly her responsibility to do so.

"She will be devastated," said Edward, referring to his sister. "I would not be surprised if my parents refuse to accept the use of your town house for the ball, and you know their means will not extend to hiring a house for the purpose, providing that a suitable one would be available this late in the season."

This part of his speech had not been rehearsed, and Edward was naive enough to think his parents might be too proud to accept such a gift from Margaret. Margaret, from her long acquaintance of both, knew otherwise, but let it pass.

"That would be up to Anne, wouldn't it?" she said mildly. "Edward, I understand your anger, but this has nothing to do with you. You don't know all the circumstances—"

"I am perfectly willing to listen to them, however," he said, making a motion to seat himself.

"No!" Margaret snapped. "I am done talking about this."

"You aren't even going to tell me why?" he asked in such a gentle voice that Margaret felt like a beast. "What could my father have done, after all his years of dedication, to deserve such treatment? Surely there has been a tragic misunderstanding. Has he no right to learn why you have turned against him?"

"He knows very well why I have relieved him of his responsibilities," said Margaret stiffly. "I am under no obligation to discuss my reasons with you. Now if you'll excuse me, I am rather busy—"

"As I can see, Cousin," he said, his dark eyes sweeping her and the empty room contemptuously. "Farewell."

He stalked from the room, his hasty exit conjuring up their mutual aunt, Martha Willoughby, who came to her niece with a question in her eyes.

"I just saw Edward—," she began.

"I know," said Margaret, rubbing her pounding forehead. "Aunt, I really have had enough for one day."

"My poor dear," said Martha soothingly. "Edward looked so angry."

"And so he was," said Margaret.

"Two more gentlemen have called—"

"Oh, lord, no," exclaimed Margaret. "Aunt, please get rid of them. Tell them I'm ill. No. Don't do that. The last time I used that excuse they started sending flowers and bringing me little notes from their mothers and sisters. I can't bear it!"

"I'll tell them you are busy," said Martha placidly.

"Yes, do that," said Margaret. Feeling foolish, she watched from the window until the carriages left. She went to her library and began writing a letter, but was interrupted with the news that her friend, Lady Shallcross, begged a few minutes speech with her. Wearily, Margaret assented.

Kate Verelst was accompanied by her son, Jeremy, aged two and a half and a great favorite with Margaret, who was his godmother.

"Aunt Marg'ret," the child exclaimed as he launched himself onto her lap.

"Jeremy," said his mother in reproof. "You'll soil Aunt Margaret's pretty dress with your dirty shoes."

"It's all right," said Margaret, caressing the crisp blond curls of the blue-eyed child who always addressed her as "Aunt" even though she was no such thing.

Every time she looked at him she reflected that had this child's uncle, Jeremy Verelst, lived, she might by now have had a child like this.

Oh, Jeremy, she thought again. Why did you have to die?

His sister's voice steadied her. Kate Verelst, cutting a dashing figure in an extremely becoming jade green traveling costume which set off her glowing chestnut hair to perfection, had her late brother's melting, celestial blue eyes but otherwise did not resemble him in the least. She had pink cheeks glowing with health, a pert nose, and, because of her great domestic happiness, a smile was rarely far from her lips.

"Are you all right, Margaret?" Kate asked, her usual smile hidden, now, in concern for her friend. Margaret could never hide her feelings from Kate, who detected the melancholy behind Margaret's cheerful manner.

"Yes, of course," said Margaret. "It is just the

headache."

"Then you do not want Jeremy bouncing on your lap. Jeremy, come to Mama," Kate said compellingly.

Jeremy looked up at Margaret out of his uncle's mischievous eyes, and Margaret melted.

"Let him stay," she said, giving the child a hug.

Kate, who saw that, indeed, Margaret had no objection to having her skirts muddied by the child's shoes and didn't wonder at it because she was equally besotted of young Master Jeremy's ingratiating ways, cut short her objections and smiled at Margaret.

"He doesn't think there is anyone in the world like his godmother, do you, my precious?" said Kate caressingly.

Margaret hugged him tighter and he hugged her back. It occurred to Margaret that when Jeremy visited he never asked for sweets, even though he knew she kept some just for him in this very room. Reminded of them, she reached for the jar and gave him a peppermint.

"You'll spoil him," said Kate with no real conviction. "My dear, all is ready. I cannot believe it myself, but we are really going! Mark and Nurse are seeing to the carriages, and I just popped over to take my leave of you. We're off within the hour."

"I hope you will have a wonderful time," said Margaret, who knew that her friend was looking forward to her trip to the Continent.

By the time the wars with that monster Bonaparte had ended, Kate was making preparations for her wedding to her cousin, Mark Verelst, who, after her brother Jeremy's death, had inherited to the honors of her late father, Lord Shallcross. She had naturally expected her doting husband to grant her wishes and

31

take her to the Continent for a month-long honeymoon. But the monster's escape from Elba made it necessary for the wedding trip to be postponed.

Then, when it was again safe to travel to the Continent, preparations for the wedding of Mark's sister, Serena, were in full swing. Serena's mother had died when she was a child, so naturally her brother and his bride hosted the wedding and thought it would be of little consequence if their own honeymoon had to be delayed for a few months. But they had no sooner seen Serena and her husband, Sir John Morgan, settled in their handsome manor house than Kate discovered she was *enciente*. Naturally a long journey was out of the question.

After Kate regained her strength, Shallcross managed to find reason after reason for delaying their journey. A former captain who had fought in Wellington's army, presumably Lord Shallcross regarded foreign travel with less enthusiasm than did his bride.

The plans were resurrected six months after Master Jeremy's birth, but were abandoned once more when Serena discovered she was pregnant with twins. Kate could not leave her sister-in-law at such a time, of course.

After Serena was safely delivered of twin sons, Kate persuaded her husband to take the journey at last, only to learn while they were in the midst of preparations that she was breeding again. Now little Amabel was a year old and deemed healthy enough to travel. Kate had been uncharacteristically firm with her husband, and they were, at last, to go.

"It will be wonderful," Kate told Margaret. "There are so many places I want to see, and while that monster Bonaparte was on the rampage, of course, there was no chance to—but that's neither here nor there. I wanted to ask—Margaret, dear, you're really the only one I can ask—will you visit Jeremy's and my father's graves while I'm gone?"

"I would have done so, anyway," said Margaret softly.

"I felt sure you would," said Kate, her eyes grown misty. "Perhaps it is foolish, but I have always done so, ever since they brought his—him home. Sometimes I feel so heartless because I am so happy, and he died before you and he—"

"I understand," said Margaret reassuringly as her vision became blurred as well, with the laughing specter of the Honorable Mr. Jeremy Verelst. For his sake she had remained unmarried, despite the efforts of various gentlemen to captivate her and add her considerable wealth to their own possessions. Jeremy was the only man she had ever known who didn't give a jot for her precious fortune.

But she had lately decided that since she wasn't getting any younger—fortune or no fortune, two-and-twenty was perilously close to being on the shelf—it was time to bury the memory of her lost love and see if she could find some happiness with another. Several months ago she had begun mixing again in Yorkshire society and made several restless dashes to her handsome town house in London in order to honor various balls and routs with her presence. Suitors, who had taken to calling her The Unattainable and sighing at the thought of the lovely lady and her equally lovely fortune being wasted, were encouraged by this behavior and renewed their assault on Margaret's defenses.

Only, Margaret didn't seem to be responding to any of the many lures cast out to her. Some of her cavaliers were quite as handsome as Jeremy. A few were as impudent, mischievous, and charming. But none were, and she had to face it, Jeremy.

"If only I could forget—," said Margaret. She broke off because she was dangerously close to tears.

"I understand," said Kate, placing a small gloved hand on Margaret's shoulder. "I pray someday you'll find someone who can make you as happy as Mark has made me. You're young and pretty—"

"And rich," said Margaret with a cynical smile. "Don't forget my most important asset. You're perfectly right. I have little reason to wallow in self-pity."

"That's not what I meant at all," said Kate, agitated. "I only meant that someday you'll find someone you will love as much as you loved Jeremy."

"Of course," said Margaret politely, not believing it possible but willing to humor her friend.

Margaret walked with Kate to the door, only to find two carriages out front and the two gentlemen who had just alighted from them in affable conversation. Their black cloaks flapped in the breeze. Margaret gave Kate a quick kiss on the cheek and hugged her little godson affectionately, then she flew back into the house before she could be detected. She really could not bear to sit trapped in one of the salons making tedious conversation with any more gentleman callers.

Telling her butler to deny her to visitors since she was on the point of leaving the house, she went up to her room, shook out her oldest cloak which she sometimes wore for walks, and escaped through a side entrance to the stables. She had no delusions that every one of her servants knew she was leaving, but she honestly didn't care. She asked the head groom to have her gig, an equipage she often used to visit her tenants' homes with remedies for sickness and alms for the needy, hitched to one of her gentlest mares. Familiar with her habits, he accepted her order without a blink, and soon she was bowling toward Crossley, Lord Shallcross's primary seat, and the fourteenth century chapel that contained the earthly remains of her lost love.

Frank Watson had had the devil of a time convincing Martin that he should not accompany him to Yorkshire. Martin was of the opinion that he and Frank should lose no time in traveling to Crossley to claim the late Jeremy Verelst's birthright. Frank persuaded Martin that his time would be better spent quietly nosing about the area alone before he approached the family with Martin's deception.

Furthermore, Frank told Martin, it would look decidedly suspicious if the lost heir arrived on his lordship's doorstep with his star character witness conveniently in tow.

Frank entered the parish of his birth late one afternoon and had no more than stepped down from the coach when he was immediately accosted by a gentleman whose garb proclaimed him to be a member of the clergy. Frank didn't have the slightest idea who he was, and he was astonished when this individual seized his hand in a friendly grip.

"Frank Watson!" ejaculated the clergyman. To Frank's relief, his memory came to his rescue by supplying the required name. "This is providential!"

"Pastor Wilkins," said Frank guardedly, returning the handshake.

"It's the answer to my prayers, your coming home like this," said Pastor Wilkins. "And not a moment too soon, I can tell you."

"I beg your pardon?" asked Frank.

"Your mother wanted to see you before she passes

on to her heavenly reward for a life of suffering," said the pastor sentimentally. "I'm sorry to be the bearer of tragic news, but she is very ill and has been unable to work for some time. Her neighbor has been nursing her, and, of course, my good wife and I have done what we could—"

"Do you mean she has been dependent on charity?" asked Frank in a mortified tone.

"Yes. Of course. No one knew what happened to you," said the pastor, carefully keeping the censure he felt the thoughtless young man deserved from his voice. "She has no one else."

"I've been at sea," said Frank blankly. "I have only just returned to England."

"Oh, that explains it," said the Rev. Mr. Wilkins. "I knew you wouldn't desert her if you knew she was in want. I'll be happy to accompany you to her house."

"Thank you," said Frank, picking up his bag. "I had intended to stay at the inn—"

The pastor wouldn't hear of allowing Frank to register at the inn before visiting his mother, and the two of them walked to the place where Fanny Watson lived. Frank removed his hat as they entered the hovel which, despite the fine spring day, was somewhat damp and drafty.

The frail, birdlike woman was lying on a nest of linens which, Frank was relieved to see, at least looked clean. A neighbor was sitting by the bed with her needlework, and a kettle of lentils simmered on the fire.

"Mrs. Purdy, as you see I have brought Mrs. Watson's son to see her," said the Rev. Mr. Wilkins in self-congratulatory tones.

"Well, it's about time," said that good woman, sniffing in disapproval at her neighbor's offensively

36

healthy-looking son. "She's had the fever. She's not herself." Susan Purdy had no opinion of ungrateful children who left their mothers to the mercy of strangers and so she would have told this Frank Watson if he hadn't looked so grave as he regarded the sick woman on the bed.

"Mother?" he said tentatively. He feared she was dead, she looked so pale and still. So he involuntarily stepped back when Fanny Watson opened her eyes and regarded him solemnly.

"Frankie? Is it you?" she asked huskily, her once-merry eyes unnaturally bright with fever. Her voice was barely a whisper.

Pastor Wilkins nudged Frank, and he answered.

"Yes," he said, adding because Fanny's well-wishers plainly expected it, "Mother."

She smiled and sighed, lapsing again into unconsciousness.

Susan wiped tears from her eyes. "She knew you," she said. "A mother never forgets her child," she added, "even if the child has forgotten her." She bent a fierce look of animosity on Frank, who was taken aback.

"It's not the boy's fault," said the pastor. "He's been at sea."

"He could have sent her a farthing or two now and again," said Susan, placing her hamlike hands on her ample hips.

"I would be happy to repay you for anything you spent —," Frank began in hopes of appeasing Mrs. Purdy's righteous indignation.

"As if she ate any more than would feed a bird," said Susan contemptuously. "What you might do now that you're here is find her a decent place to live. This place has a high wind running right through it in winter, it lets in water in the spring and

37

fall, and the roof leaks something terrible."

"I'll see about it," he said. "I intended to stay at the inn."

"So you're too good to live amongst the likes of us, eh?" said Susan belligerently.

"Please, please, Mrs. Purdy," intervened Pastor Wilkins. "Have some Christian charity. The boy has just returned from a long journey to find his mother at death's door."

"Yes," Frank said. "I'd like to be alone with her, if I may. But first, is there any food in the house? If you'll stay with my mother, I'll go out to buy—"

"Yes, that's a good idea," said Susan grudgingly. "I have my man's supper to get, but I could stay another hour."

"If you'd give me a list of what I should buy—" he broke off, knowing he had made an error.

"Lord love you, lad," said Susan, laughing. "I don't read or write. Neither does your ma. You haven't been gone as long as all *that*. Not all of us have had your fine education."

The last word was uttered with such contempt that Frank knew very well what she thought of the accomplishments with which the late viscount saw fit to endow his illegitimate connection.

"No, I'm sorry," he said. "If you'll just tell me what I should buy, I'll write it down myself."

When he finished with his list dictated by Mrs. Purdy, Frank looked up to see the pastor regarding him with a surprised look in his eye. He was later to tell his good wife that Fanny Watson's wild, reckless son had managed to grow into a proper man, after all.

After an uncomfortable night in Fanny Watson's cottage, Frank realized the truth of Susan's words. He had to find another place for the ailing woman because if he didn't, the draft and damp would hasten her end. Indeed, in the opinion of his neighbors she was as good as dead already. The doctor he brought to see Fanny agreed that a change of housing was necessary if she were to survive.

After the doctor left, Frank settled down next to the bed with a book and one of the new candles he had bought. Fanny looked restless. He bathed her face with water, but it was plain she was delirious from the fever again. The doctor had warned him about this.

"Frankie?" she croaked. He answered, then realized she was having a dream. He felt helpless to do anything for her and so he began to read to her. The sound of his voice seemed to soothe her so he continued far into the night. As he watched the thin, pallid face he realized she could be at most only five and forty years old, but she looked closer to seventy.

Before he went to sleep he counted the horde of cash he had by him. One of his first stops in London had been to a bank where he left most of the money he had earned at sea. Enough, if his calculations had been correct, to support him comfortably for a year or two, or frugally for perhaps three. But he had made these calculations before he found himself responsible for Molly Harnish, her three-year-old daughter, and Fanny Watson in the throes of a wasting illness.

He had left a sizable sum with Molly so she could live decently with her child without the fear that she would have to marry the odious creature her brother had found for her. Frank felt outrage at the thought of that pretty, brave child being forced to endure the caresses of such a repulsive beast. And he had to do something about a more comfortable home for Fanny Watson. He owed her that. At this rate, his savings would not last long. He had to find a post of some sort.

The next day he asked Susan Purdy to stay with Fanny while he looked for work. Susan was plainly skeptical. She thought it more likely he wanted to drink with low companions at the inn, but she had to admit he had bought all the food and supplies she requested of him without complaint. Fanny seemed quieter and her fever was gone down. To Mrs. Purdy's surprise, he had set a pot of bacon and beans cooking on the fire, and he had changed his mother's linen.

Somewhat mollified, Susan thought on the whole it was a good thing Frank Watson had returned, although she was reserving judgment on whether he had improved from the no-good, lazy boy he was when he left for sea four years ago. He was certainly better behaved and had a fancy way of talking like the Quality, but that didn't mean he'd ever be the strong, responsible, hard-working son Fanny Watson deserved, and so Susan Purdy intended to tell him at the first sign of his shirking of his duty.

Frank spent the day looking for work among the merchants in the village, hoping to find a situation as a clerk. He was good with numbers. He also knew French, Latin, a smattering of Greek, and was particularly fluent in gutter Spanish thanks to his travels, but he had little taste for a position as a tutor, so he didn't bother to mention these accomplishments. He'd thought one or two tradesmen had been interested in him, and was on the point of returning to Fanny Watson's house when his horse's hooves seemed drawn to Crossley, principal seat of Lord Shallcross.

Why not? he reasoned. He might as well have a look at the place. He had it on good authority that

the family was out of the country and would not return for some months. So much for Martin's bril-
liant plan to establish Jeremy Verelst's bastard
relation on the princely estate, he reflected contemptuously. He imagined that little weasel face screwed
up with anger upon finding that, instead of attempting to worm himself into the affection of the Verelst
family, his protégé was playing nursemaid to a sick
woman and trying to hire himself out as a clerk to
support her.

As he rode through the fields of Lord Shallcross's
estate he noticed many changes from when he had
last been in Yorkshire. Lord Shallcross's predecessor
had allowed the estate to become run down, mainly
because he lacked any interest in agriculture. His tenants' houses had been falling around their long-suffering ears. Now, Frank noticed with approval, the
houses appeared to be sturdy and in good repair. The
fences were mended. And the cattle he saw looked
healthy and well fed.

It didn't take him long to come to the ages-old
chapel that had been the burial place for the Verelsts
since the fourteenth century. Although most English
gentry was by custom buried at the parish church-
yard, the Verelsts always had been different. The romantically medieval chapel stood apart from the
manor house and was the only standing part of the
original keep that had once stood on the site. Pieces
of rubble from the ruin of the castle itself lay
around, forming a popular picnic spot hereabouts,
Frank knew, since the taste for gothic ruins had
come into vogue. The presence of these scattered remains of ancient masonry lent the grounds a *cachet*
that a mere rose garden or artificial lake graced with
swans could never impart.

He removed his hat and entered the chapel slowly,

41

sobered by the darkness inside. He lit a candle by the door and carried it slowly up the aisle until he was face to face with some effigies of the ancient Verelsts, all warriors, and their equally fierce women. Then he came to the last resting place of Jeremy Verelst, and, to his surprise, Jeremy had a monument of sorts, too.

Frank put his candle on an ornamental wrought-iron rail and regarded this tribute closely.

The cold, handsome marble face shone eerily in the light of Frank's candle and, absurdly touched, he felt a chuckle form low in his throat. Who could have done this?

His meditations were interrupted by a feminine voice.

"How dare you laugh in such a place, sir?" his undetected companion demanded in an outraged whisper. She must have been standing in the shadow by the nave all the time, undetected because his eyes had not yet accustomed themselves to the gloom.

He turned in surprise to confront a diminutive young lady in a slightly shabby blue cloak.

The light from his candle illuminated his face and Margaret Willoughby gasped. The marble face and the living one before her were virtually identical. The floor shifted beneath her feet and she felt herself sinking into darkness.

Chapter Two

"None of that now, miss," said Frank bracingly, grasping Margaret roughly by the shoulders. As he did so, Margaret's hood fell back and he let go of her abruptly. She staggered and would have fallen if he hadn't caught her and supported her steps to a pew that was just behind her. She sank into it gratefully and looked up, blinking at him.

She was recovering rapidly. The apparition before her, despite his resemblance to the visage of Jeremy Verelst's monument, was not in the least ghostly. He was, to judge by his grip on her shoulders, quite solid, and there had been nothing sepulchral about the robust tone of his voice.

Now he was bent before her, picking up flowers scattered from the basket in her hand. His task gave her time to regain her composure. He placed the cut flowers in the basket and set it on the pew next to her.

"Thank you. I do beg your pardon," she said, passing a hand over her eyes. "I am not usually so silly, I assure you."

"Are you ill? Shall I—"

"Of course I'm not ill," she said with some asperity. "I really must give up reading Mrs. Radcliffe's novels if they are going to make me see ghosts."

"I beg your pardon, ma'am?"

"Well, you look so much like Jeremy Verelst, and there you were, standing next to his statue. It was like his living face and his dead face confronted me all at once," she said, her lips forming a shaky smile at her own folly.

"I'm flattered that you should think so," he said, belying his words with a disparaging look at Jeremy Verelst's statue, which stood in the dignified attitude of a Greek noble whose partially exposed torso and limbs were saved from indecency by a graceful classical drape of some sort, "for I don't think I've ever seen a face so serene or so insipid except on the front of a Greek coin. At any rate, I don't think it resembles him much."

"Oh, did you know him?" she asked, swallowing the tart rejoinder she was about to utter.

"Yes, I knew him," said Frank grimly. "He was not nearly so noble, I assure you."

"How can you say such a thing!" exclaimed Margaret, indignation throbbing in her voice. She recalled that he actually had been laughing when he turned and startled her with his resemblance to her lost love. In her outrage she forgot that when she first saw the statue years ago she had reflected that Jeremy would have laughed himself into stitches over it.

"Quite easily," said her tormentor. "He was not a bad sort. A wastrel and a drunkard, of course, but he was young and I like to think he would have improved—"

"You knew him intimately, I suppose," she said sarcastically.

"From childhood," Frank replied.

"Of course. You must be a relative," said Marga-

44

ret thoughtfully. "Despite what you say, you look very much like him. I thought I had met all of the family at the funeral—"

"I've been away," said Frank, his voice tinged with wicked amusement. "You might say I am related to the Verelsts. Even so, I rather doubt that anyone would have introduced us."

Margaret was glad of the darkness inside the chapel because she felt a blush steal up her cheek. She knew exactly what he meant even though well-bred young ladies were supposed to be ignorant of such earthy matters. Margaret may have been sheltered, but she was never stupid.

"Be that as it may, I won't listen to you if you mean to slander him," said Margaret stiffly. She didn't intend to demean herself or Jeremy's memory by bandying words with this man. She rose to leave and stumbled. Frank steadied her.

"I'm sorry," he said, contrite. "You've had a nasty shock. May I help you outside? This place is enough to give anyone the vapors."

"I'm quite all right, and I *never* have the vapors," she said with chilly dignity although she allowed him to take her arm and lead her outside. "My gig is over there." She pointed to a cluster of trees. He hadn't noticed the gig before, or he probably would not have visited the chapel.

"Where is your servant?" he asked, perceiving there was no one with the gig.

"I am alone."

"Do you think that wise?"

"But of course. Everyone knows me hereabouts."

"Indeed, Miss Willoughby."

Margaret looked surprised. "How did you know my name?"

He smiled blandly.

"Did you not just say that everyone knows you hereabouts?"

"Yes. I suppose I did. And what is your name, if I may ask?"

"Frank Watson," he said. "I've been at sea. My mother lives in the village."

"And what do you do when you aren't emerging from the dark and scaring people out of their wits?" she asked. She noticed with approval that he was wearing a utilitarian navy greatcoat. In her present humor, she would have run screaming to her gig if he had been wearing a black cape.

"Actually, I'm looking for work," he said. "Do you know someone who can use a man with a good head for figures? I once worked as a clerk and I know quite a bit about estate management. I kept all of the accounts for my captain and ordered most of the provisions. I know French and Latin, a smattering of Greek, and quite a bit of Spanish but, unfortunately, not quite in the style one would use in the first circles—"

She held her head to one side, looking up at him thoughtfully.

"I wonder if you are trustworthy," she said softly.

"I beg your pardon, ma'am?"

"I do have such a post vacant. My steward had to leave rather suddenly," she said.

"I am all attention," said Frank.

"My uncle was my steward until yesterday. He had been so since I was two years old. My parents died, you see, and he and his wife brought me up and lived in my house."

"This worthy died, I take it?"

"No," said Margaret bitterly. "His reasons for leaving needn't concern you."

"I see," said Frank thoughtfully. "You dismissed

46

him, I presume?"

"Yes. I asked him to move himself and his wife back to his own house nearby, which is a modest one. You will have to take my word for it that my reasons were sound ones. My aunt has been crying her grievances abroad, and in the eyes of the neighborhood I am perceived as a cold-blooded, ungrateful viper for condemning them to live within their means."

"If you are so wealthy, why is your father's brother so impoverished?" he asked.

"It's very complicated," said Margaret, "but the wealth of the Willoughbys disappeared long ago although they were related to some of the most powerful families in the land. Uncle Robert was the eldest son, but his improvident way of life and his wife's mounting debts forced him to sell the manor and the land. Rather than see it pass from the family, my father, who was the younger son, purchased it from him, renovated the manor house, and bestowed a more modest adjoining estate upon his brother because he and his family had nowhere to live after the sale. My mother was an heiress and had brought my father more lands as well as her wealth. My father added greatly to her fortune."

Frank threw up his hands in mock horror.

"Do you mean to say he was engaged in *trade!*"

"Nothing so vulgar," she said with an answering twinkle in her eye. "Agriculture. It's perfectly respectable, I assure you. There was no entail. Nor did my parents' will stipulate anything about a male heir. My parents left everything in trust for me, and the trust ended last year."

He pictured a lonely child raised by relations who coveted her fortune.

Her voice trailed off at his look of sympathy.

"But that has nothing to do with the subject at hand," she said briskly. "What was I talking about before you asked that exceedingly vulgar question about the Willoughby fortunes?"

"You need a new steward," he reminded her.

"Ah, yes. So I do. But not one who would have as much authority as Uncle Robert was allowed," she said. "If I asked questions about how my property was being administered I was patronized and treated like a naughty child. I intend to keep the reins in my own hands from now on. I have a bailiff, but he is getting on in years, besides being loyal to Uncle Robert. I need someone I can trust to follow my orders and look after my interests."

"Why do you trust me? A moment ago you were annoyed with me for finding fault with that nightmare of classical fervor in there."

She looked at him earnestly.

"Odd, isn't it?" she mused. "I'm not quite sure why I trust you, except you look so much like Jeremy—"

"The boy who was Jeremy Verelst is dead," said Frank harshly. "I am not he."

"I know that," said Margaret, her head bowed. She had seated herself gracefully on a fallen boulder from the ruin of the ancient keep. It had been a sunny day but now the wind was rising and the sky was turning gray.

"He was important to you?" asked Frank, his voice gentle.

"Yes, although I didn't know him for very long," she said quietly. "He was the only man who—but that hardly matters after all these years."

"It matters to you." It was a statement not a question.

"Yes," she said, looking up at him. "Oh, I've forgotten the flowers! How horrid of me! I must go back into the chapel and arrange them."

"But surely you needn't—"

"I promised his sister, Lady Shallcross, I would put flowers on the graves. She always does so, but she and her family are gone to the Continent for several months."

The first drops of rain fell and the wind blew her hair around her face. She pulled at the edge of her cloak to cover her high-waisted dress of thin white muslin. She shivered.

"I may as well go back inside and arrange the flowers since it's going to rain, anyway, but my poor mare—"

"I know a shelter in the ruins where I can tie her. She'll be all right until the storm is over."

She thanked him and went back inside the chapel. There was a section of the ruins where three sides of a wall and the roof still stood, forming a makeshift shelter. Frank drove the gig into it, unhitched the mare, and tied her inside. Then he returned to the chapel, shaking raindrops from his coat. Margaret had relighted his candle and was placidly arranging flowers in two brass vases at the foot of Jeremy Shallcross's statue.

"Poor Charles Verelst," said Frank, joining her. "I see he didn't rate so magnificent a monument."

"No," said Margaret, "But you must not be laying the fault at his daughter's door. Kate was much attached to her father, and she was most distressed when he died. Still, I think he would have much preferred that small marble bust she commissioned to being swathed in classical draperies for all perpetuity."

"Did Kate Verelst commission this?" he said in disbelief, indicating Jeremy Verelst's statue.

49

"In a way. She intended for it to be a small marble bust, similar to the one she had made of her father. But then her mother got wind of the scheme and with her usual forcefulness managed to get her way."

A reminiscent smile lit Margaret's features.

"The dowager is much enamored of classical finery, I'm afraid. She redecorated Shallcross House, her husband's residence in London, with fluted columns and polished breastplates and ugly little couches on crocodile legs when Kate's sister Melanie made her debut in '13. I should not laugh at her taste, and you should not laugh at this statue if it gave her comfort to commission it. She was sincerely grieved when she lost her only son."

"But she was not quite so grieved at the loss of her husband?"

"No. The dowager would hardly build a monument to her husband," Margaret said. "She was very angry when she found out that he had left her a respectable jointure instead of a fortune to dispose of at her discretion. Arabella's tastes were always very expensive and she thought herself treated very shabbily. But she eventually married a rich merchant, so I dare say it doesn't matter now."

"Who married a rich merchant?" asked Frank, astonished. "You don't mean the dowager!"

"Yes, I most certainly do, which means I probably shouldn't call her 'the dowager' anymore. Mr. Peevers is a wealthy cit, if you want the word with no bark on it."

"I never would have thought—" Frank lapsed into a brown study. He recalled the late viscount's wife as very starched up and sensible of her own consequence, even though she took the metropolis by storm as an actress before she ensnared Charles Verelst into marriage. He couldn't imagine the proud

Arabella disparaging herself by taking a cit, however wealthy, as her second husband.

"Mr. Watson, I wonder if you are interested in the position?" asked Margaret, recalling him to his surroundings.

"Position? Oh, as your steward."

"The post comes with a house on the estate, or it did in my father's day. Uncle Robert never wished to live in it while he could board himself and his family at my expense, but the house has been kept in repair and it is quite comfortable. You probably would want to invite your mother to live with you."

"Miss Willoughby," said Frank earnestly, "I would be delighted to be your steward. But why should you offer me the post? You know nothing about me."

"That is true," said Margaret. "All I ask is obedience. I have no need for a steward who will override my wishes for what he perceives as my own good. Is that clear?"

"I will endeavor to live up to your trust," he said solemnly. "In what way may I serve you?"

"For a start," said Margaret regarding her flower arrangements approvingly and reaching for her empty basket, "if the rain has quite stopped you may help me hitch my mare to the gig."

"You probably should not travel the countryside without a maid or a groom," he ventured.

"Probably not," she said mutinously, "but sometimes one must be alone. I often visit the sick and none of the maids want to go along."

"You are young for such responsibilities."

"Someone must see to the tenants' families. Who will do so if I will not? Aunt Samantha considers the less fortunate dirt beneath her feet, and, poor dear, Aunt Martha would be of no practical use at all. Aunt Martha lives with me as my companion, and although she is a darling, she is thoroughly useless when it comes to comforting the sick. She is so sensitive that the suffering of others quite overpowers her. She is Literary, you know."

"I see. And you, I take it, are not literary."

"Hardly," said Margaret, laughing. "Are you?"

"If I were, I would never dare admit it! When shall I report for work?"

"Let's see. I'll have my housekeeper see to having the house cleaned, so you should be able to move your mother into it day after tomorrow," said Margaret thoughtfully. "Can you report to my house on Thursday morning?"

"I'll be there," he said. "Thank you, ma'am."

He hitched the mare to her gig. After giving him a mock salute with her whip, she rode off at as spanking a pace as she could persuade the placid mare to go.

Two days later, it seemed like the assembled village had turned out to watch Frank load his mother's belongings onto a cart borrowed from Mrs. Purdy's son for the journey to their new home.

He did not make the error of attributing this gathering to any particular feeling of goodwill toward himself or his mother.

Twenty-odd years after the youthful transgression which resulted in Frank's birth, Fanny Watson still was considered a Fallen Woman. This, despite the fact that she had lived like a Quakeress ever since.

Although most of her neighbors were on speaking terms with Mrs. Watson, as they called Fanny, more from courtesy than from respect for the literal truth, only a sympathetic few like Mrs. Purdy and the pastor had actually set foot in her house, which made the rest of the village's inhabitants all the more anxious to be present on this occasion. It would be their last chance to satisfy their curiosity about what kind of possessions might belong to a woman who once had attracted the amorous attentions of a viscount.

Quite apart from this irresistible lure, any kind of activity was likely to attract notice in an isolated village rather thin of spectator sports. Although members of Frank's uninvited audience had many suggestions for loading his mother's property more efficiently than he happened to be doing, there were no offers of actual physical assistance.

He was considerably surprised to see a closed carriage pull up at the door.

"Mr. Watson?" asked the driver, touching his cap.

"Yes?" said Frank shortly, piqued at the villager's refusal to help.

"Miss Willoughby sends this carriage because she thought it would be useful in conveying your mother to your new home."

"My thanks to Miss Willoughby," said Frank, relieved.

It was not a fashionable equipage, and he guessed it normally was used for transporting Margaret's house servants on her jaunts to London, but he was infinitely grateful for the loan of it. He had been wondering how he could move his ailing mother to the house without making her more ill than she already was. He had made arrangements to rent a gig from the owner of the inn, but it was a rough ride besides being open to the weather. It had been the only passenger conveyance available for hire in the village.

A murmur went around the group of spectators. This mark of favor from the heiress was most unexpected. Their gaze was more respectful after that, although no one was impressed enough to help Frank load the rest of the furniture.

53

At last the cart was full, and Frank went in to tell his mother he was leaving for the house and would be back for her shortly.

"Mother?" he said, touching her shoulder gently. She was no longer delirious, but she was very weak and spoke little although he could tell from her eyes that she understood him.

She opened her eyes and looked at him. Her bed was the only thing in the room, and he would bring the cart back for it after he had her moved safely to the new house.

"Mother, I am going to the new house with the furniture. You'll be all right alone until I come back? Mrs. Purdy can't come. Her daughter is brought to bed with her first child, and needs tending. I'll be back as soon as I can."

Fanny smiled weakly, showing him she understood.

"Miss Willoughby has sent a comfortable carriage for you. Isn't that kind of her?" Frank continued. "It's closed, so I needn't worry about your catching cold on the journey."

Fanny smiled again, and Frank touched her hand.

"You aren't afraid to be alone, are you?"

Fanny shook her head slightly and the adoring look she gave him tugged at his heart. She was very, very weak. He hoped he could get her to the new house without making her worse. At least it wasn't raining.

He stopped by the inn to tell the innkeeper that he wouldn't need the gig, then he proceeded to the sturdy brick house Margaret had bestowed upon him. The house was furnished with unfashionable but serviceable stuff, and he put his mother's belongings into an empty bedroom. Her pathetic hoard of possessions looked far too shabby for the house, which was small, but of good proportions.

It had a narrow dining room, a parlor, four bedrooms, and a kitchen below stairs. By his calculations, he had enough saved from his funds to hire a woman to watch his mother and cook their meals while he was at work. He wanted to avoid asking Margaret to give him an advance on his first quarter's wages as long as possible, and he optimistically reasoned that he could manage on the savings he had at hand until the first or second quarter if he were frugal.

When he returned to his mother's house, he found the pastor and his wife sitting with Fanny.

"Such a comfortable carriage Miss Willoughby has sent for you to ride in, Mrs. Watson," said Pastor Wilkins, rallying the ailing woman. Frank smiled a welcome and shook hands with the pastor, bowing to his wife, a plump, placid woman who was known in the parish for her kindness. She was putting Fanny's bonnet on her and trying to arrange a coat around her thin shoulders.

"Mr. Watson," said Mrs. Wilkins in relief, "if you would be so kind as to lift your mother a trifle I could get this coat on her. My husband strained his back last week—"

Frank lifted his mother and helped Mrs. Wilkins put the coat on her. Then he carried Fanny to the carriage where her neighbors called out greetings and gave Frank many helpful suggestions on how to arrange her inside. He listened with half an ear as he propped his mother up in a nest of blankets so she could see out the window. Then he got inside with her. He had left his horse tethered at the cottage, and he would collect it when he brought the cart back for his mother's bed.

When he arrived at the house he was surprised to

be greeted by one of Miss Willoughby's servants. This woman had started dinner and had made a bed ready in the second-largest bedroom for Fanny's reception.

"The mistress thought you'd be glad of a hand, Mr. Watson," said Mathilde.

"Miss Willoughby thinks of everything," said Frank, smiling, as he deposited his mother on the bed. "There, now," he said to her. "Are you all right? Not cold, are you?"

Fanny smiled at him and touched his hand. He was encouraged, since that was the first time she'd moved voluntarily. Normally she lay like an infant, allowing others to arrange her bony limbs to their satisfaction. She was getting better.

When Fanny's hat and coat were removed and she was once more enveloped in blankets and muslin sheets, the servant left the room and returned a short time later with Miss Willoughby and a basket of preserves, fruit, and two loaves of fresh baked bread.

"Miss Willoughby," said Frank, astonished. "How kind of you to come."

"I just wanted to be sure you are settled properly," Margaret said briskly, shaking hands with him. "I trust Mathilde has made you comfortable."

"Very. Thank you," said Frank. "Miss Willoughby, this is my mother, Mrs. Fanny Watson."

Fanny's eyes looked with wonder at Miss Willoughby, who reached down and touched her hand.

"I am happy to meet you, Mrs. Watson," said Margaret, smiling.

Fanny didn't reply, but she smiled and returned the pressure of Margaret's fingers slightly.

"Your son tells me you have been ill, Mrs. Watson," Margaret continued. "I hope your health will soon be restored to you. Now I will leave you to rest."

She gave the thin hand a final pat and left the room, Frank following.

"Poor woman," said Margaret sympathetically. "Pastor Wilkins tells me her improvement has been miraculous since your return."

"Pastor Wilkins gives me far too much credit," said Frank, embarrassed.

"I'm sure he does not," said Margaret. "You are a good son."

When he didn't speak, she changed the subject, perceiving that it discomfited him.

"I'd like to talk to you about Mathilde," she said. "I wonder if you would care to employ her. She is a good worker and a good nurse. She was Dr. Mason's housekeeper until his death last year. I know she would welcome the chance of keeping house for you and your mother. She has been used to an active life, and she doesn't seem very happy in my house."

"It seems there is no end to your bounty, Miss Willoughby," said Frank courteously. "I will be happy to engage Mathilde. I was just wondering where I could find a servant to take care of my mother while I am working."

"You should have a manservant as well," said Margaret thoughtfully. "I know of a man—"

"That will not be necessary," said Frank. "I can do what work is necessary. I, too, am used to an active life."

Margaret looked shocked. "Do you mean you would bring in the wood and make repairs—"

"Of course I would," he said. "Who else?"

"This is an awkward question, Mr. Watson, but is it because you cannot afford to hire a man? If so—"

"No, I could hire a man if I wished because of what I have saved while I was at sea the past four years. And if I find I need one, I shall do so," said Frank with an edge to his voice.

"I am interfering, aren't I?" she asked dolefully.

"I would never venture to suggest such a thing after your many kindnesses, ma'am," said Frank with a twinkle in his eye.

"It's true, though. I cannot help myself. I suppose I am one of those odiously managing females. Pay no attention to me when I start trying to tell you how to arrange your personal life."

"I shall steel myself to do so."

"Of course, in all matters regarding my personal property, I expect to be obeyed without question."

"Of course, ma'am," said Frank. "At what time shall I present myself tomorrow?"

"I shall expect you at 9 o'clock."

"Very good, ma'am," said Frank. Margaret began putting on her gloves, which Frank took as a signal that she wished to depart. He walked with her to the door and returned to his mother's room to find Mathilde laying in wait for him.

"Shall I sit with Mrs. Watson until you are ready for dinner, Mr. Watson?"

"I would like to talk with you, if I may, Mathilde. Would you be interested in keeping house for my mother and myself?"

"Oh, yes, sir," said Mathilde enthusiastically. "I kept house for the doctor all these years, and although Miss Willoughby is a good mistress, it is not the same, although the feel of her house has improved wonderful now that Sir Robert and Lady Willoughby have gone."

Frank was surprised by these confidences of a servant to an employer, then he remembered that in Mathilde's eyes, the only thing that separated her estate from his was that he possessed the means to pay her wages.

Frank Watson's appearance might be gentleman-like and his speech cultured, but Mathilde considered that a respectable Christian woman's birth was hardly inferior to that of the natural child of a servant, regardless of who the child's father might be. Besides, Dr. Mason dearly loved a comfortable gossip, and Mathilde, quite in the habit of repeating rumors to him, thought what was considered proper talk for Dr. Mason was quite good enough for Fanny Watson's son.

Despising himself, Frank asked her if she had known Miss Willoughby for long.

"Well, no, in a manner of speaking," said Mathilde regretfully. "Before I came to work for her she had never spoken to me in her life. Dr. Mason took care of some of her servants although Sir Robert and his lady considered the family too good to be attended by a country doctor. I was never so surprised in my life as when Miss Willoughby came to me after the doctor's death and asked me if I would come work for her. She did it out of kindness, I'm sure. The pastor probably told her I couldn't find another position. But that's like her. I heard her aunt ripped up at her proper for daring to engage a servant without her permission."

Mathilde gave an audible sniff.

"Has Miss Willoughby never been married?" asked Frank.

"No," said Mathilde, warming to her theme, "but not for want of offers. You wouldn't credit the number of gentlemen who want to fix their interest with the mistress. Scores of them, there are, although there's some that say she'll have her cousin Edward in the end. He's a fine figure of a man, besides being dotty on her."

"I see. Then their engagement is an understood thing."

"No, not by the mistress, it isn't."

"It's surprising she hasn't been married long ago."

"And so I think, too. She's pretty as can stare, besides being rich and good-natured when that old cat her aunt isn't setting up her bristles."

"Would that be the literary aunt?"

"Ah, she's mentioned her to you, has she? No, Lady Willoughby's name is Samantha. The literary aunt would be her Aunt Martha, her father's sister. She's a spinster, and wasn't left too plump in the pocket. The mistress took her as a companion because she's her only family besides her Uncle Robert's family."

"It seems your mistress has a penchant for taking in strays," said Frank, not liking the feeling that he could be classed as one of them. "So, why hasn't Miss Willoughby married?"

"Some say it's because she was in love with Mr. Jeremy Verelst from Crossley," said Mathilde, sighing sentimentally. "After he died, she never looked at another man."

Mathilde flushed slightly, which told Frank that she was well aware of his own relationship to the late Mr. Jeremy Verelst's family.

"But what about the gentlemen who are hanging about her house?" Frank asked.

"Oh, them," she said dismissively. "They just started coming around a month or two ago. Until then, it was pretty much decided that Miss Margaret intended to be a spinster. Along about then she decided it was time to get married and have some children. Since then the house has been full of jollity, with gentleman callers and flowers and gifts arriving every hour. She goes to London for parties, and it's said half the young bachelors in the neighborhood follow her there. She can have her pick, I'll tell you."

"I'm sure she can," he said thoughtfully.

"I'm glad to see she got rid of that uncle of hers. The way he has imposed on her generosity is more than flesh and blood can bear."

Frank was filled with self-loathing at having encouraged Mathilde to gossip about her mistress, and the servant's willingness to confide information about Miss Willoughby to a virtual stranger determined him to be careful what he said in her presence. He felt sure that if she would tell him all about Miss Willoughby, she would have no qualms about telling Miss Willoughby all about him. He tried to conjure up a vision of Margaret pumping Mathilde for information about him and his mother, and failed.

In his opinion, Margaret wore her dignity with such solemnity that he could not imagine her unbending enough to have a comfortable gossip with a servant. Yet it was obvious that her life was freely discussed among her inferiors. He dismissed Mathilde, saying he would like dinner in an hour, and would sit with his mother until then.

For the next quarter of an hour, he simply watched his mother sleep, glad to see her resting quite comfortably. The journey seemed, if anything, to have done her good. She woke, and her birdlike blue eyes centered adoringly on his face.

"I do believe you're feeling better, Mother," he said. "Would you like for me to read to you?"

She actually managed to produce a nod, which encouraged him more than anything that had happened to him all day.

"And so you met Miss Willoughby, Mother. Is she not a pretty lady?"

61

Another nod.

"I would say on the whole this has been a good day's work for both of us," he said, opening his book.

Chapter Three

Martha Willoughby's still beautiful hands waved in agitated arcs as her niece confronted her with the enormity of what she had done.

If her beloved young relative's outrageous words were to be believed, Margaret had engaged a perfect stranger to act as steward at her manor. Moreover, her choice was a young man whose background was, to say the least, highly suspect.

"I am afraid, my dear," said Martha, looking harassed, "that Sir Robert will be very, very angry."

She regarded with foreboding the stubborn set of her niece's jaw.

"Who I employ in my own house is none of my uncle's business," said Margaret flippantly, trying to conceal the fact that she, too, was having misgivings. "If Mr. Watson is not satisfactory, I shall discharge him. At any rate, he cannot do worse than my uncle and aunt."

Martha shuddered feelingly, and at once was repentant for the surge of joy she had felt when she learned that her brother and his wife were to be removed from her orbit. Neither had treated Martha with even common civility. She had no fortune, her late father considering it a waste of money to provide for his spinster daughter when it was naturally the duty of her surviving brothers to do so. He had considered a daughter of little beauty next to worthless in an age when an attractive daughter could be sold to a rich suitor for a generous settlement.

It was only to be expected that his son would look upon Martha as more of a liability than an asset, even though she had uncomplainingly supervised his children's schoolroom activities and willingly assumed all those homely housekeeping tasks his wife considered beneath her dignity to perform until Margaret became old enough to take an interest in her own domestic arrangements.

In youth Martha had never been beautiful, although her looks had acquired dignity and polish in later life. Not enough, however, to enable her to snag one of the few remaining bachelors in her age group, all of whom were more interested in young brides who would flatter their egos and make a better show in the eyes of the world.

Martha, who felt all the disadvantages of being long past her youth and in impecunious circumstances, was frankly astonished that her niece had so far preferred the single state to marriage. Thwarted of her natural wish for a husband, children, and a home of her own, Martha had turned for consolation to Literary Art, but she would have traded all the poets in the world to eat a meal or sleep under a roof that she did not owe to the charity of her better-circumstanced relations.

Long used to being bullied by her brother Robert and his wife Samantha, Martha marveled at Margaret's courage in flouting their wishes.

"It's no use ringing a peal over my head," said Margaret, who could read her aunt's mind with precision. "It's done. I've already installed him in the brick house, and he will be here at nine o'clock."

"But can he be trusted not to take liberties?" asked Martha in a tremulous tone.

"Liberties?" asked Margaret archly. "Are you worried about my worldly goods or my tender person?"

"Margaret!" exclaimed Martha, shocked.

The butler interrupted at this point.

"Miss, a Mr. Watson is here to see you," he said woodenly.

Although his face was perfectly impassive, it was obvious to Margaret that his phrasing, "a Mr. Watson," was deceptive. She had a shrewd notion that Sternes knew exactly who this Mr. Watson was and strongly disapproved. The butler had been hired by Sir Robert and further disapproved of the fact that a young lady, even if she was the manor's rightful owner, was now in charge of the household. Margaret reflected bitterly that if Sternes didn't become a bit more adept at masking his disapproval, he would find himself replaced as well.

"Very well, Sternes. Show him to my library, if you please," she said, subtly underlining her possession of a room considered Sir Robert's private domain since he had taken residence as his niece's guardian. It was mean. It was petty. It was decidedly unmaidenly. And it gave Margaret great satisfaction.

Martha looked at her niece hesitantly. Margaret favored her with a questioning, but not unfriendly, lift of the eyebrows.

"Do you wish to come with me to meet Mr. Watson, Aunt Martha?" Margaret asked.

"No, I thank you," said Martha, looking anxious. "Would you mind, Margaret, if I would take the carriage to the pastor's house? I have promised his wife the loan of some books from your grandfather's library. Remember, when I asked you last week you said it would be all right—"

"Of course I would not mind, Aunt Martha," said Margaret. "I have told you before, you may order the carriage any time you wish. And I've told you before you don't need my permission to use the library. If anyone on earth can be trusted to take good care of the books, it is yourself, dear Aunt."

"Sir Robert didn't approve—"

"Sir Robert," said Margaret, measuring her words carefully, "no longer lives here. His wishes hardly need concern you now."

"But what if you should want the carriage for yourself?"

"I won't. I am the proud possessor of no less than three horses suitable for a lady to ride, a gig and several other carriages besides the one reserved for family use. Or, if I am feeling too lofty to demean myself by using one of those, I can very well await your return. I will most likely be occupied much of the day with showing the new steward his duties, so don't worry about me, I beg. Go and enjoy yourself."

"Thank you, my dear," said Martha gratefully.

Margaret sighed. Martha tried so hard to please. It was a pity that her self-effacing demeanor annoyed Margaret so much. When Margaret tried to point out to her aunt that she was not a tyrant and did not require Martha to ask permission to use the carriage or have friends in for tea or purchase a new gown or place the parquet sewing stand in the parlor to suit her own convenience, Martha apologized profusely for leading Margaret to suppose she was ungrateful for Margaret's many kindnesses to her.

Because Martha was always so unfailingly considerate, Margaret felt obliged to be unfailingly considerate as well, which greatly chafed a young lady who had felt restricted all her life and would have enjoyed the freedom of coming and going according to her own whim. On the few occasions when she had followed her impulses rather than her duty and not come home precisely when she was expected from an errand or excursion, she was met at the door with questions about where she had been, lamentations because the wrap she had chosen was not warm enough, and exclamations about the lateness of the hour.

Margaret's physical needs had never been neglected as a child, but she hadn't felt particularly cherished, either.

Her aunt and uncle had treated her exactly as if she were a valuable but not particularly valued piece of porcelain. Margaret, as titular owner of the manor, was too important to be hidden in a closet. After all, his legal responsibility of serving as her guardian was Sir Robert's excuse for housing his own family in the manor. Even so, it always had been perfectly obvious to Margaret that, given their own inclinations, her aunt and uncle, though obliged to display her, would have preferred not to have had to look at her every day of their lives.

Margaret learned at a tender age that she was, in effect, the goose who laid the golden eggs, so they dared not let their resentment of her become too obvious. When she was a child, her aunt and uncle considered her high spirits tedious. When she was grown, they considered her outspoken intention of choosing her own bridegroom without reference to their wishes most unbecoming. As for her total indifference to the suit of their firstborn, they hardly knew how such an ungrateful girl could have been born.

The fact that Edward until recently hadn't appeared to like his cousin much above half was, in their opinion, irrelevant. They had raised Margaret with an eye to making her their daughter-in-law, not because they thought she and Edward would suit, but because it was only right that the daughter of the man who had bought his brother's legacy would rectify this error of fate and return it to the branch of the family to which it rightfully belonged by marrying Sir Robert's heir.

Although it was Sir Robert's own expensive lifestyle, or rather, that of his wife, which made it necessary to sell the manor, its adjoining property, and the handsome town house in London to his younger brother, he accepted none of the blame for his present impecunious circumstances. Sir Robert saw himself as the lord of the manor tragically deprived of his birthright, and he was shocked and angered that his chit of a niece would dare to defy his wishes and announce her intention of bestowing her hand and fortune elsewhere if it so pleased her.

When she entered the library, Margaret expected to find Frank standing nervously, hat in hand. After all, he was about to step into a position of importance in a gentlewoman's household, and he could be dismissed as easily as he had been engaged if he displeased her. Instead, he had seated himself comfortably in an armchair and was reading one of her father's books with every appearance of enjoyment.

"Forgive me, Miss Willoughby," he said, rising immediately when she entered. "I couldn't resist. What a wonderful collection of books! Are they your father's?"

"Some of them," she said. "But most of these are my maternal grandfather's. The bulk of my father's are at the town house in London. They were both great ones for reading, I understand. Of course, I never knew them."

Somehow the interview had not started on the footing she had wanted. She had intended to be very cool and very distant and very authoritative. This was thwarted, however, by their discussion of her grandfather's tastes in books.

"I see. That is probably why there are so many books about agriculture, but I see several classical works here that any university library would be proud to own," he said, interested. Then he brought himself up short. "I beg your pardon, Miss Willoughby. I am wasting your time. I await your orders."

She gave him an approving inclination of the head, grateful for his putting the interview back on the proper footing.

"That's quite all right, Mr. Watson," she said graciously. "There are a number of things I should like to discuss with you and perhaps we had better begin. But first, have you breakfasted?"

"Yes, I thank you, ma'am. Mathilde is very efficient."

"Excellent. Then we shall begin with the kitchens. I shall expect you to make arrangements for food to be delivered. I understand from what my cook says that our stoves are outmoded and extremely inefficient and wasteful of fuel. You will make arrangements for the necessary repairs and try to contrive with the least amount of disruption to my household. You will work closely with my cook in this endeavor. You speak French, I understand?"

"Certainly."

"Good. Marcel's command of the language sometimes deserts him, although I strongly suspect he understands English better than he wishes us to know."

"I see."

"Shall we?" she said, leading the way to the kitchens where Frank was shown the pantry and given a copy of one of Marcel's shopping lists so he could get an idea of the quantities needed. He also was given a list of all the procurers Sir Robert had used, but told not to rely too heavily upon it.

"Sir Robert," said Margaret stiffly when they were alone, "was used to give his custom to those procurers who were willing to give him the most generous — shall we call them tokens of their gratitude? As a result, I suspect we were provided with quite inferior provisions on a number of occasions at the most exorbitant fees. There was some fish served one day last week that caused both Aunt Martha and myself to — In short, I should expect that practice to stop without delay."

"Certainly, Miss Margaret," said Frank.

"Now I will show you the office in which you will work," she said, ushering him into a comfortable apartment equipped with a massive desk, a nice assortment of pens and paper, and several handsome pieces of furniture.

"My father's steward used this room whenever he was in the house," said Margaret, "and I have had it cleaned for you. My uncle discharged the poor man, of course, when he took over the property as my guardian. I hope you will find the room comfortable."

"I thank you, Miss Margaret," he said politely.

"I have placed this month's accounts on your desk," said Margaret. "I would appreciate it if you would study them carefully when I have finished showing you around. I also have moved all of the papers my uncle left behind to the large side drawer of the desk for you to examine as you get time. I didn't want any of the servants handling them because I assume they have to do with the estate."

"Very good, Miss Margaret," said Frank.

He followed her all over the house, to the stillroom, the dairy, the stables, even the attics and the cellars.

"Hmm," she said, lifting her skirt a fraction of an inch to keep it from being dirtied in the cellar, but taking great care not to expose her shapely ankles. She was suddenly conscious of the fact that she was alone in the cellar with a man who was, moreover, a total stranger, something quite new in her experience of rigorously chaperoned balls and demure outings.

"It appears my uncle has taken much of the wine with him," said Margaret wryly. "You must replenish my supply, particularly the champagne. I would see to it myself but, besides not caring for wine much above half, it would be quite unsuitable for a lady to have doings in a wine shop."

"Although I, personally, am not overfond of wine, I venture to say I am confident that I can give satisfaction, my late employer being in the business as it were, if you'll pardon the liberty, Miss Margaret," said Frank.

"Mr. Watson," said Margaret sweetly, turning to face him. "Will you do something for me?"

"Certainly, Miss Margaret."

"Do you think you could contrive to sound a little less like my butler?"

Margaret saw the flash of Frank's smile in the light of the lantern she had brought to light their way in the darkness of the cellar.

"I'm sorry," he said, amusement in his voice. "I've never been a servant and I'm not precisely certain how one is supposed to talk."

"I have not been acquainted with you for very long, Mr. Watson," said Margaret pensively, "but I

71

feel quite sure that is a shameless bouncer."

"Miss Margaret!" exclaimed Frank in scandalized accents.

"However, if I may venture to give you a hint," she continued, "you needn't address me as 'miss' quite so often. Only the servants who are old family retainers call me 'miss.' Unfortunately, that includes most of them. I am not called 'Miss Margaret,' by any of them except those who knew me when I wore short skirts and my nurse put my hair in braids. You will refer to me as 'ma'am' or 'Miss Willoughby,' if you please. And you are not precisely a servant, but my steward. There is a difference."

"I'll keep it in mind, ma'am," he said, laughing. "I am in the most dreadful quake. You have been so dauntingly lady-of-the-manorish today."

"Levity at my expense, Mr. Watson?" said Margaret, raising one shapely eyebrow.

"Never, Miss Willoughby!"

"Employing a steward is a serious matter," said Margaret carefully. "I wouldn't have you think I don't mean to exert proper control over my household. Don't make the mistake of thinking that because I am a woman you may order things as you choose in my house."

To her indignation, Frank burst into laughter.

"Are you *quite* through, Mr. Watson?" said Margaret quellingly.

"I beg your pardon, Miss Willoughby," he said. "I see I have offended you, and I truly did not mean to do so. The only excuse I can offer for my behavior is that, honestly, the thought that you would *not* mean to exert proper control over your household never entered my mind after listening to your detailed instructions for the improvement of your property for the past several hours."

"Good," said Margaret, mollified. "I see you *do* understand your position here. My uncle was inclined to underestimate my tenacity, and most of the servants were inclined to think my orders were subject to his approval. The stoves, for example, should have been replaced long ago. It is a wonder they haven't asphyxiated the cook and his staff long since. But since my uncle and his wife considered the plight of the cook and his staff beneath their notice, they saw no reason to waste good blunt, even if it was my blunt, on refurbishing the kitchens. It is not an easy task you have undertaken, for I expect you to repair the damage his neglect has caused over all these years. I hope you are equal to the challenge. Now we will return to the estate room."

They did. Margaret noticed with annoyance that she had gotten dirt on her white gown, and told Frank that since she already had soiled the hem, they might as well go out to the gardens, which she was sure were quite muddy after last night's rain, so that he might see them at their worst and hear her plans for their improvement.

The sight of these once lovely pleasure gardens gave Frank no favorable impression of his predecessor's competence. The grounds, which must have been quite excessively beautiful at one time, had been allowed to fall into neglect, although the effect was not totally displeasing in a wild sort of way. Margaret's Aunt Samantha, it seemed, deplored the necessity of ever going outdoors unless it were for an al fresco picnic or garden party, preferably at someone else's house, and the gardeners had fallen into slothful habits since Sir Robert himself never went into the gardens. Martha had once ventured to suggest to her sister-in-law that some of the less promising rosebushes might be torn out and others set in their place. She received a snub from which she didn't recover for some weeks.

"I see by your expression that you share my opinion of the gardens," said Margaret bitterly. "How could he have let it fall to rack and ruin like this? Of course, it was not Sir Robert's place to dig and plant, but his indifference allowed this neglect. I don't think I shall ever understand him, although I lived with him for twenty years."

Frank remained silent.

"You are quite right, Mr. Watson," said Margaret kindly. "It would be most unsuitable for you to venture a comment about one of my close relations, and it was most improper of me to phrase my remarks in a manner that seemed to invite one. I must try to guard my tongue in front of the servants, and in front of you as well."

"You may always speak your mind to me, ma'am," said Frank quietly. "It will never go further. I am not inclined to gossip with your inferiors."

"No," she said, much struck. "I don't believe you are."

"My reluctance to become familiar with your servants will not prevent me from ensuring that they will carry out your wishes, however."

"See that it doesn't," she said archly.

She was a bit surprised when Frank ventured no comment. It was not, as she had supposed, because he was chastened by her half-joking snub, but because a sight so magnificent had crossed his vision that he was quite distracted from Margaret for the moment.

He was facing the arched trellis that led to the gardens, and Margaret was facing him, so she could not see who had entered.

"As I live and breathe," said Frank in awed tones,

once he found his voice. "Manfred to the life."

"Manfred?" she said in astonishment. "Who is—oh, that silly hero of Lord Byron's who gnashed his teeth through an endless number of pages and finally put a period to his existence, crushed by the guilt of Unspeakable Crimes? Pray, what is he to the point?"

"And you said you were not literary," he said in mild reproach. "You are quite mistaken. There he is, and in the flesh."

Margaret spun around and saw with annoyance that the apparition was her cousin Edward. He looked magnificently angry as he strode toward them with his cloak flying in the wind and his strong, muscular thighs straining against their skintight pantaloons.

"Oh, bother," said Margaret in annoyance. "When I find out which of my servants have been bearing tales to my uncle, they will be dismissed *immediately.*"

"I beg your pardon?" said Frank, all at sea.

"My cousin Edward," said Margaret. "And I am sure I owe the pleasure of his visit to the fact that his father has found out I have hired a new steward. Sir Robert dares not approach me himself, so he sends my cousin."

"Your cousin must be *very* brave," murmured Frank.

An unwilling smile crossed Margaret's lips.

"For heaven's sake, don't make me laugh *now,* Mr. Watson."

"Laugh?" asked Frank, not liking the scowl on Edward's face. Edward was taller than Frank by a head, and outweighed him by at least a stone. While not precisely a cowardly person, Frank did not share Margaret's inclination to laugh.

"Don't let him frighten you," she said, amused.

"He really has the happiest nature when no one is annoying him. Unfortunately, I annoy him quite a lot."

By this time Edward had stopped stock still in front of Margaret.

"And you, I take it, are Watson?" Edward said belligerently, ignoring Margaret to address her companion. This breech of etiquette left her gasping with indignation.

"Edward, how *dare* you?" she exclaimed.

"Your pardon, Margaret," said Edward, without taking his eyes from Frank. "This doesn't concern you."

"Oh, it doesn't, does it?" she said, really angry now. "If not, I should like to know who it does concern! You will not address my employees without my permission. Is that clear, Edward? And I think, further, that when you leave the house you may take Sternes with you."

"Sternes?" asked Edward uneasily, tearing his eyes from his disdainful inspection of Frank to face her.

"Was he not your informant?" she said, raising her eyebrows. "Well, you may take him, anyway, along with any other of the servants who don't seem to recollect which Willoughby is paying their wages. I will tolerate no spies in my household, Cousin."

Edward's eyes fell before her. "Margaret—"

"Do you deny that someone in this house informed your father that I have engaged a new steward? Otherwise, how would he have known?"

Edward maintained his silence.

"You may as well take Betty, too," said Margaret tartly. "The girl did little enough before you turned her head with your attentions. She does virtually nothing now."

Edward's mouth dropped open at that.

"Margaret!" he exclaimed, shocked. Betty was one of the parlormaids, and Edward believed his gallantry toward that damsel had been discreet. Apparently he had been mistaken.

He was not so much embarrassed by Margaret's discovery of this liaison as he was shocked to hear a maiden of good family allude to matters about which she should have known nothing. At any rate, modesty should have prevented her from admitting she knew anything about them, particularly to a gentleman. It just went to show what a hoyden his cousin was, and he was further injured by her having confronted him with his indiscretion in front of an inferior.

"Edward!" retorted Margaret, mimicking his tone.

"Surely we should have this discussion in private," said Edward, giving Frank a sour look.

"I quite agree," said Margaret, "and we shall do so when I am not busy. In case it has escaped your notice, I am presently occupied with initiating Mr. Watson into his duties and I don't have time to argue with you, Edward. I will thank you not to interfere in my affairs. And if you will pass this message on to your father as well, I will be your debtor."

Outraged to see that instead of being prostrated with embarrassment Frank seemed to be enjoying their exchange, he was restrained by Margaret's presence from teaching the fellow a lesson in manners. Edward stalked from their presence, his dignity much compromised by the unpleasant sound of the soft, sluggish suction of his boots slogging through the soggy earth.

Margaret sighed.

"He's really not a bad sort," she said.

"If you say so, ma'am," said Edward, obviously unconvinced.

77

"No, I am quite serious," she said. "Edward is probably the best of my family, and I should hate to have an open breach with him, mainly for the sake of his younger sister, Anne. She will make her debut late this season. It's irregular, but she was too ill to be presented at the start of the season with the rest of the debutantes. I shall expect you to go to London with me in a week's time to help me open the town house and prepare for her ball. I promised her she would be launched from the London house, even though one of her mother's relations will be her actual sponsor."

"You will take me to London with you?" he said, surprised. "Who is going to supervise all the repairs you want me to make?"

"You will not have to remain in London beyond a few days, I should think," said Margaret. "Just long enough to make sure all is in order, and make arrangements for meat and produce to be delivered."

"Is the town house, by any chance, also in need of refurbishment?"

"No," said Margaret. "My aunt and uncle are fully sensible of how important an asset a town house is, and, since they were used to spending most of the season in my town house while Edward, Anne, and I were confined in the country with our governess, have kept it in tolerable repair. I might wish to change some of Aunt Samantha's furnishings. She has extremely flamboyant taste."

"Greek columns and armor?"

Margaret's eyes crinkled with amusement. "Like the dowager Lady Shallcross? I am surprised you remembered that. No. Nothing so sedate. Aunt Samantha, if you please, is very fond of chinoiserie. Like the Regent."

"Dragons and daggers? And masses of blood red

lacquer?"

"Something like that. Fitting, I must say."

Frank remained silent.

"There, you've made me do it again," she said accusingly.

"What?"

"Criticize my family in front of you as if you were an acquaintance of longstanding."

"I am flattered, ma'am."

"As well you should be," said Margaret lightly. "Come, let us return to the estate room. I would like to show you some plans for the gardens drawn up by my father. You would never think it to look at the gardens now, but there was once orange blossom in a hedge by gate. . . ."

Molly Harnish wandered with satisfaction through her new house. Of course it was not precisely a *new* house, being at least fifty years old. But it was the finest house Molly had ever expected to live in.

Since their arrival an hour before, Molly and her daughter, Rebecca Francine, had been going from one room to the other exclaiming in delight at each architectural wonder.

"Mama," said Becky, sounding very grown up for her three years, "where will I sleep?"

"With me in the square bedroom at the front of the house until you're old enough to have a room of your own, love," said Molly grandly, swelling with pride at her beautiful little girl.

Becky was a thin child, but Molly was confident that she would put on weight now that she was with her mother. She had big blue eyes and long, tangled flaxen curls like Molly's own, and an indefinable sweetness of expression like that of her unnamed sire's. She was more beautiful, Molly thought to herself, than any of the pampered, aristocratic children she saw taking their airings in the park with their nurses. Although the garment Molly wore had faded from its original hue long ago and hung rather limply on her body, she had somehow contrived to dress her daughter in blue figured muslin, crisp in its newness, and the tiny white velvet pelisse, an impractical extravagance according to Molly's scandalized mother, set off the child's petal-perfect skin.

Molly knew that her little Becky was destined for a better life than her own, and if it took every breath and every drop of blood in her body, Molly would see that her darling got it.

Molly caressed the reassuringly solid finish of each piece of furniture in fascination. The master bedroom boasted a fine brass bed with a handsome wool spread, not an ill-smelling, lumpy pallet like the ones she had slept on all her life. A smaller bedroom had been fitted with a child's white, narrow bed and pink muslin hangings, but Molly, after so long a separation from her daughter, intended for Becky to share the big bed with her.

There was food in the kitchen. Her benefactor had been somewhat apologetic because he hadn't had time to hire a servant for her, but she had laughed heartily at that.

What did he think? That she was one of those fragile, ornamental, useless ladies she saw going through the streets with a servant to hold each bandbox and another to hand milady down from her carriage lest she stub her dainty little toes?

Molly, rapt in her good fortune, would positively enjoy scrubbing these floors and cooking in her own kitchen. She would keep every surface clean and shining so her precious darling would never soil the pretty dresses Molly intended for her to have when she played with her dolls on these floors. She would cook her little one delicious food rich with cream and butter and eggs to make her big blue eyes shine and her round little cheeks glow. They would be happy, safe in their love for one another. It would be perfect.

Now if only—but he had made it clear that although he was willing to support her and little Molly, he had no intention of entering into a more permanent relationship with her. Molly knew he found her attractive. Although he was meticulously polite to her, there was no mistaking the look of admiration in his eye. It was a look Molly saw often on the faces of men, but she knew better than to succumb to it.

She knew what it was to have a child out of wedlock and to be dependent upon relatives for charity in order to survive. This would never happen to her again. Whatever she had done in the past, she was a wiser woman now. She would live chastely with her child in this lovely home that had been provided for her.

It would not always be easy, because Molly was a passionate woman for all that she had spurned the many advances made to her since Becky was born. She had a child to think of now.

Any man who wanted to enjoy her favors, Molly vowed, would have to marry her and give her daughter a good home. She had learned her bitter lesson well. Unless, of course, *he* would express an interest in her. For him, she might make an exception.

Would it be so unsuitable for them to make a match of it? Whoever his father had been and for all his fine education, he was only an unemployed seaman now. His position was above her own, but not *that* far, after all.

He'd promised to call on her to see how she did whenever he could get away to London.

And when that time came, Molly thought, smiling to herself, he would find her at her most alluring. She may not have a fine carriage and a different dress to wear every day of the week, but she could teach those highborn maidens a thing or two about pleasing a man.

Chapter Four

Frank was puzzled when the door to Margaret Willoughby's manor was opened to him by a frightened-looking housemaid after he had applied the knocker a good half-dozen times at genteel intervals.

"Mr. Watson," stammered the girl.

"Good morning," he said, sorry he did not know the servant's name. He waited, expecting her to stand aside and let him enter.

She didn't.

"Miss Willoughby is expecting me," he said with raised eyebrows.

"Oh, lawd a mercy," the girl wailed, opening the door wide and turning her back on him to run through the door that separated the hall from the rest of the house.

Frank entered, plainly wondering what was happening. Could Margaret have discharged Sternes after all? Even so, surely someone other than the housemaid should have been left to answer the door? Unless, perhaps, Margaret fired all the footmen, too?

Well, he didn't intend to stand in the hall for the rest of the day. He knew the way to the estate room which Margaret said was his to use while he was in the house. He thought his behavior might be interpreted as encroaching if Margaret learned he had simply walked into the house and taken possession of the estate room without sending a message to her that he had arrived, but there didn't seem to be anyone available to take that message to her.

He could hardly make his way to her private apartments and knock on her bedroom door. The day before she had had all the appearance of someone who rose early, but that may have been for his benefit only. For all he knew, she might still be in bed. He knew of some ladies with pretensions to fashion who never appeared outside their boudoirs before noon.

So he left his hat in the hall and began slowly to walk to the estate room, where he was met by Sternes. The butler's usual frozen composure was considerably impaired.

"Sternes," said Frank in concern. "Is something wrong? The door was opened to me by a housemaid or I would have—"

"Good morning, Mr. Watson," said Sternes. "We're all at sixes and sevens today."

"So I see," said Frank patiently, assuming that if he gave Sternes a moment to collect himself he would tell him why the house was in such disorder. "Is Miss Willoughby at home? She told me yesterday that—"

But at that moment Miss Willoughby herself, dressed in a very becoming but sadly crumpled morning gown of white muslin and her brown curls in wild disarray, stalked by them without speaking and entered the estate room. Frank exchanged a startled look with the butler and followed her in. Her distraught aunt, who had been following Margaret with a purposeful look on her face, cried out sharply as Frank prepared to close the door, and was admitted ahead of him.

"Ah, Mr. Watson!" said Margaret, "I am glad to see you. There is something you must see to without delay. How it has been allowed to deteriorate—"

"Margaret, my dear, I think we should send for the doctor!" said Martha with, for her, unaccustomed authority in her voice.

"There is nothing wrong with me except for a few scrapes and bruises. I am perfectly all right, Aunt Martha," snapped Margaret in annoyance. "But I think *you* should lie down for a few minutes. You look as if you might faint."

"I have never fainted in my life!" said Martha indignantly.

"No, of course not," said Margaret placatingly. "Don't mind me. I'm just upset—"

"Of course, you are upset," said Martha. "That is exactly why I want to send for the doctor—"

"No doctor!" said Margaret firmly. "Now I must speak with Mr. Watson."

"Yes, ma'am?" said Frank, hoping she was going to tell him what was happening. He perceived that Margaret's upper arm revealed by her gown's short puffed sleeves was scraped, and her fingers looked bruised. She had a small scratch on one cheek and her jaw was a trifle swollen.

"Ma'am, what has happened to you?" he exclaimed, perceiving the extent of her injuries.

"Don't *you* start," said Margaret in despair. "Mr. Watson, if you begin clucking all over me, too, I shall scream, and so I warn you."

"Well," said Martha affronted, "if you call it *clucking* simply to suggest a doctor—"

"No, Aunt Martha, I don't mean you. But Sternes looks as if he were presiding at a funeral and that blasted maid is shrieking the house down. You'd think the balcony railing had collapsed under *her* instead of—"

"What balcony railing?" exclaimed Frank. "You don't mean yours!"

"That's exactly what I *do* mean," said Margaret, "and I want you to have it repaired immediately, and all the other balconies and railings inspected as well."

"I should think so, ma'am," said Frank vehemently. "Are you sure you're all right? You look a trifle pale. Maybe you should sit down."

"Thank you, I think I will," said Margaret, who, now that the shock had worn off, was feeling decidedly shaky. Her shallow, rapid breathing caused Frank to look over her head at Martha and mouth the word "doctor." Martha nodded and ran off to order a footman to fetch Dr. Wilson.

"What have you done?" asked Margaret sharply.

"I have asked your aunt to send for the doctor, of course," said Frank matter-of-factly. "This is no time to be stubborn. Your color is not good, and I don't like the way you are breathing, if you want the truth. Now I am going to tell one of the servants I expect to find loitering in the hall with their ears to the door to bring you a glass of sherry."

Margaret sank back in the chair and closed her eyes.

"I think I should like that," she said.

"That's better," he said approvingly. He opened the door and singled out a footman.

"Tell Sternes to bring Miss Willoughby a glass of sherry," he said severely. "And the rest of you will go back to work, if you please."

Margaret heard the scurry of footsteps and smiled faintly.

"What a ramshackle household you must think this," she said. "A trifling accident and we all—"

"A trifling accident, do you call it?" he said, his eyebrows raised. "I call it a case of criminal neglect. You might have been killed."

"I *do* wish people would stop saying that," said Margaret. "It makes me feel quite sick."

"I am sorry," said Frank. He heard a discreet knock on the door and opened it to find Sternes with a glass of sherry on a tray.

"Thank you, Sternes," said Frank, taking the glass.

"Shall I bring something for you as well, Mr. Watson?"

Of course, thought Frank venomously. You'd love to be able to tell the rest of the household that I was tippling in the estate room at an indecent hour.

"No, I thank you, Sternes," said Frank. "Just be sure to deny Miss Willoughby to visitors except for the doctor, of course."

"Very good, Mr. Watson," said Sternes majestically. He lingered hopefully but, encountering the unmistakable look of dismissal in Frank's eyes, reluctantly left the room.

Margaret regarded the glass of sherry with distaste.

"Sherry at this hour!" she said ruefully. "Even Aunt Samantha was never so depraved as this."

"Don't joke about it," said Frank, handing the glass to her. "Here, drink this."

She did. In one gulp.

"Oh, blast," she said, coughing. "And if you *dare* laugh—"

"I assure you," he said, "I have rarely felt less like laughing. Do you think you can tell me what happened? *Which* balcony? As I recollect from the dia-

87

grams of the house which your father had drawn up, you have a corner suite with balconies outside your bedroom and sitting room."

"It was the one outside my bedchamber window," she said. "I was just about to go down to breakfast. I opened the French windows and went out on the balcony. I often do so in the morning. From up there the gardens don't look so bad. I leaned on the railing and it just fell off the side of the house. Thank heaven I managed to recover my balance and throw myself backward before it went. Oh, lord. I just lay there trying to get my bearings for what seemed like hours, only it couldn't have been. One of the maids walked into the room, calling my name. I had just rung, you understand, and she was answering the bell and didn't know where I was."

"My God," said Frank.

"You may well say so," said Margaret. "Well, I had just about recovered enough to begin crawling toward the French doors — I was afraid the whole thing was going to collapse and me with it — and she saw me and started shrieking the house down. It fair curdled my blood. Here I was, shaking and scraped, and I had hit my jaw. Oh, lord. It will probably turn purple and —"

"Good God! How you can care about that when you might have been — but then, you asked me not to say that," said Frank penitently. "I wonder how many other unsound balconies you have in the house."

"There. You are the first sensible person I've talked to today," said Margaret in approval. "There they were, clucking and whimpering all over me, and all I could think was, where next? Part of the stone floor of the balcony itself actually crumbled and came off with the railing."

Another rap sounded on the door and Martha entered without waiting to be admitted. By this time Margaret had closed her eyes and was leaning back in the chair again, Frank standing before her anxiously.

"I've sent a footman with a message for Dr. Wilson. How is she?" asked Martha.

"She'll do," said Frank.

"Why, thank you, Mr. Watson," said Margaret with a tremulous smile. "You will see to having the balconies inspected right away?"

"Immediately. I will send one of the servants to the ironworks in the village now, with your permission."

"Of course," said Margaret.

He sat down at the desk and began to write the message asking the master of the foundry to call on him at Miss Willoughby's house at his earliest convenience, a phrase which the man, as would any other craftsman residing in a county so dependent on the heiress's good graces, interpret to mean that he had better show himself without delay.

"On no account, Aunt," said Margaret, sitting up suddenly, "are you to go out on the balcony from your room."

"No, of course not, child," said Martha soothingly. "Don't worry about me. And I shall tell all the servants. I cannot see how the railing could have come loose. Surely it was bolted."

Margaret shrugged her shoulders, which had finally stopped shaking.

"The bolts rusted, probably," Margaret said.

"Would that explain why the stone floor gave way?" asked Frank thoughtfully, sealing an envelope.

"Possibly. I don't know," said Margaret. "That is for the man at the ironworks to say."

"Perhaps you should come with me to your room and lie down, dear," said Martha.

Frank noted that Martha, too, was looking rather pale.

"Perhaps you would like a glass of sherry, too, Miss Willoughby?" he asked her.

"Certainly not," said Martha stoutly. "I am not so poor a creature as to require stimulants because Margaret has met with an accident and been fortunate enough to escape serious injury. I have no patience with such foolishness."

"Yes, Aunt Martha," said Margaret apologetically. "You have remained calmer than all of us, except for Mr. Watson who wasn't here at the time, after all, and all I've done is snap and snarl at you. Poor dear, how do you stand me?"

"Very easily, I assure you," said Martha, smiling gratefully at her. "Now if you want to please me, you'll come upstairs and lie down on your bed until the doctor comes."

"Perhaps Mr. Watson will be so kind as to clear the hallway?" Martha added with a glimmer of humor.

"With the greatest of pleasure, ma'am," said Frank purposefully as he opened the door and proceeded to deliver a tongue-lashing to those servants who had nothing better to do than loiter about, hoping to be a witness to Margaret's distress.

He had no doubt that a much improved-upon version of a rumor that the mistress had narrowly escaped death in a spectacular accident already was known at Sir Robert Willoughby's nearby estate, and he wondered how that gentleman had received the news.

He was to know an hour after the doctor had come and administered a sleeping draught to Margaret, who protested, but swallowed it at her aunt's insistence.

A heavy knock sounded at the estate room door and, without waiting for an invitation to do so, Edward entered, looking grim.

"Good morning, Mr. Willoughby," said Frank with narrowed eyes. "How may I serve you?"

"You may tell me what the deuce has happened to Margaret!" he said. "Not a half-hour ago her head groom's daughter who happens to be my father's kitchen maid came carrying some tale about my cousin's being injured in a fall from a balcony. The maid said Margaret was found in a pool of blood. I came to determine the truth before the tale reaches my father's ears."

"The tale has been greatly exaggerated, but has some foundation in truth," said Frank dryly, not surprised that Edward should be on cordial terms with his father's kitchen maid. "Won't you sit down, Mr. Willoughby?"

"Yes," said Edward, grudgingly adding, "thank you."

"Miss Willoughby has sustained some scrapes and bruises," said Frank, "but other than that she is unhurt. She was badly shaken, however, and the doctor has administered a sleeping draught or you could see her for yourself. The pool of blood, I am happy to say, was pure invention."

"You relieve my mind," said Edward earnestly. "My parents greatly regret the estrangement that has grown up between themselves and my cousin."

"I am sure they do," said Frank, reverting to the dry tone with which he had begun the interview. He was thinking rapidly, trying to think of a way to get rid of his visitor. Edward was looking very presentable in correct morning attire and for reasons he

91

refused to examine, Frank was strangely reluctant for Margaret to see her magnificent cousin in this guise while she was in a weakened state.

But even if Edward hadn't been looking so damnably handsome, Frank still would have been anxious to get rid of him. Frank had only been acquainted with his employer for a few days, but he already knew her well enough to be certain that despite the fact that she had been incapacitated for most of the morning, she would, upon awakening, expect an accounting of his time, and he had better make it good.

"Do you happen to know when your father last had the balconies inspected?" asked Frank abruptly. "Miss Willoughby's injuries occurred when the balcony railing outside her bedchamber collapsed while she was leaning against it and nearly carried her with it to the ground."

"Good God!" said Edward, shocked. "I have no idea when the balconies were last inspected. I don't live with my parents, you know."

"Hmm. A pity," said Frank.

Edward turned an angry eye on Frank.

"See here, what are you implying?" he demanded. "If you are trying to suggest that my father neglected his duties—"

"I have done nothing of the kind," Frank said mildly. "Surely you understand that it is my responsibility to investigate what happened."

"Don't adopt that top-lofty tone with me, Watson," said Edward furiously. "I know very well what game you are playing."

"Indeed?" asked Frank. "Then perhaps you will enlighten me. I wasn't aware that I was playing any particular game."

"Oh, come now! To what do you think you owe

your sudden elevation?"

"Well?"

"To your resemblance to that poor, silly gudgeon, Jeremy Verelst, and well you know it. Margaret fancied herself in love with him just before he died, although I could have told her, if she'd been interested in *my* opinion, that any length of time in his company would have proved to her how unsuited they were. He was the wildest rake in town, but she refused to look at another man for years after he died. Now, just when she's beginning to recover from her morbid obsession and mix in society again, you intrude upon her, wearing his face, and plotting to ingratiate yourself with an impressionable, vulnerable young woman—"

"Impressionable? Vulnerable?" mused Frank. "Are we discussing the same young lady?"

"Damn you!" shouted Edward. "I won't be trifled with! You know very well what I mean. You've wormed your way into her confidence and influenced her to drive my parents away—"

"Oh, come now," said Frank, keeping a leash on his temper with great difficulty. "You're doing it a bit too brown, Mr. Willoughby. Your father and his wife had already vacated the manor before your cousin was aware of my existence."

Edward rose and looked down menacingly upon Frank, still seated at the desk.

"You won't get away with it, you know. Someday Margaret will come to her senses and regret her estrangement from her family. And you'll be out in the cold. I'd watch my step if I were you, Mr. Frank Watson. Don't think the whole county doesn't know what you are."

"If you are referring to my parentage," said Frank, rising to face his enemy, "I have never made a secret

93

of my origins. Miss Willoughby was perfectly aware of them when she hired me. And now, if you will excuse me, I have a great deal of work to do."

"With the greatest of pleasure," said Edward furiously. He turned on his heel and prepared to leave.

"I will tell Miss Willoughby you called," said Frank, sorry that he had angered his employer's visitor. After all, he reasoned, the man was probably so belligerent because he was worried about his cousin. "Your aunt is sitting with her. Perhaps you would like for me to send one of the servants to tell Miss Martha Willoughby you would like to speak with her."

"Why the devil should I want to do that?" said Edward, making it plain that he thought his aunt's feelings of little importance and, at any rate, was not about to waste his precious time on a dependent relation he and his parents hardly noticed was in the house during the twenty years of their residence.

The merest courtesy demanded that Edward send a message of reassurance to his aunt. Frank, who had heard Margaret's name linked romantically with Edward's by far too many people, hoped with all his heart that they'd never make a match of it. He couldn't imagine how she possibly could be attracted to him. As for Edward himself, Frank had no doubt that it was the lady's wealth and position, and not the lady herself, that attracted her rather self-centered cousin to her.

After Edward left, the master of the ironworks in the village called on Frank in some alarm, having heard a garbled version of the tale that had sent Edward posthaste to investigate. The honest soul thought it tragic that the young lady had thrown herself off the balcony in her melancholy over a love affair gone sour.

"No, Miss Willoughby has sustained no serious injury," said Frank, disabusing the man of his conviction that Margaret had self-destructive tendencies. Lord, Margaret would have a fit when she heard that one, thought Frank, wondering that he could be amused by the thought. "But perhaps you can tell me when the balconies were last inspected."

"Well, sir, that would be two years ago," said the man thoughtfully. "Remember it well. Sir Robert told me to concentrate on the rooms on the first floor and the third."

"Not the second floor?" asked Frank, surprised. Margaret's room was on the second floor, as was her aunt's, and most of the guest rooms. "What excuse did he give for not having the second floor inspected?"

"He said that the ironwork on those balconies was exceptionally fine, which I suppose you could say it is, if," he added with a sniff of distaste, "you have a taste for flowers and birds, which I don't, and Sir Robert wanted the ironwork on the first and third floor made to resemble it. The railings on the other floors were plain, and Sir Robert thought they detracted from the appearance of the house. He wasn't concerned about the safety of the railings. Only the appearance. I did the others the way he wanted 'em, much as it went against the grain. But custom is custom, my father always said."

"I see," said Frank. "How old are the railings on the second floor? Did you make them? I've inspected the one that fell, and it didn't look particularly old. I would guess that the railings were made in the lady's father's time."

"You would be right," said the man. "They were made about thirty years ago. I didn't make them. I was just setting up in business then, and I wanted the commission. But Miss Margaret's father had the other ironworker in the village do it. He's been out of business for twenty years now. He had a weakness for drink, just between you and me, sir."

"I see," said Frank thoughtfully. "At any rate, Miss Willoughby is most anxious to have you begin the inspection of all the balconies without delay, and to repair her own balcony at once, of course. The other inhabitants of the house have been instructed not to go out on any of the balconies until after you have pronounced them safe."

"We can begin this afternoon, if you like, sir."

"That would be most satisfactory," said Frank. "And I would be interested in your opinion of what made that particular balcony collapse."

"Yes, sir."

After he left, Sternes let himself into the room after a courtesy knock, giving Frank the distinct impression he had been listening at the door. Frank sighed. It was obvious he wasn't going to get much work done that day, and he wondered what his fiery employer would have to say about that.

"Mr. Watson, the cook asks would you like a tray brought to you here or will you have your luncheon in the breakfast parlor? Or perhaps you would condescend to eat in the kitchen. Marcel would like to consult you about the new stoves," said Sternes, making it plain that in his opinion the kitchens were far too good for this unwelcome interloper.

"The breakfast parlor will do very well. Then I shall meet with Marcel in the kitchen after I have eaten, if that is agreeable to him," said Frank.

Sternes looked at him with grudging respect.

"I'll tell him, Mr. Watson," he said.

Frank ate an excellent luncheon of cold, sliced sirloin of beef, crusty bread, and fresh asparagus in solitary state and visited the Frenchman in his domain after he had finished the last of the fruit and cheese. The bright-eyed, wizened little man greeted him with acclaim.

"Ah, Mr. Watson. You will build for me a beautiful new stove, yes?"

"Er, yes, indeed, Marcel."

"It is most remarkable! I have here several drawings of models which I think will be of the most perfect."

Frank examined the drawings carefully.

"Which would you prefer?" he asked the cook.

"This one," said Marcel eagerly. "It is very like the one Miss Willoughby bought for the London house. I asked at that time if one could be bought for this kitchen, too, but Sir Robert refused probably because, between you and I, Monsieur Watson, he and his wife spent more time in London than hére. And, if you please, the best time to install the new stove will be when Miss Willoughby is in London next week. We will have to prepare the cold meals while this is happening and we would not want the lady to be inconvenienced, no?"

"No. Or, at least, that will be a clever plan if the lady still is going to London next week. She has had a nasty shock, you know."

"If the little Miss Margaret say she will be in London next week," said the cook fondly, "she will be in London next week. She is a young lady of the most determined."

"So I have learned," said Frank. "The only problem is, I will be accompanying Miss Willoughby to London. And won't you be going as well? Who will cook for her?"

"She has that Jacques," he said disparagingly. "He does well enough when I am here. The young cousin's ball is not for some time, and, of course, I, my-self, will go to London *then*. The so-clumsy Jacques alone cannot be trusted to prepare for so important an event, although he can produce a palatable meal for the little Miss Margaret while she stays in town as long as she has no company and does not need to make too fine an impression. She will be dining out with friends much of the time, is it not so?"

"Quite possibly," said Frank, wondering at Marcel's command of the language. Surely Margaret told him the man spoke little English. Or, Frank thought, it was likely he pretended to speak little English so he could ignore any instructions which he found unacceptable.

"About the food, monsieur," said Marcel. "Do you permit that the fish be ordered from the shop of my choice? Sir Robert, he choose the shop of an inferior quality for reasons I could not say, but the fish, she smell bad, do you comprehend?"

"Yes. I trust your judgment, Marcel. I will order the food from the shops of your choice until Miss Willoughby has reason to be displeased with them."

"Oui, monsieur," said Marcel, clapping his hands. "For the little Miss Margaret, we will—"

"Don't misunderstand me, Marcel," said Frank, his tone light but his eyes stern. "I deplore the practice of accepting bribes from merchants in order to extract full payment from Miss Willoughby for inferior merchandise. I will not tolerate that practice whether it be exercised by Sir Robert or by any other of Miss Willoughby's employees. You *do* understand me, do you not, Marcel?"

"Monsieur!" exclaimed Marcel, shocked. "You would accuse me! It is an insult of the most serious! I overlook it because it is plain that this so crafty Sternes has been whispering lies into your ears about me, yes? I would never cheat the little Miss Margaret. Her uncle? He is a pig. I spit on him. But the little Miss Margaret shall always command my most inspired efforts. And her good aunt, also, the kind lady. Two ladies of the most sensitive and delicate, I shall serve with the last drop of blood in my body—"

"Yes, yes. Quite right, Marcel," said Frank hastily. "It was only a hint, you know."

"Tonight I have for Miss Willoughby and her aunt after their so terrible experience a little soup of chicken and fresh scallions, a breast of chicken sautéed just *so* in fresh butter, egg, and bread crumbs so delicate that it—"

"I'm sure they'll be grateful," said Frank, ruthlessly interrupting these raptures. "I will visit you again tomorrow after consulting Miss Willoughby about the stove. May I take these to show her?"

"Yes, monsieur. I am sure we will deal well together."

"Yes, so am I," said Frank, impressed by his rather effusive loyalty to his mistress. For the most part the cook's speech was rather too florid, but Frank detected more than a note of sincerity in it. "I enjoyed my luncheon very much. I thank you."

"You are most welcome, monsieur," said Marcel genially.

Frank passed through the hall to see a positive florist's shop being assembled in the entrance. The inevitable silver salver upon which visitors leave their cards was filled to overflowing. Margaret's suitors, no doubt, he thought dismally. Some were lingering in the parlor in hopes of catching a glimpse of their goddess. They reminded Frank of a pack of crows in their black capes.

Frank politely but firmly sent them about their business, assuring them that he would convey their compliments to Miss Willoughby in person, then spoke rather sharply to Sternes because he had allowed them entry.

"Miss Willoughby is not to be disturbed, Sternes," he said. "She cannot have those nodcocks kicking their heels all over the house."

At that moment Margaret, looking heavy eyed but rested, furtively put her head around the door to the hall.

"There you are," she said. "Mr. Watson, what progress have you made with the balconies?"

"Miss Willoughby! Should you be up?"

"Probably not," she admitted. "I feel rather stiff, but I will go demented if I have to lie in bed and pretend to be an invalid a moment longer. Let us go to the estate room. And Sternes, we are not to be disturbed by callers unless it is really important. Or, you might admit my cousin Edward if he calls. I shall never hear the end of it if he is refused."

"He has been here already," said Frank, displeased by her willingness to see her cousin and Sternes's obvious satisfaction at hearing that Edward was to be preferred over any other visitor. Sternes permitted himself a small smile of triumph that made Frank itch to wipe it off his face.

Then Margaret was leading Frank away from the hall and toward the estate room. She turned around and looked at him.

"Was he very rude?" she asked. "Edward, I mean?"

"Very," said Frank, but he was smiling.

"I'm sorry," said Margaret. "I hope he wasn't too outrageous."

"Well, he was. But he had reason to be agitated. It seems he heard some wild tale about your being found in a pool of blood."

"Oh. How rather interesting," said Margaret pensively. "A pool of blood. But *so* excessive, don't you think?"

"Then the master of the foundry heard you had thrown yourself off the balcony because of a failed love affair."

"What the devil!" exclaimed Margaret. "Mr. Watson, you made that faradiddle up! Please tell me you made that up!"

"No, upon my honor. That one is going the rounds of the village even as we speak."

"I shall die of mortification."

"Nonsense. It's perfectly obvious you did *not* throw yourself off the balcony or you wouldn't be alive to give them the lie."

"That is a comfort," said Margaret when she reached the estate room and seated herself in the most comfortable chair. "On the whole, I think I brushed through the business tolerably well, although I shall have this dreadful bruise on my jaw for a while."

"My dear Miss Willoughby," said Frank lightly. "You have only to appear in that face abroad for bruised jaws to become so fashionable that young ladies throughout Yorkshire will be wondering how they may follow your lead. Will they have their maids paint their faces in purple, do you think, or will they deliberately walk into doors to achieve the desired effect?"

Margaret sat bolt upright and stared at him.

"I was joking," he said mildly, disconcerted by her stare. She had paled slightly. He rose and walked toward her. "Are you all right?" he asked anxiously. She looked very strange, all of a sudden, and it had nothing to do with the bruise on her face.

She continued to stare at him, her lips parted.

"Miss Willoughby!" he said, beginning to be alarmed.

"What? Oh, forgive me," she said, smiling shakily. "It was only—" She broke off, in some confusion.

"It was only?" he prompted.

"I'm being silly," she said. "But when you were joking about the neighbors taking my lead, you suddenly looked and sounded just like Jeremy Verelst. He used to tease me in just that style because the other girls in the neighborhood were inclined to imitate the way I wore my hair and they copied my gowns. When I was eighteen I enjoyed setting the fashion in the neighborhood, and I wore the most outrageous gowns and jewels. I blush to think of deplorable figure I must have cut. My aunt encouraged this, partly, I suspect, because she was powerless to stop me from decking myself out like a jeweler's window if I chose, and partly because she secretly hoped I would make such a cake of myself that no one but her precious Edward would have me. I lost heart for the game after Jeremy died. But you never knew me when I was wearing peacock feathers and rubies the size of duck's eggs. So how could you have known?"

"I didn't," he said gently. "I was only joking. There are no ghosts here, Miss Willoughby."

"Of course. I know that," she said, rubbing her eyes. "It must be that horrid medicine the doctor gave me. It has made me stupid."

"Never," said Frank.

"Well, what have you accomplished today?" she asked, getting control of herself.

"Besides giving your accounts a cursory look, hiring the owner of the foundry to repair your balcony, and throwing your anxious suitors out of the house at intervals, I have inspected some drawings of the different models of stoves Marcel prefers and tenta-

102

tively made plans for the stove to be installed while you are in London next week. That is, if you are going to London next week."

"Of course I am," she said, eyebrows raised. "Why ever not?"

"Well, the thought did occur to me that you might still be overset by —"

"The accident? Nonsense. I am perfectly fit, although I probably look a bit worse for wear. I refuse to skulk at home because of a trifling disfigurement. Besides, I think most of it will fade before next week, don't you?" she asked anxiously.

"Very likely," he said, smiling. "I have found this pile of unpaid bills in the desk. Doubtless your uncle never got around to settling them. I assumed you would wish me to do so, but naturally you will want to look at them first. I will leave them here, for your inspection. Tomorrow I will send payment for those you approve. There seem to be a great many for cigars, wine, and clothing, presumably for your aunt because I cannot imagine what you would want with a silk turban decorated with diamond chips and ostrich feathers, or with such a great number of paisley shawls. Perhaps you will want me to send those to your uncle's home. Is there anything else you require of me before I leave the house tonight?"

"No, I think not," said Margaret.

"Then I'll take my leave," he said, standing. "Here are the sketches of stoves Marcel thinks will be most suitable. He likes that one," he added, pointing to a grotesque black iron model. "He says it is similar to one you had installed at your London house several years ago."

"And he must have as good a stove as Jacques's or lose face," she said sagely. "I see it is by far the most expensive, but we'll have it. He deserves it for tolerating the present condition of the kitchens for so long. Speaking of Marcel, I hope he has prepared something for Aunt Martha and me. I'm starving."

"He has made for you a soup of chicken and fresh scallions," he began in a villainous French accent, "and a breast of chicken of the most delicate—"

"Invalid fare," said Margaret, laughing, "but it sounds delicious." She rose. "Until tomorrow, Mr. Watson."

"Good evening, Miss Willoughby," said Frank.

As Margaret had hoped, the purple bruises faded within a few days and life returned to normal. She went all over the house with Frank, pointing out improvements she wanted him to make; visited the tenants with gifts of food and advice; and drank endless cups of tea with her suitors and visiting neighborhood gentry.

"I think I favor the silly chub in the puce waistcoat and the yellow pantaloons," Frank told her one day. "You never need fear attack by wild animals once he starts that infernal caterwauling."

"Philistine," said Margaret with a twinkle in her eye. "He wrote that song for me, I'll have you know, and I thought it very affecting. He compared me to a rose, and has somehow contrived to find azure depths in the bottomless silver seas of my delicate orbs."

"How perfectly revolting," said Frank.

"I know," Margaret said sadly. "I am afraid my eyes are a sore trial to him. There really isn't much that can be said for plain gray eyes, after all."

Frank, who could think of a number of more accurate ways to describe the subtle coloring as well as the delightful shape and expression of Margaret's eyes, strongly disagreed, but didn't dare say so.

She was wearing a very dashing riding habit in a

shade of velvet that resembled a ripe pumpkin and was carrying a tall green hat frosted with veiling in her hands. She was very fond of long rides through the countryside although she couldn't abide the thought of fox hunting, and she intended to enjoy a canter before she had to endure tea with the pastor, his wife, and Martha at the rectory.

"The gardens look better already," said Margaret into the awkward silence. "I saw you outside directing the gardeners."

"I'm glad you approve. I was going to have them plant some more rosebushes next."

"Good," she said, rising. He rose and remained standing until she was out of the room.

Then he began wading through more of the seemingly endless piles of paper that had accumulated in the office during Sir Robert's tenure. It was well after noon when he heard a timid knock on the door and opened it to Martha, who was looking anxious.

"Mr. Watson, have you seen Margaret?"

"No, ma'am," he said. "She was to have gone riding before having tea with you and the pastor."

"I know," said Martha, "but she hasn't returned. She should have been back before now. It isn't like her to be late. She has always been most careful to show proper respect to Pastor Wilkins and his wife."

"Do you know where she rides, ma'am?"

"She often goes by the chapel at Crossley," said Martha hesitantly.

"I'll just ride over that way and see if she has been detained," said Frank. "I'll probably find her meditating among the ruins. Isn't that what romantic young ladies do nowadays?"

"Oh, I would be so grateful," said Martha. "I hesitate to go myself unaccompanied. I'm a very indifferent rider. But I don't want to take a groom because the news will sweep the house that Margaret is missing, and you know how—"

"Yes, I know very well. I will find her. Why don't you send a message to the pastor saying you and Margaret have been detained?"

"Yes. I have already thought of that," said Martha.

Frank rode off toward Crossley fully expecting to find that Margaret had stopped somewhere along the way to pick wildflowers or visit with one of the tenants or, if she had reached the chapel, was staring at that ridiculous statue and wallowing in elevated thoughts.

So he was very surprised when he had ridden no more than a mile from the manor to find Margaret sitting glumly on a rock. She waved at him, her face lighting up with relief.

"Never have I been so happy to see anyone! I couldn't have walked much farther," said Margaret. Her beautiful riding habit was embellished here and there with leaves and twigs. Her hat was sadly crushed.

"What has happened to you? And where is your horse?" asked Frank, dismounting at once and drawing her to her feet. "Are you all right?"

"Of course. Mirabel threw me. Can you imagine? My gentlest mare. I have never been so deceived by an animal," she said, laughing.

"You're limping," he said.

"Yes. I think I hurt my ankle. Was there ever anything so provoking? The blasted mare must have run straight for the stables. No sugar for *her* when I get back. I do hope she isn't hurt."

"And I hope she is," said Frank. He bent and cupped his hands so she could place her boot on them in order to mount Sulieman. She hesitated for a moment with her hand on his shoulder and he returned her regard solemnly. Then she lowered her eyes and sprang lightly to the saddle.

Frank turned the horse's head around and began leading the animal toward the manor.

"What is his name?" she asked.

"Whose?" asked Frank, who had been absorbed in his own thoughts.

"This horse."

"Oh. Sulieman."

"That's a nice name. How old is he?"

"I really have no idea. He's not mine. I hired him from the innkeeper in the village."

"Oh," said Margaret thoughtfully. She was no judge of horseflesh, but perceived that Sulieman had seen better days. "You know, if you need a horse you could very well borrow—"

"No, Miss Willoughby, I cannot very well borrow one of yours," said Frank firmly. "Sulieman answers my purpose very well. And the day he stops answering my purpose, I shall make other arrangements."

"I am interfering again," she said penitently. "Don't be vexed."

"Certainly not. I am sure you meant it kindly," he said. "I didn't mean to be abrupt. Have you ever had any trouble with that particular animal?"

"Mirabel? Never. She's the best-mannered of my saddle horses, or so I thought. I bought her two years ago, and she's always been my favorite."

"This isn't a particularly rough piece of track," he said thoughtfully. "How did you happen to fall?"

"I do appear to have a tendency towards accidents lately, don't I?" she said ruefully. "She was restive ever since we started. Then she simply reared up and threw me. I wasn't expecting it and I fell into some underbrush. My beautiful habit! And my new hat!

107

I'm sure the pastor would say I have received my just desserts for thinking so well of my appearance in them this morning."

"You were fortunate again," he said grimly.

"Yes," she agreed.

Before long they arrived at the stables and Frank talked with the head groom while Margaret pretended to scold Mirabel and gave the mare a lump of sugar from her pocket.

"She came in not twenty minutes ago, Mr. Watson," said the groom. "We were about to organize a search for Miss Margaret when the young lady's aunt told us you were already gone looking for her. The boys and me would have been on your trail in another few minutes."

"Was Mirabel all right when she came in?"

"Yes," said the groom. "She fretted something fierce until I found the thorn. It was a big one, lodged under the saddle. Peculiar something like that could get worked so far in, ain't it?"

"Yes," said Frank thoughtfully. "Peculiar."

"Miss Willoughby," Frank said, addressing his employer. "Your aunt is waiting for you to go to tea with her."

"The pastor!" exclaimed Margaret in a conscience-stricken tone. "At least I know nothing shocking can happen to me at the rectory."

She turned away and started for the house, carrying her crushed riding hat and favoring her right foot. Frank turned abruptly to the groom.

"Have there been any strangers loitering about the stables lately?" he asked.

"No, sir. No one. Only a few of Sir Robert's men who came to see if we could accommodate some of his guests' mounts. Part of the stable roof collapsed years ago at his house and he never seemed to get around to having it fixed."

"Sir Robert's men," said Frank slowly.

"They're all right, though," said the groom. "I know them. But as for strangers, no, sir. There haven't been no strangers."

"Thank you," said Frank, not liking the thoughts that were going to keep him awake most of the night.

Chapter Five

Frank Watson had spent four years routinely forti-
fying a merchant ship with provisions for nearly a
hundred men on sea journeys lasting for months between ports. Naively, he thought that this endeavor
had strained his ingenuity to the limits.

He was greatly mistaken.

In fact, the effort of negotiating with various
thieves throughout the Seven Seas for manifests that
included items such as three hundred live chickens, a
hundred salt hams, twenty kegs of rum, and several
hundred dozen lemons to keep the scurvy at bay was
mere child's play compared with the superhuman effort required to transport the prodigious number of
servants, bed linens, ball gowns, and saddle horses
deemed essential to the minimal comfort of one
small lady on a visit of a mere six weeks to her London town house.

It would have been a trying week, even if it hadn't
been for the backbreaking labor involved in preparing for the journey. Frank also supervised the refurbishing of the gardens and kept a watchful eye on the
repair of Miss Willoughby's balcony.

In addition to his official duties, he had assigned
himself an unofficial one—that of keeping a protect-

110

ive eye on Miss Willoughby herself. He was highly suspicious of the accidents she had had since he took up his post in her household.

Miss Willoughby was not a clumsy person, yet she had met with a number of potentially serious mishaps, ranging from the spectacular ruin of her balcony to a narrowly prevented tumble from the stairs leading to the third floor because of a loose runner. If he had not been following her up the stairs and managed to catch her, she might have broken her neck on the treacherous, nearly vertical steps with their sharp angles.

She dismissed the incident with a blush at finding herself so abruptly captured in his arms and a shaky apology for her clumsiness. He set her on her feet carefully and made a notation in a little notebook he carried with him, an action which allowed her time to regain her composure. A short time later, the steward was seen with a hammer and nails on the stair, fixing the runner himself.

Despite an attempt on both their parts to minimize the incident, Margaret had fallen with enough momentum that she easily could have swept them both to their deaths, and they both knew it.

Frank's disquiet was heightened by the knowledge that Margaret was the only one who used that particular stairway. The servants used the plain wooden, but infinitely safer back stairs. The only room in use on that floor was the schoolroom library, where Margaret kept her personal collection of books because she considered it somehow disrespectful for her copy of *The Mysteries of the Udolpho* to rub shoulders, as it were, with her father's more scholarly tomes, and her grandfather's practical ones. Her aunt never ventured to the third floor, having more literary tastes and preferring to keep her private

111

cache in her own room.

Frank's attempt to organize Margaret's journey also was greatly complicated by the fact that Margaret's servants were strongly divided into two camps: the pro-Sir Robert forces led by Sternes, the butler, who thought it undesirable as well as unnatural for the young lady to hire an unknown steward in the place of her devoted uncle; and the pro-Watson forces, led by Miss Poole, Margaret's dresser, who always had been jealous of Sternes and would have allied herself with the devil himself to confound him.

So, on the morning of the journey while Frank should have been checking items off the long list he carried in order to ensure nothing would be left behind, he was in the ridiculous position of arbitrating a pitched battle between Margaret's superior, city-bred dresser, and Sternes, an old campaigner who had a gift for reducing dressers and ladies' maids to tears without speaking a single word that could be construed as evidence against him.

But Miss Poole was made of sterner stuff than any of the butler's former victims, although she was on shaky ground in this encounter. The adversaries stood their ground and uttered their insults with all the dignity of their relative positions and enough venom to bring about the demise of a good-sized elephant.

It took all of Frank's patience not to discharge both of them on the spot. The only thing that stopped him was uncertainty as to whether he had the authority to do so.

He had no difficulty in breaking up the small knot of servants that had formed a sort of Greek chorus to the hostilities as the group underscored the remarks of their respective champions with smug exclamations of approval at verbal slashes which cut skillfully close to bone. But dislodging the combatants themselves proved more difficult.

Frank was astonished and thoroughly disgusted when he learned the nature of the earth-shaking issue that had precipitated the crisis.

"Miss Poole," said Sternes with his usual dignity, "this carriage is reserved for the upper male servants of the household and I would not demean the tone of the company by conveying that filthy creature in it. Permit me to say that only a female devoid of the least sense of propriety would even suggest it."

Miss Poole, brandishing the birdcage menacingly, was recalled to herself by a squeaking protest from her feathered charge, which had been thrown off its perch abruptly by her agitation.

"Mr. Sternes," the dresser said coolly. "Miss Margaret never goes anywhere without her pet. She even had a gown made to match the creature. It would be most unaccommodating of you not to convey it for the mistress. You have always performed this small service for her in the past."

"And I assure you I would have done so this time, as well, if you were sharing the family carriage with Miss Willoughby," returned Sternes haughtily. "Naturally Miss Willoughby herself cannot be inconvenienced by the bird's noise on such a long journey. However, on this journey there is no reason why the bird should not accompany you in the carriage with the parlormaids. There can be no question of the bird's disturbing anyone of any consequence in such a company."

A tic manifested itself at the corner of Miss Poole's mouth.

Miss Willoughby's failure to include her dresser with the passengers of the family carriage rankled, but Miss Poole had been confident that her dignified way of receiving the news had hidden the dismay she felt at the slight.

"You know very well, Mr. Sternes, that Miss Willoughby is taking her aunt with her to London this time," said Miss Poole, "and that is the only reason why I am traveling elsewhere."

"Far be it from me to call any female a liar," said Sternes, eyebrows raised. "Let me assure you that no one attaches any special significance to your fall from Miss Willoughby's favor. I haven't heard it mentioned in The Room above a half-dozen times, and so your loss of face, which seems so severe now, will not be remembered above a fortnight."

"It was no such thing," said Miss Poole, her cheeks growing red and her jowls quivering.

"I am told that in town the more superior dressers often accompany their ladies everywhere," said Sternes, malice dripping from his voice, "but in the country ladies fall into the habit of consulting their own wishes rather than what is strictly proper. Of course, there is no question of Miss Margaret Willoughby's aunt not taking precedence over a mere dresser, but Miss Martha Willoughby's maid, certainly, being so much younger than yourself, could have ridden with the parlormaids. No one could blame Miss Willoughby for procuring the company of an attractive young female on the journey instead of one so worn down by her many long years of service that she is inclined to fall asleep in the coach and offend the sensibilities of her mistress with her snores."

"Well, none of us are what we once were, Mr. Sternes," said Miss Poole with an edge to her voice. "I would not be surprised if Miss Willoughby wishes to engage a butler more conversant with the ways of polite society. After all, you had never been employed in a house of good ton before your engage-ment here, and certainly it was fortunate for you that your brother was in service with Sir Robert Wil-loughby before his retirement and provided the proper reference. I have often heard it said that town polish is as essential to a gentleman's butler as it is to the gentleman himself. *You* appear to be the proof."

Frank felt it incumbent upon him to intervene at this point, as Sternes looked about to forget himself and commit violence toward a female.

"Sternes," he said, despising himself for his petti-ness but despising the butler even more for his cruel baiting of a woman who had been slighted by her mistress and was attempting to survive the disgrace with a modicum of her dignity intact, "take the cage."

"Of course, Mr. Watson," said Sternes, sniffing in a haughty way, "if you say so."

"I say so," said Frank.

Sternes, utterly defeated, took the cage and en-tered the coach containing two footmen, who were so unsuccessful at controlling their grins that Sternes made their entire stay in London quite hideous with his bullying and unreasonable demands. However, both thought being privy to the spectacle of Sternes playing nursemaid to a bird well worth the price.

Frank turned to the triumphant dresser, who smiled at him so gratefully that instead of delivering himself of the dignified lecture he had intended, he merely accompanied her to the coach filled almost to capacity with female servants and handed her in with a grace that would have done justice to an earl. He was amused to see from the expressions on the faces of her traveling companions that this personal atten-tion from Miss Willoughby's protégé did much to el-evate Miss Poole's consequence, although the maids might reasonably have resented sharing their limited space with her. The addition of a noisy bird in an elaborate cage to these cramped conditions would have rendered the coach intolerable.

He saw the coaches containing the servants and the linens off a good hour before he dispatched the coach containing Margaret's gowns and hats.

And it was two hours after that when he respectfully handed the elder Miss Willoughby, her maid, who watched Frank out of the corner of her eye with a roguish look which he steadfastly ignored, and Margaret herself into the beautifully upholstered traveling coach and stood back so Marcel could present his parting tribute to the mistress, a basket of fruit and sweets to give her and her companions sustenance on her journey.

He estimated that the servants, who would be traveling straight through to London while Margaret and her party would break their journey several times for refreshment on the way, would have ample time to ready the house to receive its mistress.

Then Frank mounted Sulieman and gave the signal for the last coaches to depart. He intended to ride by the side of Margaret's coach the whole way along with four stalwart outriders, which surprised Margaret, who had expected him to ride in one of the other coaches. As far as she was concerned, his responsibility for the journey itself would not resume until they arrived at the town house. However, she assumed he merely wanted to enjoy the exercise in the fresh air and sunshine, and dismissed the matter from her mind.

But the journey was not to go smoothly. To Frank's vexation, they had only been on the road three hours when an outrider from the front of the cavalcade rode back to tell Frank that the first coaches were being prevented from continuing their journey by an obstruction across the road, and that a dispute had grown up concerning how best to remove it and, as a consequence, the men were engaged in arguing instead of remedying the situation.

With a smothered oath, Frank told Margaret what had happened and rode on ahead with the four brawny grooms to supervise the removal of the object, whatever it was. They were far from any town or posting house that could afford the ladies shelter or refreshment, so Frank hoped the obstruction could be moved quickly. It would not do for his employer to waste her whole day kicking her heels in the coach.

He soon found that the impediment consisted of a number of trees which were lying in the road, and was disgusted that the footmen in one of the coaches could not have dislodged such a simple barrier without his supervision.

He had dismounted and instructed the men to attach ropes to the trees and have the horses pull the trees out of the way when he noticed something curious. All the trees were sawed off evenly, giving the impression that the obstruction had been placed across their path quite deliberately. There were fresh stumps by the side of the road.

Now who would go to the trouble of cutting down trees only to . . . He had the answer. To the astonishment of the men, he mounted his horse quickly and rode back down the road toward Margaret's coach, hoping he'd be in time.

He wasn't.

"Stupid, stupid fool!" he scolded himself as he rode to the rescue. "The oldest trick in the world!"

Margaret's coach was stopped and in front of it were two masked men demanding that the passengers

117

alight from the coach. Frank had drawn off the able-bodied grooms who should have protected Margaret from attack and rode off like the damnable fool he was to investigate a red herring that shouldn't have fooled a child, leaving his principal charge exposed to the mercy of predators.

Martha Willoughby and her maid, whose frightened screams reached Frank distinctly, had already gotten out, and one of the men was making a menacing gesture through the open door of the coach, presumably toward Margaret. Frank didn't have a weapon, but he didn't think of that. He rode straight for the intruders and would have knocked one down if the man hadn't had the presence of mind to jump out of the way. A third foe was on horseback, and brandished a purposeful-looking weapon at Frank.

A bullet whizzed by Frank's ear, and Frank prepared himself to meet his death, only to realize the shot came not from direction of the man on horseback, who had been so startled by it that he had dropped the pistol, but from the coach.

"Blast it, Mr. Watson," Margaret exclaimed furiously, her lips white. "I almost shot you! Why did you have to come riding in like a hero? I was only going to scare him, and then you got in the way. You could have been killed!"

Frank stared in disbelief at the small but serviceable pistol in Margaret's dainty, gloved hand.

"Where the devil did that come from?" he demanded.

"My reticule," she said blandly. "I always carry it. Holdups on the London road are quite common, you know."

Frank, feeling foolish, turned to see the horseman ride away as if all the fiends of hell were on his trail.

"He's escaping," Frank said, entertaining visions

of handing the robbers over to the Bow Street Runners if only he could have thought of a way to convey them to town.

"Oh, let him go," said Margaret crossly. "And Bessie, stop that screeching at once! We were never in the slightest danger!"

She glanced at Frank, and his thunderstruck expression made her laugh, although the sound was accompanied by an edge of hysteria. The two other culprits were looking rather alarmed because in the confusion their horses had run away, leaving them stranded.

The drama was ended, and the farce begun.

"Poor Mr. Watson," said Margaret. "You thought you were riding to my rescue and I, ingrate that I am, almost shot you for your pains. I am much obliged to you. Now stop looking as if you'd like to murder me."

"I had not thought I was so transparent, ma'am," said Frank grimly.

"Oh, but you are. In fact, you are very much in the way. My 'real' hero will be very much annoyed with you. You see, I recognized these poor men as Mr. Stanhope's grooms. I saw them on a visit to his home several weeks ago and I rarely forget a face. I wonder what can be keeping my rescuer—ah, here he is."

At that moment, a man in a swirling black cloak rode up to them, brandishing his own weapon.

"Stand aside, vermin!" he shouted. "Unhand those ladies and come receive your punishment, if you dare!"

Obviously, he mistook Frank for his third accomplice and nearly fell off his horse when he got a glimpse of Frank's face. Frank recognized the young man as one of Margaret's more persistent suitors and comprehension dawned, making him feel almost as ridiculous as the silly cawker who had tried to win his lady's hand by staging a bogus robbery and rescue.

Instead of swooning into his manly arms as Mr. Stanhope had anticipated, the object of his ardent devotion was instead regarding him with decided disfavor.

"Mr. Stanhope, you deserve that I should shoot you here and now," said Margaret indignantly, "but I will refrain because there is little harm done. What a silly scheme! You should have chosen your tools more carefully if you expected me to imagine myself in deadly peril. Surely you didn't think this schoolboy's prank would succeed."

Stanhope's eyes boggled at the sight of the small lethal weapon in his beloved's hand.

"Miss Willoughby!" he exclaimed.

"Are you afraid I'll do myself an injury?" she asked scathingly. "Don't be. I am quite a competent shot. My cousin Edward taught me one summer when he had nothing better to do. Would you care to challenge me in a show of sharpshooting? I'll engage to hit as many wafers as you do. No? Mr. Watson, perhaps you will hand Mr. Stanhope his hat before his horse tramples it. Thank you."

Frank handed Mr. Stanhope his much abused headgear with a flourish, and he wasn't surprised by the look of unadulterated hatred that he received for his pains.

Mr. Stanhope disappeared in a fine cloud of dust, leaving his two embarrassed servants to find their own way home. They departed from Miss Willoughby's entourage on foot, looking extremely foolish. One of them even attempted a stumbling apology, which was cut short by an exclamation from Frank that he'd be damned if he would leave the horses standing in this wind any longer while he listened to their prattling.

Frank bent a fiery eye on Miss Willoughby's coachman and the groom, who barely had been suppressing their laughter at Mr. Stanhope's discomfiture. The smiles were wiped abruptly from their faces when they perceived the forbidding look on Frank's face.

"I hope you enjoyed our little entertainment," Frank said savagely. "Perhaps when we reach London you will explain to me how it is that your mistress was compelled to defend herself with her own weapon against presumed attackers while you kept to your seats like a pair of stuffed fowls and waited for *her* to protect *you!* Did you not remember the firearm I gave you before your departure?"

After much stammering, the coachman admitted that he wasn't much of a shot, and he had feared he would hit one of the ladies.

"But, Mr. Watson," Margaret protested. "I didn't want them shot! They were only a pair of grooms who were taking part in a ridiculous prank!"

"Your coachman and groom didn't know that," said Frank stubbornly. "We shall continue our discussion in London," he added to the squirming miscreants.

"Shall we proceed?" asked Frank, offering his hand to Martha and assisting her into the coach. Bessie, quieted now and looking oddly appealing with her pretty face streaked in tears, followed the older woman, who had been whispering soothing sounds in her direction since their "rescue."

"Oh, lord," said Margaret ruefully when her companions were inside, with the door closed behind them. It was obvious that Frank had something on his mind, and it would be a dashed unpleasant interview. Inexorably, he led her a little way from the coach, out of the driver's and groom's hearing. Margaret rambled on, hoping to distract him from giving voice to his indignation. She was oddly reluctant to alienate him, even if he was a paid employee and was compelled to swallow his sense of injury.

"Remind me never again to prefer Bessie's company to Miss Poole's on a journey," she said. "I only had Bessie because she occupies less space in the coach, and she is usually perfectly willing to perform simple tasks such as unraveling Aunt Martha's needlework, whereas one could *never* ask a dresser of Miss Poole's stature to do so homely a task."

"I am sure Miss Poole would be delighted to hear you say so, ma'am," said Frank, his good humor quite restored by the thought that Margaret would be well served for scaring him half out of his wits by being compelled to share the rest of the journey with a watering pot. He was further mollified by the thought that Margaret, despite some of the truly frightening things that had happened to her in his presence, had never yet succumbed to vapors or hysterics.

"It is too late to exchange companions now, however," he added. "I have every confidence that the obstruction has been removed from the road and Miss Poole will reach London in good time to bully the footmen and the maids witless in the handling of your ball gowns. Was it necessary to bring so *many* of them, ma'am? They took up a whole coach."

"Poor Mr. Watson," said Margaret with a twinkle in her eye. "Do you begin to perceive that my uncle's lot, though an enviable one, was not always an easy one?"

"Indeed, yes," he said feelingly. "If he has been organizing your journeys to and from London for the past several years, he's a stronger man than I, and I owe him an apology for the aspersions I've been casting upon his competence."

"Actually," Margaret admitted, "he saw to few of the details himself. He trusted the servants to go about the business on their own, which resulted in some hideous journeys and much of the baggage being left behind. I must compliment you. I don't think I have ever journeyed to London with so organized an entourage."

"You gratify me, ma'am," said Frank. "Now if you'll excuse me, I'll ride on ahead to make sure your admirer's barricade has been removed. Be forewarned that if I ever again find him floundering at your feet like a lovesick whale, I shall personally throw him out of the house!"

"Why, Mr. Watson," Margaret admonished him. "I hired you as a steward, not a chaperon. I shall find my court quite fallen off if you mean to do violence to every gentleman who pays attention to me. I want no dragons guarding my gate, sir. Especially since I expect to be married within the year, and so I haven't much time in which to make my selection."

"You are funning, of course," he said curtly. "I wish you would not joke about such a subject. If your idle words get abroad we'll have every old court card within miles—"

"But I'm quite serious," she said lightly, a smile curving her lips at his obvious dismay. "I will be quite on the shelf if I remain unwed much longer. And society will pity me, and I'll have to take to wearing caps and purple gowns. That would *never* do for the dashing Miss Willoughby, don't you agree?"

"You mean it, don't you?" he said, appalled. "You

really are going to marry one of those silly cawkers—"

"Yes, I am," said Margaret with determination in her voice. "Just as soon as I find one who is content to take the advantages I can offer without expecting me to love him in return. It wouldn't be fair to lead a man to expect—in short, I don't think I'm capable of that tender regard a gentleman has a right to anticipate in the lady he marries.

"Fortunately," she added in a brighter tone, "it shouldn't be difficult to find a man who would be willing to enter a loveless marriage for the sake of a fortune."

"What fustian nonsense is this?" said Frank, barely restraining himself from taking her slim shoulders between his strong hands and shaking her until her teeth rattled. "My considerable respect for your intelligence has been misplaced if you would close yourself off from every chance of happiness because of your attachment to a dead man. Jeremy Verelst was never worth even one of your tears, Miss Willoughby."

"How would *you* know?" she asked, affronted.

"I know," he said grimly. He looked toward the coach, and was annoyed to see that both of Margaret's fair companions were peering curiously at them from the window, obviously wondering what they were discussing so heatedly when it was time to resume their journey. "I must leave you to go see if they've managed to remove the barrier. I'll ride back and bring some of the other outriders with me to flank your coach the rest of the way."

"Don't worry," Margaret said, her tone dripping with sarcasm. "I don't think there will be any more daring rescue attempts today."

They arrived at the London house very late the

next day, Margaret's party being forced by an unexpected thunderstorm to take shelter in an inn for the night and most of the following morning. Despite the warmth of the spring evening, Margaret was glad to see a fire burning cheerfully in the grate of the parlor.

After removing her light pelisse and hat, she sank gratefully into an armchair and sighed with relief. She would have gone straight to bed if she hadn't known that Jacques the cook was at that very moment preparing a special dinner for her delectation. Jacques had every intention of impressing Margaret with his skill before his rival, Marcel, arrived to prepare for Anne Willoughby's ball in a few weeks, and Margaret was far too good-hearted to spurn the meal he had labored upon all afternoon in anticipation of her arrival.

She also knew that if she went to bed and had a tray sent to her room, Martha would do likewise even though Martha hated eating in her room. But Martha, who feared the stigma of being thought an encroaching poor relation above all else, would never dream of allowing the servants to set the dining room table for herself alone, and there was no one in the house her equal in social rank to share her meal except for Margaret.

Margaret allowed a pleasant languor to steal over her body and anticipated an early night abed once the long ceremonious dinner was over. Martha, she knew, was upstairs doing her own unpacking because she considered it encroaching to let any of the servants do it for her. Martha clung tenaciously to her small shows of independence, which left the maid Margaret had so considerately hired for her with little to do.

So Miss Willoughby expected to be quite alone

with her thoughts in the interval before dinner. She closed her eyes and let herself be lulled into a light doze by the comforting sounds of the town house coming to life under the practiced ministrations of her servants.

She was surprised, therefore, to be interrupted by Frank's voice as she dozed. She opened her eyes with a start, possessed of the most horrid feeling that he had observed her asleep, with her mouth open.

"Forgive the intrusion, ma'am," he said politely. Had she imagined his earlier anger? "Do you require anything from me before I go to the inn?"

The note of stiffness in this very proper speech told her that she had not imagined his anger, and she wondered why her intention of taking a husband should so annoy him. Then she thought she knew. But of course! When she took a husband, she would no longer need a steward. Her future husband would manage the estate himself, or have his own steward do so. Margaret felt something like disappointment sink her spirits, then quickly stifled it when she realized what Frank had just said.

"The inn? Whatever are you talking about?" she asked, rubbing her eyes. "I am not usually so slow-witted. I don't remember anything about an inn, and why would you be going there at this hour?"

"To retire, of course, ma'am," he said, surprised.

"But surely you will stay here," she said. "There is plenty of room."

"You cannot be serious," he said.

"Why not?" she asked.

"Because it would not be proper," he said. "You are an unmarried woman and I am an unmarried man."

"Do you think people would talk?" she asked, laughing. "Why should they? You're my steward.

126

And Aunt Martha is here."

Frank's mind boggled at the thought of Martha as the stern chaperon protecting her niece's virtue, even if Margaret *was* perfectly safe from him.

"You will forgive me for saying so, ma'am, but I doubt if your meek aunt, much as I esteem that lady, would be of much use in protecting your reputation if it became known that an unmarried man was housed under your roof."

"Why, Mr. Watson," said Margaret, wide-awake now, "I had no idea you were so stuffy. Whose reputation are you worried about, really? Mine or your own?"

"Both," he said, looking injured, "and it isn't a laughing matter."

"Well, then, I must be very stupid because I think it is *very* funny," said Margaret. "Now I've offended you."

"Not at all," he said politely.

"Yes, I have. I can see it all over your face. Why can't we deal together today, Mr. Watson? We were in such complete accord all last week. That is, except when you became so tiresome about my refusal to take a groom out riding with me."

"You won't go out riding alone in London, I should hope," he said, shocked.

"No, I won't do that," she said soothingly. "I am not *totally* dead to convention. I suppose you gave my coachman and groom a thunderous scold. I wish you would not."

"On the contrary," he said, rising to the bait. "I would have discharged them if it were left to my discretion, which you made perfectly plain was not the case."

"Ah, that rankles, does it?" asked Margaret. "You'd like to turn them both off without a character, I have little doubt. Well, I forbid it. They have been with my household these past fifteen years. Henry Coachman even taught me how to drive my gig when I was in my teens."

"As you wish, ma'am," said Frank, much affronted. "I am only concerned for your safety."

"Oh, for heaven's sake," said Margaret, nettled, "I wish you would stop acting as if there were a gang of forty cutthroats outside my parlor door."

He looked down at her enigmatically for a moment.

"What now?" she asked, feeling strangely vulnerable under his unblinking regard.

"Nothing, ma'am. I was only thinking. Have I your leave to go?"

"Of course," she said coolly. "Good evening, Mr. Watson. Shall I expect you in the morning?"

"I am at your service in this, as in all things, ma'am," he said formally.

"Very prettily said, upon my word," she said approvingly. "You need not come *very* early in the morning. I plan to sleep late."

"If there is nothing else—"

"Oh, go, blast you," she said in high dudgeon.

He raised his eyebrows and went.

The next day he took her at her word and, instead of visiting her town house early in the morning, he made his way to the quiet street where Molly and her daughter resided in the house he had rented for them.

Becky greeted him with acclaim. He had been her idol since that wonderful day when he had driven up to her grandmother's house in a hired carriage with her mother on the seat beside him to take her to this jolly house which was always clean and smelling of wax, and where food was always bountiful.

128

He had bought her a doll and a pretty new dress. He had bought her something this time, too. A white hat with pink ribbons under the chin.

"Oh, thank you, sir," said Molly when she saw her daughter prancing excitedly in the middle of the floor in this confection. "How pretty it will look with her new pelisse!"

"Sir?" he asked quizzically.

"Frank, then," Molly said, lowering her eyes.

"You are most welcome, Molly," he said, handing her a little bunch of flowers done up in paper. "This is for you."

"Oh, how lovely," she said. She regarded him with grave eyes. "You spoil us."

"Well, you can do with a little spoiling," he said lightly. "So, does it feel like home to you? Are you sure you can manage without a servant?"

"Oh, yes," she said, glad she had put on her new blue muslin dress with the white lace trim. She raised a nervous hand to smooth her hair. "I wouldn't know how to talk to a servant. I hope you don't mind. I'd rather do my own work and use the money for other things."

"Like your pretty dress and toys for Becky," said Frank. "I approve wholeheartedly. But you'll let me know if the work becomes too much for you."

"It won't," said Molly, pleased by his compliment on her dress. "Will you have a cup of tea?"

"I can't stay long," he said. "I just wanted to see how you are. I must go now to wait on my employer, but I wondered if you would like to go for a ride in the park and have dinner with me, and Becky, too, of course, if I manage to have the evening free?"

"Oh, yes," said Molly, her eyes sparkling.

"Good. I doubt if my duties will extend much past the morning. Miss Willoughby will most likely be occupied with exchanging visits of ceremony with her many friends. I shall call for you at two o'clock, if that would be agreeable."

Later, Molly wasn't sure how she had answered his question, she had been so dazzled at the thought of being seen in his company. Her heart began to sing.

He does like me — at least a little, she said happily to herself.

She began fidgeting with her hair and dress, and wondered how she could bear to wait until two o'clock.

Chapter Six

Frank spent a long, frustrating morning in the bowels of Margaret's town house, making an inventory of the pantry with Jacques. Jacques was plainly amazed. Sir Robert had never bothered with an accounting of the foodstuffs in the house, and Jacques was affronted by what he perceived as Frank's interference in his domain. Dealing with Marcel was bad enough. Now there was another interloper.

At first he put one obstruction after another in Frank's path. But Frank won his cooperation halfway through the morning when he complimented Jacques on the state of the pantry. He was pleasantly surprised that Jacques had been conscientious about rotating the pantry items so that the oldest was always used first, and nothing was allowed to spoil. This evidence of frugality on the part of a culinary artist was a good sign.

Jacques eyes took on a hopeful sheen. Until now, Marcel had been considered the primary cook by Margaret, while Jacques was favored by Sir Robert and his lady.

His fear was that Margaret would banish him to Yorkshire and install Marcel in the London house. Jacques hated the country.

Jacques considered it a good sign that Margaret had not brought Marcel with her to London on this visit, even though he surmised it was only because she wanted Marcel to oversee the refurbishment of the Yorkshire house kitchens.

Perhaps all was not lost for Jacques, even though Margaret had taken control of her own household. He found Frank's words encouraging.

"I see evidence of very little waste," Frank was saying approvingly as he flexed the muscles of his tired arms.

He had removed his coat, which Jacques considered unsuitable behavior in a man of Frank's position, and his face shone with the labors of his exertion. He had insisted upon removing and inspecting every last barrel of flour in the pantry, and every last smoked ham. Then he made notes in a mysterious little book he carried with him.

"You have my congratulations," Frank continued. "I did not find the pantries at the Yorkshire house in so good a state, I don't mind telling you, although it is probably unfair to compare your kitchen with Marcel's since your facilities are so much superior. We are remedying that, however."

Nothing could have endeared him to Jacques's heart more effectively than this mild aspersion on his rival. Jacques declared himself, in an excess of Gallic passion, at Frank's service to the end of his life.

About one o'clock, Frank tidied himself and donned the fresh shirt he'd had the foresight to bring with him from the inn, then he went upstairs to see if Margaret would receive him.

He was tired, but pleasantly so, feeling that he had accomplished much. He had arranged to have regular provisions delivered to the town house and his inspection of the entire structure told him that it was in good repair and would not need nearly as much work as the country house. He intended to take his leave of Margaret and return to Yorkshire first thing in the morning to supervise the last of the spring planting and inspect the tenants' cottages for needed repairs.

A glimpse into Margaret's parlor as he walked through the hallway did much to impair his good mood. He found her apparently just returned from riding since she was still wearing one of her many jewel-hued velvet habits and her cheeks were still flushed becomingly. She was smiling up at one of her besotted admirers, who was holding out to her a sheaf of paper tied with pale pink ribbon and a white rose.

This worthy was wearing a green swallow-tailed spencer and the most revealing of nankeen pantaloons. His sandy hair was swept into the Brutus, and his other hand held a curly-brimmed beaver.

Margaret took the offering with a pleased expression on her face and held out her hand to be passionately kissed by her ecstatic swain.

The fact that there were interested observers in the room, two demure young ladies and an older, more fashionable one, and two other gentlemen all, like Margaret, dressed in riding habits and watching this tender scene with varying expressions of thinly veiled amusement and jealousy, disgusted him further. This was Margaret's world, and he thought it the most abominable of wastes for a woman of her intelligence and humor to squander her considerable gifts in the company of such painted dolls.

She was smiling at her infatuated admirer exactly the way one would smile encouragement at a precocious child.

Frank stalked to the library, a little surprised by his own dudgeon, and asked Sternes to convey a message to his employer that he would be grateful for a word

133

with her before he left the house. Sternes, not forgot
ting the score he had to settle with this encroaching
young man, maliciously pointed out that he hesitated
to interrupt his mistress's pleasure when she was entertaining guests.

"Since Miss Willoughby will be dining with friends
before the ball," said Sternes, an oily smile on his face,
"it may not be possible for me to deliver your message
until tomorrow."

"It is my intention to return to Yorkshire tomorrow," said Frank with a shrug, "and I must begin my
preparations for my journey. Miss Willoughby will be
much put out if she discovers that you refused to deliver my message and I have left London without performing some service she had in mind for me to
dispatch for her. But you will, of course, use your own
judgment in the matter."

Sternes reluctantly left to do his enemy's bidding.
He was well aware that he was not in the good graces
of his mistress because Miss Poole, who had somehow
risen in Miss Willoughby's esteem, had complained to
her of him. He could not afford to give offense to Miss
Willoughby, he realized regrettably, by omitting to deliver this upstart's message. The upstart seemed to be
high in her esteem as well.

While Sternes was gone on his errand, the ladies
and gentlemen who had witnessed the tender scene in
the parlor decided they were very much in the way and
tactfully withdrew from the tête-à-tête. Unfortunately,
they chose to walk from room to room, the ladies
amusing themselves by criticizing the furniture and
hangings, and getting much in the way of the servants
who were not accustomed to guests wandering
through the house unless accompanied by their hostess.

Soon the party came into the library and surprised

Frank in his inspection of one of the late Mr. Willoughby's books.

"Well, good afternoon," said the sophisticated lady with what Frank considered quite unbecoming interest in his person.

He bowed, but remained silent. The gentlemen joined them, one friendly chap going so far as to extend a white, flawlessly groomed hand and introduce himself.

"Sir Miles Smythe," said the gentleman, deluded by Frank's gentlemanlike appearance and immaculate linen into thinking he was addressing a fellow guest.

"Frank Watson," said Frank, shaking the hand because he didn't know what else to do with it.

"I was not aware there were other visitors in the house," said the lady, sidling rather closer to Frank than was entirely proper and enveloping him in a cloud of overpowering ambergris scent.

He drew back with unflattering haste.

"I am not a visitor, ma'am. I am Miss Willoughby's steward," Frank said coldly.

As he expected, his mild explanation resulted in a state of embarrassed confusion.

The gentlemen, perceiving they had been led into the grave solecism of attempting to converse with one of their hostess's menials as an equal, abruptly took themselves off, muttering and sweeping the two confused young ladies with them, possibly from a chivalrous desire to save their fair charges from contamination.

The remaining lady, whom Frank had hoped in vain would go with them, continued to regard him with that unnerving, speculative gaze. He'd seen that look often in his travels and had even occasionally responded to it. He just never expected to see it in Margaret's library. The lady licked her discreetly painted

135

lips. Her eyes mirrored her hunger.

"Stuffy creatures, aren't they?" she said with a sound that suspiciously resembled a purr.

Frank returned no answer.

"So, *you* are Margaret's steward. I thought her uncle, that spindle-shanked little man with the overbearing wife, was minding her affairs for her."

"It is not my place to comment upon Miss Willoughby's arrangements, ma'am," he said, his voice expressionless.

The lady continued thoughtfully, as if he hadn't spoken.

"Dear Margaret attained her majority last year, did she not? Imagine Margaret having the spirit to give old Spindle-Shanks the *congé* and make her own 'arrangements,' as you so euphemistically put it."

Frank regarded her with acute dislike.

"Top-lofty, aren't you?" she said, walking up to him and delicately tracing the angle of his strong jaw with one gloved finger. He stepped back and favored her with a blank stare.

"I like that," she continued, following him. "And you do resemble a certain young man, unhappily deceased, whom Margaret once fancied. Well, she certainly pulled the wool over everyone's eyes. For the past four years she has been sighed over and called The Unattainable by every besotted swain in London because she buried herself in the wilds of Yorkshire in order to mourn her dead hero, and all the time she had been consoling herself with you. How perfectly delicious!"

He remained silent.

Despite her light tone, she was infuriated because he was treating her exactly the way any gentleman would treat a social inferior who had been presumptuous. His face was frozen in an expression of mingled indifference and repugnance so insulting that she wanted to scream obscenities at him. She knew she was not showing to advantage, but she couldn't help herself.

"You don't look like any steward I've ever known," she fairly shouted. "Pray, what kind of services do you *really* perform for dear Margaret? Whatever they are, I am certain she finds them enjoyable."

"That remark is so vulgarly suggestive that I wouldn't demean myself by responding to it," he said coldly.

"Why, you—"

"Chloe."

It was softly spoken, but both participants in the ugly little drama broke off to look toward the speaker, whose calm voice was belied by her angry eyes.

"Ah, there you are, Margaret," said Chloe sweetly, intending to brazen it out. The spots of high color on her cheekbones betrayed her mortification. It was shockingly bad form to be caught hurling insults at a social inferior.

Frank said nothing. He might have been a statue.

Margaret advanced into the room.

"My dear Chloe," she said quietly. "I see you have lost your way to the door. Allow me to show you the way."

"Of course. Thank you, my dear," said Chloe, favoring Margaret with a look of loathing only slightly less intense than the one she gave Frank.

They left the room and Frank remained standing by the fireplace, looking straight ahead, until Margaret returned.

She did so at once.

"Perhaps you will tell me the meaning of the rather extraordinary scene I appear to have interrupted," she said, sitting down and giving a nod toward another chair. He remained standing.

137

"I would rather not repeat what she said. I trust the lady is not a close friend."

"No. I dislike her excessively," said Margaret. "She is wild to a fault, but she is an intimate of Melanie Bentley's, so I can't very well give her the cut direct. She has led Melanie into all sorts of mischief, and Melanie's husband nearly divorced her over a scandal she caused several years ago at Chloe's instigation."

"She seems to think I am something other than your employee," said Frank, his expression wooden.

"I don't understand," said Margaret blankly.

"I was afraid my position in this house would cause gossip. She thinks that you have been finding consolation in my arms for the loss of Jeremy Verelst," he said bluntly.

"Why, that's—untrue," said Margaret, appalled. A slow blush crept up her cheek.

"Yes," Frank said with a note of regret in his voice.

She glared at him suspiciously but his expression was bland.

"She tried to make up to you, did she?" asked Margaret.

"I believe that was her intention, ma'am," said Frank. "I trust you don't think I gave her any encouragement."

"She has the most venomous tongue in London."

"I should not be surprised," he said mildly. "Perhaps it's just as well that I have come to take my leave."

"What? Oh, you're going to the inn again, I suppose. Very well. You may have tomorrow morning off and wait on me at midday. I have several commissions for you."

"I had intended to leave for Yorkshire in the morning, ma'am. Don't you remember? There is the late spring planting, and the work on the railings of the

138

house—"

"No," said Margaret.

"No?"

"No. I need for you to remain a few days longer. Besides, if you leave tonight and Chloe starts whispering poison in the town, it will look as if we're guilty of whatever ugly accusations she is making."

"But, ma'am—"

"Mr. Watson, do I or do I not employ you?"

"You do."

"Very well. Then follow my instructions. We must discuss this further. Blast! It is almost time for me to dress for tea at Lady Lynton's. How very tiresome. And I have just remembered I am engaged for most of tomorrow, too. It had better be tonight, I suppose. Come back tonight at, let's see, I have promised to attend a ball at—oh, I can always claim the headache and leave early. Come back at ten o'clock. I should be home by then."

Frank firmly closed his mouth on whatever objection he had been about to make.

"Very well, ma'am," he said. He turned to leave, but her voice stopped him at the doorway.

"Mr. Watson!"

He turned, an interrogative lift to his eyebrows.

"I beg your pardon for the insult you have suffered in this house," she said.

"I must say," he said, looking surprised, "that is very handsome of you, ma'am. But you needn't apologize for her. And it was a rather interesting experience. I think now I know how your cousin Edward's parlor-maid felt."

"My cousin Edward's—?" repeated Margaret, perplexed. Then she gasped. "Mr. Watson! How *very* improper of you to mention Edward's, er, predilections in my presence."

139

"But, ma'am," he said, his eyes opened wide in innocent reproach. "I would have known nothing about it if you hadn't mentioned it in *my* presence first."

"Oh, you mean that day in the gardens when he came stalking up to us. I hoped you had forgotten that," she admitted. "It *was* most improper of me. Edward made me so angry I said the first thing that came into my head—but that is beside the point. I should have kept an eye on Chloe."

"It wasn't your fault, ma'am," he said.

"Yes, it was," she admitted. "If I had not been wasting my time on that ridiculous creature and his silly poem—it was a poem, you know. I saw you when you looked into the parlor. You looked so disgusted that I couldn't forebear flirting with him a little out of sheer spite. It was horrid of me, I know. You looked so disapproving. Then the others left me alone with him."

"And?" he prompted.

"He made me a declaration!" she blurted out.

"Indeed," said Frank, his sense of humor restored. "May I be the first to felicitate you, ma'am?"

"You may *not*, I thank you. His verse compared me to a daisy. He might as well have called me commonplace at once. And this time my eyes are, if you please, 'simmering pools of moonlight.'"

Repugnance was written in every line of her body.

"I beg your pardon?"

"I *believe* he meant to write 'shimmering.' At least I hope so."

"It was decidedly ill-advised of him," said Frank, suppressed laughter causing his eyes to water slightly.

"You may well say so," she said wryly. "It was *horrid!* And then I come in here to find Chloe fondling you—"

"It was not, thank God, quite so bad as that," he said, his voice heavy with distaste.

140

"I am relieved to hear it," said Margaret. "Still, I am sorry you were so annoyed in this house. And if I had not given into my shameful impulse, you would not have been. But how was I to know the five of them would start roaming about the house like cattle let loose in pasture? I have never met with such ill-bred behavior in my life."

"I shall return tonight," Frank promised, much mollified by her apology. He *had* been annoyed by Chloe's attentions. It was unusually perceptive for Margaret to notice it. Perhaps she didn't think of him as only another menial, after all. Dare he hope he saw jealousy in those "simmering pools"?

It was with a greatly lightened spirit that he went to Molly's house to take her to the promenade in the park.

She met him at the door, her smoky blue eyes sparkling excitedly and an extremely becoming pink hat tied around her chin with white ribbons. Her little girl was dressed in the white velvet pelisse and looked like a confection in a bakery shop window. He had rented an open carriage for their ride and, with courtly grace, handed both ladies into it.

They had made a turn or two around the park when he caught sight of a most unwelcome face among the pedestrians. Martin stared at him long and angrily, his jaws champing, as Frank swept by with his small harem.

"It's *him*," said Molly, alarmed.

"He won't bother us," said Frank indifferently.

"I don't like his looks."

"Nor do I," said Frank. "Well, are you enjoying yourself, Molly?"

"Oh, yes," she said, forgetting Martin. "To think it's really me, plain Molly Harnish, riding in a carriage with a real gentleman among all the nobs."

The "nobs" were giving them some strange looks. Frank very much resembled a gentleman and was wearing acceptable, though by no means fashionable, attire for the promenade in the park. But Molly's pelisse and hat, though becoming, were obviously ready-made, and not from the best stores. Frank treated both of his fair companions to a spanking dinner at a modest inn. Molly was almost embarrassingly grateful.

He took them home and carried little Becky, who had fallen asleep, into the little room with the narrow bed, which he mistakenly thought was hers. Then he came back downstairs and joined Molly, who was twisting her hands in her lap and looking nervous. She started and blushed when he reentered the room.

"Is something wrong, Molly?" he asked, surprised.

"No. Nothing," she said, a bit too quickly.

His eyes narrowed.

"Something *is* wrong," he said softly. "Do you want to tell me what it is?"

"No. I mean, I'm nervous."

"Nervous? Why?"

Molly's cheeks burned crimson because it was obvious he had no idea what she was talking about. She had assumed his invitation was a prelude to a seduction, and she had welcomed it. But, after all, he was a virtual stranger.

Molly was a young, passionate woman, but she was no wanton. She had not been with a man in That Way for four years, not, in fact, since the night when Becky had been conceived. She had steeled herself for the delicious moment when she would find herself alone with him, only to find that lovemaking apparently was the farthest thing from his mind.

She didn't know whether to feel relieved or insulted. These emotions warred with one another on her face, and relief won. Her companion, who had never been an obtuse person, immediately realized what she had been expecting. A few weeks earlier, he would have been tempted to oblige.

"My poor dear—" he began, the pity so strong in his voice that she thrust out her lower lip and put her hands on her hips, unconsciously imitating the one of her mother's many homely gestures she hated above all others.

"Well, never mind," she said in a husky voice. "I should have known you were not for the likes of me. But why, then, did you rent this house?"

"Out of a sense of justice, Molly," he said. "Nothing else. I owe you and Becky. And I will take care of both of you as long as you need me. But I'm afraid that's all I have to offer you."

"Why?" she asked. "I'm not expectin' you to marry me."

"I know that, although it will be a lucky man who does marry you, Molly."

The girl looked crushed, and Frank felt like a monster.

"It's *her,* isn't it?" she said accusingly.

"Who?" he asked warily.

"That Miss Willoughby you work for."

"My good girl—" he said, appalled. Had he been so transparent?

"You're afraid she'll find out about me and turn you off," she said shrewdly, causing him to breathe a sigh of relief. "That's the Quality for you. Their little games are all right and tight, but just let one of *us* take a fancy for one another and they come across all morallike. Well, I can't blame you. She's the one who calls the tune, and no mistake. You'll still come see Becky and me now and again, won't you?"

"Yes. Of course," he said. "Any time I can. But I'll

143

be leaving for Yorkshire soon."

She paid him the compliment of looking disappointed.

"Then this is good-bye."

"For now," he said, taking her hand and kissing it.

After he left, she sat in her favorite chair and stared at her hand for quite five minutes, lost in a dream that she knew quite well was never to be.

It was close on eight o'clock when Frank left Molly's house, and he estimated that he had plenty of time to return to the inn, give the carriage back to the innkeeper in exchange for Sulieman, and have a wash and a change of clothes before waiting on Miss Willoughby at ten o'clock. He intended to do his utmost to persuade her that he should be allowed to return to Yorkshire as planned the following morning. He was convinced that once he was out of sight, the vicious gossip that the scheming Chloe intended to circulate would die a natural death.

He was so wrapped up in these thoughts that he almost walked right past Martin, who lay in wait beyond Molly's doorway, without seeing him.

"Not so fast, your high-and-mighty-ship," said Martin, stepping in front of Frank with a belligerent stance. "Do you mind telling me why you're sniffing around that little ladybird's skirts instead of getting arm-in-armly with the nobs in Yorkshire like you're supposed to?"

"The 'nobs' are on the Continent," said Frank reasonably. "I can't very well worm my way into their good graces unless I follow them, can I? I haven't that much blunt, I'm afraid. So, I've taken employment with their neighbor, Miss Willoughby, until they come back."

"She's the one who was going to marry him, you clodpole," said Martin. "She'd know you were an im-

144

postor as soon as she clapped eyes on you."

"No. She thinks I am very like," said Frank. "She may be my chief advocate once I decide to unveil my identity, as it were."

"Hmm. Damned if you're not playing too deep for me, boy," said Martin. "But if she were to vouch for you—maybe you aren't so thick-skulled at that. But why are you wasting your time with—"

"That's my affair," said Frank. "Rest assured that when the Verelsts return to Yorkshire, I will put our plan into execution. Until then, I will dance attendance on Miss Willoughby and learn all I can about the neighboring gentry. If you'll forgive my saying so, there are probably many details about Yorkshire's first families that I can't learn from Jeremy Verelst's valet."

"You might have a point," said Martin thoughtfully. "Why don't we discuss it over—"

"No. I'm expected back at Miss Willoughby's town house tonight, and I don't dare be late. And, begging your pardon, Martin, it won't do for us to be seen together. Your 'recognition' of me as Jeremy Verelst at the proper moment will be decidedly unconvincing if it is known that we have met in London."

Defeated, Martin agreed and disappeared into the shadows of the early evening. Frank got into the carriage and drove it to the inn. After washing and dressing himself in his best dark coat, light pantaloons, and a white linen shirt and stock, he started for the stables to fetch Sulieman but instead impulsively decided to take a hackney. There were many of them in the street, and he saw no reason to get the reek of horse on his spotless pantaloons when it could be avoided.

He dismissed the hackney a few blocks from Margaret's house. It was a beautiful, clear night, and he thought the walk would clear the cobwebs from his overactive brain. He wondered what fresh exertions Margaret would expect him to perform in her difficult but vastly entertaining service.

These thoughts occupied him so thoroughly that he almost walked into the threatening figure that blocked his path.

"Ho, there, my bully," said a gruff voice. "It wasn't so smart to dismiss the hack, now, was it?"

"Who goes there?" asked Frank, peering into the darkness.

The man was a complete stranger.

"I haven't any money," Frank said calmly, "unless you fancy my watch."

"Gawd," said his adversary. "You should get off so lucky."

"Well, what do you want then?" asked Frank patiently.

"I'm goin' to beat you to a bloody pulp, that's what!"

"Why should you want to do any such thing?" asked Frank, bewildered.

"Well, if that don't beat the Dutch!" exclaimed the man. "The man gets my sister with a brat, then runs off to sea for four years, then comes back and sets her up in a house for his own pleasure—"

"Are we talking about Molly Harnish?" asked Frank, enlightenment dawning.

"Damned if I won't kill you for that," screamed Molly's furious brother. "Pretendin' you don't know me! After I put you up in my own house when you didn't have anywheres to go, and you repaid me by seducing a girl that weren't no more than a babe herself. Then, instead of marryin' her proper, you go runnin' off to sea to let the girl, her ma, and me face the disgrace."

146

"Now, see here —" said Frank, backing away.

"I'm goin' to beat you to a bloody pulp," Tom repeated, showing every one of his broken, discolored teeth, and proceeded to make good his threat.

When Frank returned to consciousness, he was dimly aware of having given as good as he got and wondered what happened to his attacker. He shook his head to clear it and stood, wincing. His body felt as if it had been beaten by cudgels which, indeed, it had.

Frank had not, at first, seen his opponent's companions, who had come along for the sport of helping their crony beat up a solitary man. Still, they were the worst for drink and weren't giving him too much trouble until one of them pulled a sword stick on him while he was occupied with another of his attackers.

He felt a sharp pain in his back, and when he put his hand to it, it came away sticky. Frank hoped it wasn't blood, but without much conviction. He staggered through the dark street and practically collapsed against Margaret's door.

It was after eleven. He applied the knocker and it was opened by Margaret.

Frank was fighting to remain on his feet, but even in his brain-clouded state he could practically feel her anger. He didn't doubt that she had sent the butler to bed so she could rail at him for being late in privacy.

"Where have you been?" she demanded as he lurched through the door.

She stared at him, amazed. He shook his head as if to clear it.

"You're drunk!" she exclaimed, outraged.

"No," he gasped, catching at the door for support. "I was set upon —"

"Sternes!" she shouted. "Come help me!"

She put one arm around him and his hand closed on her bare shoulder. He could see by the light of several

147

candles in the hall that she was wearing a revealing white ball gown with an overdress woven in some silver threads that resembled a spider web. A wave of dizziness practically floored him.

"Stop that!" Margaret commanded. "Don't you *dare* faint!"

"I won't," he said. "You'd better let go of me. I appreciate the gesture, but one of them pulled a sword stick on me. I don't want to get blood on you."

"Oh, *do* be quiet!" she said, trying to support him as he sagged.

"Stand back," he said, trying to fend her off. "If I fall on you, I might hurt you."

"Then don't fall," she said tartly. "Sternes! Where the *deuce* are all those servants who are always underfoot when I don't want them!"

"Shhhh," said Frank. "You'll rouse the whole house. This is humiliating enough without—"

"It's about time," she snapped as Sternes hurried into the hallway followed by several footmen who looked as if they had donned their livery in a hurry. They helped Frank to a chair in one of the salons off the hallway and pressed a glass of brandy to his lips.

"That's enough," he said after he swallowed a thimbleful and felt the rest spill down the front of his once spotless shirt. His head was clearing.

"I'll send for a doctor." said Margaret.

"No. He won't be needed," said Frank. "The wound isn't deep. All I need is for someone to dress it."

Margaret's aunt, wrapped in a puce dressing gown and her hair in curling papers, chose that moment to make her appearance.

"What is the meaning of this melee?" she asked, the soul of dignity despite her unorthodox attire. "Mr. Watson! You've been *drinking!*"

"No, he hasn't, Aunt," said Margaret, rushing to

148

her much abused steward's defense. "He was attacked in the street."

"How dreadful!" said Martha, drawing close to the sufferer. "But, my good man, surely you don't mean on *our* street!"

"I think we should send for the doctor." said Margaret.

"Perhaps," said Martha. "But I think we should have Bates look at him before we turn the poor doctor out of his bed."

Bates was an old servant who had served during the first of the Napoleonic Wars as a doctor's assistant. He often patched up the hurts of the servants and horses when a doctor wasn't available.

"Of course. Where have my wits gone begging?" exclaimed Margaret. "Sternes, summon Bates at once."

"There is nothing very much wrong with me, you know," said Frank. "The dizziness has passed, and the bleeding has all but stopped, I am sure. I'm afraid I am in much better case than your gown."

Margaret looked down to see that her gown was bloodstained across the bodice where she had tried to support Frank and gotten too close to his back.

"Well, there's no sense in worrying about that now," she said with a shrug. "Yesterday you complained because I had brought so many."

"I didn't mean it," he said, closing his eyes for a moment.

"You aren't getting dizzy again, are you?" she asked anxiously.

"No," he lied.

"We'll put you to bed after Bates sees you," said Martha.

He opened his mouth to object but Margaret forestalled him.

"You are not, I repeat *not,* going back to that inn

tonight," said Margaret, reading his mind with unnerving accuracy. "You are going to stay in this house and you aren't going to leave until you are fit to do so, is that clear? If the tabbies want to gossip, let them gossip."

"I think it is very proper for Mr. Watson to be concerned for your reputation, my dear," said Martha approvingly, "but one must be practical. He is not fit to go anywhere tonight. Anyone can see that."

"Nonsense," said Frank. He would have objected further if Bates had not entered, followed by one of the footmen with a supply of cloth for bandages and a bowl of hot water.

"Ah, you must be the unfortunate young man," said Bates purposefully. "Now, if you'll just remove your coat and shirt—"

"Not in front of the ladies, if you please," Frank said, indicating Margaret and Martha.

"You are quite right, Mr. Watson," said Martha. "I will get a room ready for you. Come, Margaret. While Bates is tending to Mr. Watson, I think we should get you out of that bloodstained gown."

"Oh, yes. Of course," said Margaret. Her eyes were huge with concern. She knew it was going to hurt when Bates peeled the shirt and the dried blood away from the wound. She had the most absurd desire to hold Frank's hand and murmur endearments to him, which she firmly repressed.

The ladies defected in good order, and Margaret, after washing herself and donning a soft blue wool dressing gown which covered her from neck to ankle, made her way back to the salon door, intending to conduct Frank to his room herself so she could make sure he wasn't entertaining any wild ideas about going to the inn instead.

On her way upstairs she had instructed Martha to

150

prepare the room in which her solicitor usually stayed when visiting the house. Now that Frank was going to stay the night, it occurred to her that he couldn't very well be put below stairs with the servants. Although he was a paid employee, she never thought of him in the same category with Sternes and the footmen. On the other hand, he was certainly not a guest. High sticklers would say that he had no place above stairs, either. But then the room which Martha had prepared was never used for principal guests.

She rapped lightly at the salon door, assuming that Bates's ministrations were over, and was surprised to receive no answer. Instead, a low groan elicited from the room. Alarmed, she rapped again, and was answered with silence.

"Bates!" she called, assuming that Frank had passed out from pain or loss of blood. "Do you require assistance?"

Still no answer. She opened the door and went in, astonished by the tableau that confronted her.

Frank was seated on a low wooden chair facing away from her. Hovering over him was Bates. The normalcy of their postures would have reassured her if she hadn't gotten a good look at Frank's back.

The long jagged wound left by the sword stick was, as Frank himself had said, superficial. Bates was dabbing at it with a cotton cloth, and the bowl of water on the table next to him was a sickly shade of pink.

What arrested her attention was Frank's back itself. It was muscular and deeply tanned, his shoulders broad and tapering to a narrow waist. But marring his skin was a series of large, ugly, puckered patches. There were scars on the back of his upper arms, too.

She felt as if she had gazed upon that sight for many minutes, but it could only have been a second or two. She gasped, and both men turned to look at her.

151

"Miss Willoughby," said Bates disapprovingly. "This is no sight for a lady's eyes."

"I heard Mr. Watson groan and thought you might require assistance—"

"The groan was mine, miss," said Bates apologetically. "I was unprepared for—but, after all, I've seen much worse on the battlefield."

Frank looked positively furious. She had never expected to encounter that look from the eye of an employee.

"Get out," he said, his tone leaving no room for argument.

She obeyed.

A few minutes later, the two men left the room and she stood her ground as Bates filed by her.

"I'll conduct you to your room, Mr. Watson," she said.

"Thank you," he said. "I'm sorry I was sharp with you."

She nodded her head stiffly.

"I'm not tired," he said. "May I borrow a book from your father's library? There is one I saw there this afternoon which I especially wanted to read."

"You should rest—" She stopped and realized she had been officious enough for one day. If she had not insisted that he wait on her tonight, he would be safe, at this very minute, in his room at the inn. "Of course," she amended.

She accompanied him to the library, and he made his selection. He turned to leave the room and saw she was blocking the door.

"Miss Willoughby?" he prompted.

"Oh, I'm sorry," she said, standing aside.

"What is it?" he said softly, arrested by the look on her face.

"Those scars."

152

"They are old ones, Miss Willoughby."

"Four years old? In Hampshire?"

"Yes. I thought you knew I was there."

"You tried to save them."

"Foolish of me, was it not?"

"It was very brave," she said, a catch in her throat.

"Yes. And if I had died instead, he would be here with you today. Is that what you're thinking?"

"No. Of course not," she said guiltily.

He seated himself in an armchair. "I can see you want to talk about it," he said wearily. "What do you want me to describe for you? The stench of burning flesh? Their screams?"

"No! Stop," she said, tears welling in her eyes.

"Miss Willoughby," he said calmly. "It is time you realized something that no one has had the courage to tell you in the whole of your spoiled, pampered existence. You are not the only one in the world to have lost someone you loved. This country is only now recovering from a series of wars that has practically denuded it of its young men. There are many, many mothers in this country who have lost their sons, and probably every one of them was as good a man as Jeremy Verelst. There are widows with small children who will never know their fathers. And they must earn their living by laboring in the homes of others because the husbands who would have provided homes for them have died in that cursed war and left them nothing."

"So my suffering doesn't matter," she said stiffly.

"I did not say that," he said. "Your devotion does more honor to his memory than anything he ever did in his short, ineffectual life. But the fact is, you didn't know him very well, and he didn't know you. If he had lived, you might have discovered you didn't suit at all."

"Then again, we might have been married and had

153

children and died in each other's arms after fifty years of ecstatic happiness," she said.

"Yes," he agreed reluctantly, "you might have at that. But you'll never know, will you? Meanwhile, you are closing yourself off from the likelihood of forming a real attachment—"

"I wish you would make up your mind!" she snapped. "First you don't like it because I am entertaining suitors with an eye to getting married. And now you're saying I should forget Jeremy and find consolation elsewhere. You are a trifle inconsistent, Mr. Watson."

"Yes. I did say that, didn't I?" he admitted. "It just shows how muddled my own thinking has become. As you so properly pointed out at the beginning of our association, I am hired to take care of your property, not to act as the dragon before your gate. It seems to me, however, that the suitors you have entertained so far are callow, besotted boys who you could tie to your apron strings with little trouble. I find it difficult to believe that a woman of your intelligence would have any real interest in that type of husband."

"On the contrary," she said, "that is exactly the type of husband I want. I have no desire to lead the life of a Patient Griselda with a masterful husband who would dispose of my fortune as he sees fit, oversetting my arrangements and allotting me pin money from my own coffers while he plunders my estate for his own selfish purposes. Once I am married, I will have no rights, no more than I did when my uncle was my guardian."

"Was he so stern a guardian?" he asked.

"No, not in the sense you mean," she said. "I was not mistreated or abused. But he and his wife did not raise me, as they did their own children, with affection. Rather, I was carefully maintained. They could

154

not very well neglect me for fear of causing talk in their circle. They had to present the heiress—pink, healthy, accomplished and well-dressed. And they did."

"Who inherits if you die?" he asked.

"What a singularly odd question! However, according to the terms of my will, Uncle Robert would get the house and the land that was part of the original estate since he is my closest male relative. Aunt Martha would be comfortably provided for in an establishment of her own. There are some relations on my mother's side who will come in for small legacies. And pensions for the older servants, of course. My young cousin Anne will have my jewels and a legacy, because knowing my uncle's improvident ways I cannot believe her portion will be anything but meager. And then there will be some family heirlooms for Edward, because he has an income of his own and needs no legacy from me."

"I see," he said thoughtfully.

"Why do you ask? It hardly matters since I will most probably live for a great many years yet. In any case, when I marry it will probably be changed to provide for my children."

"Of course," he agreed politely.

"I am the most selfish toad imaginable," said Margaret, standing up. "You have had a horrid experience and you should be in bed recovering. Come with me."

He followed her up the stairway to the clean, well-appointed room, uncomfortably aware of the fact that she was wearing nothing under the all-concealing wool dressing gown. It was absurd, he told himself firmly, to be so sensitive to her state of dishabille considering that this garment revealed far less of her figure than was visible in the ball gown she had worn earlier in the evening.

155

They faced each other solemnly across the bed and he noticed that her face was flushed delicately, as if she were aware of his disturbing thoughts.

"I hope you sleep well, Mr. Watson," she said formally.

"Thank you, Miss Willoughby," he answered.

She hesitated a moment, then lowered her eyes and left the room. He watched her retreating figure until she was out of sight, and wondered what she had intended to say before she thought better of it.

He lay awake for a long time, but although the book lay open before him he didn't read more than a page or two. Then he fell deeply and dreamlessly asleep.

Chapter Seven

Frank thought it ironic that he had the misfortune to encounter possibly every one of Margaret's many servants on his short walk from his bedroom to the breakfast room at the ghastly hour of seven o'clock.

The maid who served him was hard put to keep a smile from her face every time she looked at him. Sternes looked obscurely triumphant. And Jacques, with quite insensitive cheerfulness, offered him a beefsteak for his eye.

Frank informed him dryly that he would much prefer to have it sizzled in butter and served to him with some fresh bread and eggs, and Jacques handsomely assented to his request.

Miss Willoughby's steward was decidedly disgruntled. His employer was going to be occupied for most of the day and had left not so much as a message for him.

She apparently had such a low opinion of his recuperative powers that she expected him to lie in bed all day and eat thin gruel, he thought wryly. He decided that he might as well get some work done, so he made his way to the library where he expected to immerse himself in some of the papers he had found stuffed into the drawers of the massive desk his predecessor used when he was staying in the house.

Frank emerged from this exercise with an even poorer opinion of Sir Robert's competence. He was particularly annoyed because since entering the house he had been struck by the perfectly hideous red patterned wallpaper and tasteless chinoiserie furniture, and now he discovered that, according to the documentation he found in the library desk, not one of these dubious improvements had ever been paid for. To add insult to injury, the carpets and draperies were already showing signs of wear.

He thought it the outside of enough that Margaret, whom he felt quite sure had not endorsed these expenditures, should be required to settle them. So it was partially on her account that he was uncharacteristically grumpy with all of the house's inmates.

His mood was not improved by the sounds of cheerful speech that floated to him from the hallway. He recognized Margaret's musical tones and her cousin Edward's deeper ones.

Much as his eyes longed for the sight of Margaret, and he rigorously repressed an examination of his reasons for being out of curl whenever he was deprived of her company for very long, he wished to avoid her cousin.

It turned out to be a vain wish.

It wasn't long before the three of them spilled into the room, bringing youth, beauty, and a cheerfulness that set his teeth on edge.

Margaret was dressed in a dashing scarlet riding habit with gold braid and a ravishing hat à la hussar worn at a rakish angle over her deliciously tumbled curls. Edward, impeccable as always, wore riding dress and lightly held Margaret's elbow in what appeared to Frank's disapproving eye to be an unnecessarily possessive posture. They were accompanied by a small, dark, pretty young woman with a shy smile and wide, trusting amber eyes.

Sourly, Frank reflected that despite a superficial resemblance to Margaret, the girl looked insipid.

"Mr. Watson!" said Margaret brightly. "I didn't expect you to be up so early."

Edward gave her a disapproving look. Obviously he hadn't known that Frank was staying in the house, and he wasn't happy about it.

"Anne, my love," said Margaret, drawing the pretty girl forward, "I must make you acquainted with my steward, Mr. Frank Watson."

"How do you do, Mr. Watson," said the girl politely, holding out her hand. Frank took it.

Despite the civility of the proceeding, Frank could feel Edward's eyes burning a hole through him. Frank had rarely felt at such a disadvantage, and it annoyed him no end that it mattered to him.

"I say, Watson," said Edward tactlessly, interrupting Frank's introduction to his sister. "Have you been in a brawl?"

"Yes," said Margaret, "isn't it dreadful?"

"It certainly looks like you came off the worse for the encounter," said Edward, looking pleased. "Did you walk into a door or tumble down a flight of stairs?"

"Edward!" said Margaret indignantly. "He was set upon by footpads."

"A pity," said Edward, without much conviction.

"Your servant, Miss Willoughby," said Frank to Anne, ignoring Edward, who had interrupted before he could reply to his introduction to Anne. She answered suitably, then the party fell silent.

"Edward, why don't you take Anne into the breakfast room? I'll join you after I have a word with Mr. Watson," said Margaret.

Edward looked reluctant, but he took Anne's elbow and led her away.

159

Margaret turned to Frank. She tried valiantly to keep a straight face, but when Frank's lips began to twitch as well, she couldn't repress a gurgle of laughter.

"Levity at my expense, Miss Willoughby?" he asked, trying to look severe and failing abysmally.

"I'm sorry," she said, trying not to laugh. "What must you think of me? Last night I was so distressed about your injuries, but by the light of day—"

"You find my misfortune vastly amusing," he said.

"No, of course not," she said hastily. "It's just that—"

"And when I am sporting a black eye and bruises over most of my body, *must* you bring round your disgustingly well-favored cousin to share your enjoyment of my battered state?"

"It really was too bad of him," said Margaret, sobering. "Who would have thought he could be so rude?"

"If you'll pardon my saying so, ma'am, your own demeanor is somewhat lacking in feminine compassion and sympathy."

"I know," she said, conscience-stricken. "Your poor face, and your eye. I feel *terrible* about it, especially when I reflect that it's all my fault for asking you to wait on me last night."

"You seem to be deriving an inordinate amount of amusement from this poor, broken face, just the same."

"It is *not* broken," she said. "Besides it's not your face that is so amusing, it's that *appalling* suit. I don't think I've ever seen anything so dreadful."

"You can say that after living with this wallpaper and this hideous carpet?" he asked.

"I see your point," she said, "but one expects such things from Aunt Samantha, and one does become accustomed. You, on the other hand, have always appeared to have such excellent taste that —"

"Softly, I beg of you," said Frank. "If you hurt his

feelings I shall never forgive you."

"Whose?"

"Peter's, of course. He's the only one of the footmen who even approaches my size, and I had persuaded myself that it would do well enough before you undermined my self-esteem with your ridicule.

"I'll have you know," he added with awesome dignity, "it is his *Sunday* suit."

It was too much for Margaret. She dissolved into gales of laughter, and he joined her.

"You're wearing the footman's suit?" she said, when she regained enough composure to speak. "Whatever for?"

"Because some interfering busybody removed all my clothes from my room," he said in an injured tone. "I'd have been there yet with the sheets up to my chin if Bates hadn't come along to check on my injuries."

"Your clothes were torn and bloody," she said, sobering. "One of the servants must have removed them for cleaning."

"That's all very well," said Frank, "but there was nothing for it but to borrow some clothes."

"How shocking," she said, apologetically. "I'll send someone to the inn for the rest of your things immediately."

"No."

"You surely won't go back—"

"Of course I will. I am not going to hide in your house for the rest of my stay in London," he said.

"Will you hide in my house just until tomorrow?"

The appeal in her eyes was irresistible.

"Yes," he said.

"Good. I must take Anne around to all the shops. I want to buy her some new clothes for her come-out because she can't be seen in that schoolgirl's wardrobe her mother provided for her. Then I am going to a ball to-

161

night. It's such a bore. Will you wait up for me to return? We never did talk last night. And will you have everything you need while I'm gone?"

"I will have plenty to do while you are gone. Don't worry about my running out of work."

"That's not my concern and you know it. You should be resting."

"It looks much worse than it is, I assure you, ma'am," he said.

"If you say so," she said in a dissatisfied tone. "I will talk with you tonight."

"Very good, ma'am," he said. "I may leave the house later today if it is all right with you."

"Certainly," she said, restraining herself from asking him where he intended to go. "Oh, I'll have someone bring your horse, too."

"Thank you, ma'am," said Frank solemnly.

At that moment, Martha erupted into the room clutching a small book to her bosom.

"Margaret, the most wonderful thing!" she exclaimed. "Oh, good morning, Mr. Watson. I didn't expect to see you up so early."

"Good morning, ma'am," said Frank.

"What is it, Aunt?" asked Margaret, smiling. "Something that pleases you very much, I collect."

"Yes, indeed," said Martha. "A book of Lord Byron's poems has just arrived. Remember, you told me I might order it — "

"Oh, how nice," said Margaret with a convincing show of enthusiasm. Frank, who knew her true opinion of Lord Byron's poetry, stifled a grin.

"I knew you would be delighted," Martha said. "If only we had a male voice to read it to us. Lord Byron's poems positively *plead* for a male voice, don't you agree, Mr. Watson?

"Or, I suppose, persons in your way of life do not

162

have much occasion for the reading of poetry," she added apologetically.

"I like poetry very much," Frank said. Margaret gave him an incredulous stare.

"There is nothing like the male voice for the reading of poetry," Martha said, beaming approval on Frank. "My brother has a very good voice for reading, and he used to indulge us evenings, did he not, Margaret? I declare the excellence of his voice almost made up for—but that is neither here nor there," she finished hastily.

Then she turned upon Frank, moved by a sudden inspiration.

"Mr. Watson," she said, "if you are to stay tonight, perhaps you would like to read—"

"Aunt Martha! We must not impose on Mr. Watson's good nature," said Margaret, embarrassed. "He is still recovering from his injuries of last night, you know."

"Well, he looks quite well except for his discolored eye," said Martha naively, "and I should think Lord Byron's divine words would be a treat for—"

"Indeed they would, ma'am," said Frank hastily. "I should be delighted to read to you tonight."

"But have you forgotten, Aunt Martha, that we are to dine early and go to the ball at—"

"Oh, my dear!" said Martha. "I could not enjoy myself knowing there is such a treasure at home waiting to be discovered. Pray excuse me from the ball. You shall have plenty of company with your young friends and their mother. You needn't take me along."

"But, Aunt, you get out so seldom," said Margaret. "I made sure you would want to go since Mrs. Darlington is a friend of yours from school days."

"I had a comfortable coze with Elvira a few weeks ago when she and her daughters came for tea," said Martha, "and no one actually gets to talk at a ball. I would much rather stay home. Unless, of course, my

163

dear, you really want me to —"

"No, of course not," said Margaret. "You must do as you wish, of course."

"Splendid," said Martha. "I shall leave you to the discussion which I interrupted. I hope you'll both pardon me."

"Of course, Miss Willoughby," said Frank politely.

"It is of no account in the world, Aunt Martha," said Margaret. "I was just about to go into breakfast with Anne and Edward. We've just come in from riding. Have you breakfasted yet?"

"No, my dear. I had just come down when I saw the post," said Martha. "I'll go with you if my presence won't be too much of a damper on a party of young people."

"Of course not," said Margaret warmly, accompanying her aunt from the room.

"Oh, my dear!" exclaimed Martha when they were almost to the parlor.

"Is something wrong?" asked Margaret.

"Mr. Watson! What shall we do with him tonight?"

"Do with him?"

"Well, if he is to stay here we cannot very well expect him to dine with the servants. What shall we do? Are you to have company tonight?"

"No, Aunt," said Margaret.

"Good. Then I suppose it would be all right to have him to dine with us, if you have no objection."

"None in the world. Why should I?" asked Margaret.

"Well, my dear. Dining with your steward. I know occasionally one must show some consideration for one's employees and servants and tenants as on public day, but to have them to dine at your table —"

"My uncle's lawyer has frequently dined with us," said Margaret stiffly.

"I know that, but Mr. Eccles is a younger son of good

164

family. Mr. Watson, on the other hand, for all that he seems to be an excellent young man in his way, isn't, well, you could hardly call him a person of family. One cannot vouch for such a person's, er, habits at table."

"Oh, is that what is worrying you?" said Margaret, her brow clearing. "I am willing to wager Mr. Watson will give us no cause to blush for his manners. And if he does, no one will see him, after all, except us."

"Well, if you say so, my dear," said Martha, looking uncomfortable, "but people might think it so *odd* if it were known you dine with your steward."

"Is there some particular reason why we should *not* have Mr. Watson to dine, apart from your fears that he will disgrace us by making slurping sounds with the soup?" asked Margaret quietly.

"No, my dear! I never said—" said Martha, looking extremely unhappy.

"Of course not," said Margaret, smiling. "I was only funning. I quite see, though, that some persons might presume too much after being shown such favor. But I am confident that Mr. Watson would never do so."

That evening Margaret entered the dining room to find Martha and Frank enjoying an animated discussion about poetry. It was obvious that Martha couldn't have been more amazed if one of the roasted fowls on the table had stood upright and begun a conversation with her. Margaret noticed with approval that the rest of Frank's clothes apparently had been brought from the inn, and he now wore an unexceptional dark coat and spotless linen instead of the footman's garish Sunday suit.

"Mr. Watson!" said Martha, enthusiastically. "You enter into my exact opinion of that particular verse. And to think that someone of your—" She broke off, red-faced.

"Background?" guessed Frank with an amused smile

165

on his face.

Martha looked aghast. She had been thinking, of course, of the fact that he was illegitimate and born in the village to a servant.

Frank chose a different interpretation.

"Actually," he said modestly, "although I didn't precisely go to Harrow, I was fortunate enough to receive an education above my station, for which I am extremely grateful."

"And so you should be," said Martha approvingly. "The appreciation of learned works is a far more valuable thing than mere wealth."

"Indeed, yes, ma'am," said Frank absently. While he had been discussing poetry with Martha, he never once allowed his eyes to stray from her face, a courtesy which didn't often come her way. But now that they had finished discussing Lord Byron, the full glory of Margaret's appearance in a low-cut ivory spangled ball gown with emeralds glimmering in her hair and softly at her slender throat burst upon him. The gleam in his eye when he looked at her so dazzled Margaret that she was forced to ask her aunt to repeat the remark she had just addressed to her.

Dinner passed without incident, although Margaret could have strangled her well-meaning aunt for the way she watched Frank eat with such patent approval. It's a wonder, Margaret thought furiously, he doesn't feel like a performing dog, she is plainly so surprised to see him eating with utensils instead of with his feet.

Any hope she might have had that Frank hadn't noticed the older woman's regard died stillborn when she saw the bland look he gave her as he reached to hand her a plate of bread. Margaret had rarely been so mortified in her life. After Frank skillfully dismembered a roasted hen with the carving knife and sliced several thin slices for the ladies from the breast, Martha

166

flashed Margaret an approving look that plainly said, "Did you see that? Isn't it wonderful?"

"You did very well," said Martha in congratulatory tones. "Very well, indeed, Mr. Watson."

Margaret's breath hissed inward at her aunt's insensitivity. Martha plainly expected Frank to be gratified by her praise of his table manners, as if he had been a small child who had mastered a particularly clever trick.

Margaret felt ready to sink, but Frank's consideration robbed her aunt's thoughtless observation of any offense.

"Thank you very much, ma'am," said Frank, smiling at Martha. "I enjoy discussing poetry very much."

Then he turned the conversation in such a way that before long he was regaling them with stories about his adventures at sea, contriving to convey the impression that being constrained to share a ship with a hundred men in various stages of despair, drunkenness, and rebellion is a vastly entertaining experience.

Margaret gave him a shy, grateful look and he returned it with such a gentle smile that she couldn't help but smile tentatively in return.

Then the spell was broken when Sternes appeared in the doorway.

"Miss Willoughby," he said. "Mrs. Darlington, Miss Darlington and Miss Amelia Darlington have arrived."

"Show them in, Sternes," said Margaret. "Perhaps they would like to join us for dessert."

"No, no, my dear," said Mrs. Darlington, a plump, pretty matron wearing far too much rouge and a gown that made the best of her rather top-heavy figure. "We have already dined, and we could not eat another thing, I promise you."

Her eyes were wide with curiosity when they fell on Frank. Her regard was so pointed a request for an introduction that Margaret had no choice but to oblige.

167

"Mrs. Darlington, may I introduce my steward, Mr. Frank Watson?" she asked.

"Have you just come up from the country, too, Mr. Watson?" asked Mrs. Darlington, giving Frank a look only slightly less thorough than the one Chloe had given him.

"Yes, ma'am," he said. He turned as Margaret introduced him to the younger Darlington females.

To Margaret's chagrin, Mrs. Darlington quickly herded her tender maiden daughters as far away from Frank as she could, obviously under the impression that he could be a danger to them. Margaret noticed that both girls seemed impressed by him, and quickly joined forces with Mrs. Darlington to remove the fragile, blond, blue-eyed damsels from his orbit.

"We must go or we'll be late," said Margaret, kissing her aunt on the cheek. "I wish you a good evening, Aunt."

"What Martha? You are not joining us?" asked Mrs. Darlington in surprise as she tore her eyes with difficulty from Frank's well-made person.

"No, my dear," said Martha. "Pray, excuse me. I hope you will have an agreeable time."

"I'm certain we shall," said Margaret. "Mr. Watson, we will discuss those matters I spoke of later."

She had used her very best employer to employee voice. He replied in kind.

"Yes, ma'am," he said with a brief, subservient bow.

Margaret bit her lip. She had quite effectively put him in his place, underlining his function as a menial. She might just as well have snubbed him, and she knew he didn't deserve it. In her weakness, she only thought of what Mrs. Darlington would think to see her dining *en famille* with her steward. If he had a paunch and a bald dome of a head like her uncle's lawyer, she wouldn't have thought it necessary.

168

She herded the Darlington ladies out of the house and into their carriage.

"He is quite good-looking," said Mrs. Darlington in so unconcerned a voice that Margaret knew she was about to pry for information.

"Mr. Watson?" said Margaret indifferently. "Yes. I suppose he is."

"How long has he been with you?"

"Only a little over a week. Why do you ask?"

"No reason." Mrs. Darlington glanced at Margaret slyly. "My dear, I hope you don't mind my asking, but is there an understanding between you and your cousin Edward?"

"An understanding?" asked Margaret, surprised by the shift in conversation.

"Yes. I mean, do you have an interest in that direction?"

"No, of course not," said Margaret. "We have been raised as brother and sister, after all."

"I see. Then does he have an interest in another young lady?"

"Not to my knowledge, ma'am," said Margaret, wondering what her companion was driving at.

"I am happy to hear it," said Mrs. Darlington with a complacent sigh. "Only a few nights ago he danced twice with my Elizabeth. He was quite charming to us all afterward, was he not, Elizabeth?"

"Mama, please," said the elder Miss Darlington, blushing.

"He couldn't seem to take his eyes off her," persisted her fond mother.

Margaret made a sound that might have been interest or assent, depending on how one wanted to interpret it. To her knowledge, Edward had never shown a serious interest in a young woman of his own class except for herself, and even then, she suspected, it was at his parents' instigation.

Edward was not interested in marriage except to a fortune, preferably her own, and Margaret had not been even remotely tempted when he laid his hand and heart before her the previous summer. Even if she had been susceptible to his type of charm, which she most definitely was not, she would have thought twice about committing herself to a man who was likely to share his favors quite impartially between his wife and half the opera dancers in London, not to mention the parlor-maids.

Margaret wished Elizabeth Darlington a good deal of luck if she wished to attach him. Edward, if left to his own devices, Margaret was quite sure, would live and die a bachelor. His penchant for young, buxom servant girls was no secret in their corner of Yorkshire. He thought dancing at balls and fetching lemonade for demure schoolroom misses pretty flat entertainment.

So Margaret was surprised and not particularly pleased upon her arrival at Lady Marsdon's flower-bedecked town house to be accosted by Edward almost as soon as the footman had taken her wrap.

"Hallo, Coz," he said, kissing her hand. "I am delighted to see you. We must have a comfortable chat later."

"You last saw me at breakfast," she hissed under her breath. "Why the sudden interest in my company?"

"May I have the honor of this dance?" he asked formally.

"Of course," she said, conscious of many eyes upon her as she laid her hand on his arm. They moved into the set and had little opportunity for speech until the dance was over.

"Now, what was all that about?" she asked suspiciously as he escorted her to a small sofa and seated himself beside her. "You never dance. You prefer to

170

stand by the side of the room cynically surveying the company."

"That sounds like a quotation. I hear quite enough of that sort of thing from our mutual aunt," grumbled Edward, who not only was not bookish, but also resented people who were bookish making elusive references to things they read in books while he was present. He considered alluding to literature bad manners, like conversing in a tongue a third party doesn't understand while in company.

"So why are you suddenly dogging my steps?" she asked.

"Since that Darlington harpy has been trying to throw her yellow-haired chit into my path."

"For shame, you trifler," said Margaret, amused. "At the last ball, I have it on good authority that you couldn't take your eyes off her—"

"I swear," Edward objected, "I hardly looked at the chit. Her mother kept forcing her on me, and I didn't want to embarrass the poor thing, so I danced with her."

"How unfortunate," said Margaret. "However, you can easily remedy the situation by flirting with every young lady in the room so that Mrs. Darlington thinks you'd be no great loss, after all."

"But I don't want to flirt with every young lady in the room," Edward complained.

"Then why did you come?"

"Lady Marsdon's son is a friend of mine, and asked me to come because his mother and sisters were afraid the affair would be short of men. We were sharing a bottle at the Daffy Club when he put it to me, and so I agreed. I couldn't very well get out of it."

"I see," said Margaret, laughing. "Well, try not to look so miserable."

"I wasn't aware that I looked miserable. You look

"devilishly pretty tonight, Cousin."

"How very kind," Margaret murmured.

"I would have a better time if I could sit in your pocket all evening."

"Much as I regret wounding your vanity, my dear Edward," said Margaret lightly, "I didn't come to this ball in order to protect you from the Darlingtons."

"No. You came because Lady Marsdon is one of our neighbors in Yorkshire and not to do so would have been a cruel slight."

"Yes," said Margaret. "but that's no reason why I can't try to enjoy myself a little, and I cannot do so if you will glare at every man in the room who even *looks* as if he might want to dance with me."

While she talked with Edward, she had the peculiar feeling that she was being stared at by several pairs of eyes. This was not an unusual feeling. The heiress was quite used to being pointed out to others. But somehow this was different. She was used to looks of admiration or speculation, but the sly looks and barely hushed whispers made her very uncomfortable.

Then she thought she knew the reason. Her aunt and uncle were standing across the room, looking at her and Edward expectantly. Her aunt gave her a flirtatious little wave of her plump, be-ringed hand, pursed her lips in the shape of a kiss and simpered.

Margaret turned accusing eyes upon Edward. Her aunt and uncle rarely attended balls. Yet there they were, looking at her with fatuous smiles of greeting on their faces. It appeared to Margaret as if everyone in the room had hushed, watching expectantly to see how the heiress would greet the kin she had just evicted from her home.

She realized that Sir Robert and his lady had deliberately stalked her to the ball (there was really no other word for it) in order to force a reconciliation. Margaret

172

sighed and placed her hand on Edward's arm, hating his smile of triumph. He escorted her to his parents, who greeted her as if she had returned from the dead.

"My darling, my precious girl," gushed her Aunt Samantha, a formidable lady of expensive, though not particularly attractive appearance. She was wearing a lavender silk dress that clung with rather unfortunate results to her massive figure and a silk turban over her abundant false curls. Her smaller husband, following in her wake, often gave the appearance of a tugboat trying to catch up with a battleship in full sail.

"Good evening, Margaret, my dear," said Sir Robert, kissing Margaret's brow.

Margaret was not deceived by their affection. In the whole time she was a child, she could remember perhaps a half-dozen times when her uncle had kissed her and every one of them was in the presence of persons outside their family circle whom he wished to impress with his devotion to his niece.

"There's our good girl," crooned Samantha. "Sir Robert feared you would give us the cut direct," she continued rather too loudly, "but I told him, 'My love, our little niece would never be so cruel to her aunt and uncle who have raised her from a child.' "

"No, indeed," said Sir Robert, looking as if he might kiss Margaret again. Margaret took the precaution of moving closer to Edward, and jumped when his hand closed on her elbow as if to keep her confined. People were openly staring.

"You look well," said Margaret hesitantly.

"Do you really think so, love?" asked Samantha mournfully. "It is like your kind heart to say so. But I have been suffering the most dreadful palpitations. Of course, it gave me a pang not to be going to my own room in a place that has been home to me for so many years —"

"We are staying," said Sir Robert in a tone of censure, "with Samantha's brother Gilbert. We are, of course, too late in the season to rent a town house of our own. Gilbert's house is rather snug, so we're all very crowded with the children and all, but we are tolerably comfortable, I assure you."

"Yes, my dear," said Samantha with a small, brave smile. "Don't worry about us. I dare say we will become accustomed. The important thing is that you're comfortable, although it must seem strange with you and Martha rattling about in that big house all alone. But I am sure you had good reasons for wanting solitude, and if your uncle and aunt are in the way, of course you must do as you see fit. Your happiness, dear child, is all that matters."

Margaret could have sunk through the floor. Her aunt and uncle had made sure everyone within earshot knew that they living in less-than-luxurious accommodations, and it was all their heartless niece's fault. Aunt Samantha's brother Gilbert and his wife were delightful but unpretentious individuals who lived in a good, but not particularly fashionable, quarter of London and who had been gracious enough to open their home to Sir Robert and his lady for the season. Even so, neither Robert nor Samantha could resist twitting Margaret about the inferiority of their present dwelling.

Anne, who had just come from the dance on the arm of her brother's friend, Anthony Marsdon, greeted Margaret with a smile of pleasure.

"Dear child," said Samantha with a tender sigh as she put a plump arm around her daughter's slender waist. "How she misses her cousin, don't you, my dear?"

"Well, of course," said Anne uncertainly.

"Far be it from me to criticize," said Samantha. "After all, it is your house, Margaret, and you must do as you wish, even if it is vastly inconvenient to your

174

nearest kin, but our poor Anne had been so looking forward to staying with you in London—"

"Mother!" exclaimed Anne, embarrassed.

Edward, with great presence of mind, led Margaret into the waltz.

"I wish you would not hold me so closely," Margaret complained.

"Such ingratitude," he said with a saturnine lift of one shapely brow.

"Why should I be grateful? You planned this. Now I look like the most unnatural beast in nature. Well, it won't work. I am not going to invite your parents to move into the town house. I have already invited Anne to stay with me after her ball in three weeks, but she said her mother refuses to let her come."

"That is true," said Edward uncomfortably. "Mother says if we're not all welcome in your home, Anne cannot avail herself of your hospitality, either."

"She must do what she thinks best," said Margaret, as the waltz ended. "You may escort me to Lady Marsdon. I haven't greeted her yet."

"I was going to ask you for the next dance."

"Three dances in a row? Thank you, I have more care for my reputation than that."

"Indeed? If you ask me, your association with me can only improve it."

"Whatever do you mean by that?" asked Margaret, puzzled.

"I mean I've heard some pretty nasty rumors about you this evening."

"I didn't know Chloe was just in your style," she murmured.

Edward flushed and tightened his grip on Margaret's wrist.

"She's a dangerous woman, and no mistake," said Edward. "If you truly cared for your precious reputa-

175

tion, you'd discharge Frank Watson."

"Everyone knows that Chloe is a spiteful liar," said Margaret. "I, for one, would never believe a word she says. She's only bent on creating mischief because Mr. Watson snubbed her."

"*He* snubbed *her?* That fellow is capable of anything."

"He is an excellent steward," said Margaret with great dignity, "and I am not going to discharge him because some idle minds have nothing better to do than gossip about my personal affairs. On second thought, before I greet Lady Marsdon, I must find Mrs. Darlington and her daughters. It was very rude of me to walk away from them without a word at your instigation. If you'll excuse me?"

"As you wish," said Edward coldly.

Margaret regretted that he was angry, but there wasn't really much she could do about it. She saw Mrs. Darlington by the tea table and made her way toward her. She noticed the woman facing her tried to convey a wordless message to Mrs. Darlington, but the lady was oblivious and her words came to Margaret's ears with disastrous clarity.

"He was actually *dining* with them," Mrs. Darlington was saying with relish. "I couldn't believe my eyes. I only half-believed Chloe's nonsense about a dead ringer for Jeremy Verelst, but you should see him. Blonde and handsome as a Greek god. I wonder where she found him. It's plain he's more than just a steward, my dear."

The message being urgently conveyed to her by her companion's eyes finally got through. Red-cheeked, she turned to see Margaret looking at her with a cynical expression on her face. Mrs. Darlington had hoped that becoming intimate with the heiress would mean great things for her girls, and she had traded shamelessly upon her acquaintance with Martha Willoughby in order to gain entry to Margaret's circle. Since all the eligible men continually competed for Margaret's regard, it only made sense that a friendship with Margaret would afford two very young ladies ample opportunity to become acquainted with a great many bachelors.

Margaret and Lady Darlington stared into each other's eyes for a long, pregnant moment, during which Mrs. Darlington bid a sad farewell to all the hopes she had engendered for this carefully nurtured friendship. Mrs. Darlington and her daughters had already received cards for Anne's ball, so they were safe on that account. But there would be no more elegant teas at Margaret's house, nor would Mrs. Darlington's daughters ever again be invited to ride through Hyde Park in Margaret's open carriage, which was always accompanied by a small court of London's more eligible bachelors during the fashionable hour of the promenade in the park.

Unsupported, Chloe's vindictive character assassination would have been attributed to sheer spite once its novelty had worn thin. But now that Mrs. Darlington had chosen to corroborate it with consistent, though less damning, evidence of her own, Chloe's gossip might be believed by persons who may have otherwise dismissed it as the pure, malicious mischief-making it was.

Margaret's head began to throb.

"There you are, Mrs. Darlington," she said mildly. "I hope you will forgive me, but I believe I will go home. I have the most shocking headache."

"How unfortunate," said Mrs. Darlington, anxious to make amends. "I will collect the girls and we will leave immediately."

"No, I pray you won't bother," said Margaret. "I will

find some other escort. Your daughters should not be expected to forego their pleasure for the sake of my headache."

"Well, if you're sure," said Mrs. Darlington hesitantly.

"Quite sure," said Margaret crisply.

Edward was dancing with his sister and tried to catch her eye as she left the room. Blast! If he caught wind of the fact that she meant to leave, he would probably insist upon escorting her and she would have to listen to him make pointed remarks about her steward all the way home.

Smilingly, she turned down several solicitations for her hand to the dance and went in search of her hostess, Lady Marsdon.

"I am so sorry you have the headache," said Lady Marsdon in response to her excuses. "I suppose your cousin will be taking you home."

"Perhaps. I haven't asked him."

"How fortunate. My son Anthony would be honored to escort you," she said with a twinkle in her eye. "You know he is quite one of your most devoted admirers."

"You're very kind," said Margaret, horror-stricken, "but I couldn't put your son to such inconvenience at his sister's ball."

"No, it would be a pleasure," said Lady Marsdon, who felt it expedient to sacrifice the presence of her eldest son at his sister's ball rather than deprive the company of Mr. Edward Willoughby, whom she had hopes would show some interest in her own daughter. And if Anthony managed to captivate the elusive Miss Willoughby, well, that would be beyond all Lady Marsdon's hopes.

Imperiously, she lifted her hand and caught Anthony's eye. He excused himself from the small knot of men about to go into one of the salons for a game of

178

cards and came to her side.

"Ma'am?" he said to his mother. He turned to Margaret. "Good evening, Miss Willoughby."

"Good evening," said Margaret.

"Anthony, Miss Willoughby has the headache and wishes to go home without inconveniencing Mrs. Darlington and her daughters who brought her. I told her you would be happy to take her home in the carriage."

"With the greatest of pleasure," said Anthony enthusiastically. Not only did he look forward to having the enchanting Miss Willoughby to himself, but he was beginning to find his sister's ball poor sport and was happy for an excuse to leave it.

"You are too kind," said Margaret tentatively. Now she'd really done it. The last thing she wanted was a tête-à-tête with Anthony, a young man of whom she had never been fond. He was one of Edward's intimates, and he had not a thought in his head that wasn't concerned with hunting, drinking, and playing cards. He was excruciatingly dull company, and she didn't like the wolfish way he leered at her, as if he could swallow her in one bite.

She accepted his escort because she really couldn't see any help for it, and she flinched a little as all eyes turned to watch their departure. Anthony made hearty conversation all the way home, and laughed far too often and too loudly for the sake of her aching head.

When they arrived at her town house, Margaret turned to him and offered her hand after he helped her from the carriage.

"Thank you so much for your escort," she said politely. "There is no need to accompany me inside."

"Nonsense," he said. "I can't simply drop you off in the street, as it were."

He punctured the night air with a loud laugh at his

179

own wit. Margaret led him to the door, which was opened by Sternes, who greeted them majestically and turned to escort them inside the house.

"That's all right, my good man," said Anthony jovially. "I'm not staying."

Sternes bowed and withdrew.

Margaret viewed with alarm Anthony's obvious intention of making her a speech of some sort. His adam's apple was bobbing up and down, and he had a fatuous expression on his face. He took a step toward her, and it took all of her resolution not to turn and run to the safety of her parlor and her aunt.

"I guess you know I'm head over ears in love —"

"Please, I beg you will not —," said Margaret at the same time, backing away from him. Unfortunately, she had her back to the wall, and he continued to advance.

"How fortunate I am to have you alone," said Anthony, moving so close she could smell the wine on his breath. He put a hand on the wall on each side of her as if to prevent her escape. "There are so many fellows buzzing around this particular honeybee —"

"No, Anthony," said Margaret, trying to dodge his kiss. She knew instinctively that his lips would be moist and loathsome, and they were.

He was about to kiss her again, and she had recoiled and tried to avert her face, when suddenly her besotted beau was snatched away. She opened her eyes, which she had closed in revulsion, to see Anthony struggling in Frank's grip. Martha, who apparently had followed Frank into the hall, was gaping in astonishment.

Frank, by this time, was shaking Anthony so hard that Margaret could hear his teeth rattling.

"No, Mr. Watson," said Margaret, horrified. "Let go of him at once."

Frank paused and raised one quizzical eyebrow.

"Perhaps I misunderstood the situation," he said

coldly. "Did you welcome his attentions? If so, I apologize for interrupting."

"How dare you suggest—," said Margaret, flushing. Repugnance was written so plainly on her face that any compunction Frank might have had about laying unfriendly hands on the impetuous Lothario was erased. So, with his usual graceful economy of movement, he opened the door and threw Anthony out of it. Then he closed the door and brushed his hands together with satisfaction.

"Now, then," he said comfortably. "If that will be all—"

Emotions warred on Margaret's face for a moment, then she covered her face with shaking hands. Martha, who had remained transfixed with embarrassment through the whole distressing scene, put motherly arms around her afflicted niece.

"Miss Willoughby—," exclaimed Frank, horrified. He started forward, then checked himself.

"My poor dear," crooned Martha. "Don't cry, love. He won't bother you again. *I'll* have something to say to Lady Marsdon, and no mistake if—"

She broke off in astonishment as Margaret's face emerged from her hands and showed her concerned audience an expression convulsed with laughter.

"Forgive me, Aunt Martha," said Margaret in an unsteady voice. "I don't know what's come over me."

"Poor child," exclaimed Martha in alarm. "She's hysterical," she added sagely to Frank, who had turned to stone, in an undervoice. "Perhaps some brandy—"

Frank moved as if to act on her suggestion but Margaret held out a hand to stop him.

"No, please don't," she told him. "There is nothing wrong with me. But when you said 'Now then, if that will be all—' for all the world as if you spent every day of your life throwing people out of my house—"

181

She again dissolved into laughter, and Martha tightened her grip on her shoulders, exchanging a long look of comprehension with Frank.

"I don't know why I'm behaving like this," said Margaret helplessly. "Pray, forgive me."

"It's all right, child," said Martha, "you must lie down on your bed and—"

"No," said Margaret, gently disengaging herself from her aunt's sheltering arm. "I'm better now. It has been such a *horrid* evening. But I am not at all tired."

"Well, if that's so," said Martha, hesitantly. "Perhaps you would like to join Mr. Watson and me in the parlor. Mr. Watson was reading "Manfred." It will be just the thing . . ."

Margaret looked trapped. She *loathed* Lord Byron's dramatic poem. Frank, who remembered her caustic reference to the work when he suggested that her cousin Edward was the living image of the tortured hero, met Margaret's eyes and nearly laughed aloud at the dismay in them.

"Very well," said Margaret. "I'll just go change and get my needlework."

"Shall I go with you, dear?" asked Martha. "Perhaps you should rest—"

"No, that isn't necessary," said Margaret. "I am accustomed to keeping much later hours, I assure you. I shall be with you in a trice."

She left, and Martha looked at Frank for a pregnant instant.

"I would never have expected such behavior from Lady Marsdon's son," said Martha as she led the way back to the parlor.

"It was the emotion of the moment, perhaps, or the wine served at the ball," said Frank, who, much as he deplored the young man's depravity, could readily understand the mental state of a man made reckless by the vision of the enchanting Miss Willoughby clad in a garment that revealed so much of her lovely shoulders and bosom. "He is one of your niece's suitors, I collect."

"Not a particularly persistent one," said Martha, shrugging. "Margaret is the fashion at the moment and a few of the young men pay court to her simply because it is the thing to do. He is one of them. But it is quite another thing to presume—"

"Quite," said Frank. "Most ungentlemanly."

"Exactly my own opinion," said Martha. "Fortunately, the tone of dear Margaret's mind is much too high to be taken in by the compliments she has cast at her daily. But my greatest fear is that she will end up alone and friendless like me."

"Alone, perhaps," said Frank kindly, "but hardly friendless, if I may presume to say so."

"No," said Martha, brightening. "There is her fortune, after all."

Frank was about to point out that he wasn't referring to Margaret at all. When he made the remark he had meant to emphasize Martha's own good fortune in having the obvious affection of not only her niece but also a circle of friends that included the pastor and several other intimates, when he recollected that it was extremely improper for Martha to discuss either her niece's or her own affairs with him. Martha apparently came to the same realization at that moment and changed the subject.

Martha was reluctant to allow Frank to resume his reading of "Manfred" until Margaret joined them, which amused Frank because he knew that his employer would have been delighted to miss as much of the poem as possible.

"What a pity that we have progressed beyond the middle of the second act," said Martha. "Would you mind very much if we resumed at the beginning of the poem, Mr. Watson? I declare, I could listen to his words forever, and poor Margaret — "

Margaret entered the room in time to hear her aunt's suggestion and hastened to assure her with some alacrity that it was unnecessary for Frank to start at the beginning of the poem for her benefit.

"I should not dream of imposing on poor Mr. Watson in such a way. I remember the first act perfectly well, I assure you," she said firmly, "and my enjoyment will be in no way abated by going to the second."

"Well, if you're sure, dear," said Martha skeptically. "We were just at the place where Manfred has entered the Hall of the Arimanes, but perhaps we should repeat the beginning of the second act — "

"No, I pray you," said Margaret, whose eyes transfixed Frank's amused ones with a command not to argue with her, "do not repeat *any* of the poem on my account. I would not spoil your enjoyment, and I am the latecomer after all."

Martha was about to make another polite protest, confident that her niece was only being considerate, when Frank resolved the matter by resuming.

". . . Many a night on the earth,/ On the bare ground, have I bowed my face,/ And strewed my head with ashes; I have known/ The fulness of humiliation — for I sunk before my vain despair, and knelt/ To my own desolation . . ." he intoned.

Such stuff, thought Margaret tolerantly as she placidly jabbed a square of white linen with her needle. Still, Frank's voice was deep yet melodious, and his phrasing was quite good. She wondered what his singing voice was like. Then she caught herself up guiltily on the manner of her thoughts and forced herself to concentrate on her needlework.

She was not particularly fond of embroidery, but she had always depended on it to help her pass the tedium of her uncle's readings. She would not for the world have had her aunt guess how little to her taste was Lord Byron's work for fear of hurting that lady's feelings. Watching Martha's simple enjoyment of the poem and recollecting her animated conversation with Frank, Margaret reflected rather guiltily that Frank had shown more attention to that affectionate lady's entertainment than had Margaret over the past few months. She and her aunt were fond of each other, but not intimate. Their conversation always tended to be a trifle stilted, whereas with Frank, Martha could talk more freely and naturally about subjects that interested her.

Margaret realized that her aunt was really a very intelligent woman with a great deal to say, only Margaret had never really listened. Martha was lonely, and Margaret didn't realize it until she saw the hungry way Martha responded to Frank's kindness.

Had Margaret been so wrapped up in her own concerns and her own desires that she had neglected the only one of her relatives who had given Margaret unconditional love throughout her life? Margaret had to admit, to her shame, that the answer was yes. Although Sir Robert and Lady Willoughby were fond of telling acquaintances that they had unselfishly saddled themselves with Margaret's upbringing, it was Martha, and not they, who had provided the practical aspects of parenting.

She resolved to be more considerate of her aunt from that time forward. It was too disgraceful that it took the example of her steward to make her more sensitive to a woman who had been the only softening influence in her life.

Absorbed in these thoughts, the words passed through and around her as the evening progressed.

At one point, her aunt yawned and stood up.

"Pray, forgive me," said Martha. "I am so sleepy. I

must retire. I don't know when I have so enjoyed an evening, Mr. Watson, and I thank you."

Frank stood up at once and made as if to close the book.

"The pleasure has been mine, ma'am," he said politely.

"No, no," Martha protested. "Do not stop on my account unless, of course, you are very weary of reading. I am sure Margaret would like to listen to the rest."

"Very true, ma'am," said Frank, his eyes dancing.

"Good night, dear," said Martha, bending to kiss Margaret's cheek.

Margaret had been so immersed in her needlework that she suddenly realized her aunt was leaving. Before she could recover from her astonishment that her sleepy aunt was about to go up to bed, very improperly leaving her unchaperoned in the company of a single gentleman at an indecent hour, Martha was gone.

Margaret looked at Frank in surprise. He smiled wryly. He understood the workings of Martha's mind all too plainly. Although Martha would never have left her niece in the company of a gentleman from her world, she didn't think it mattered in the least that Margaret was left in the company of her steward. Frank, to Martha, was simply an agreeable young menial who happened to be staying at the house. Despite Martha's obvious respect for Frank's intelligence and cultured tastes, the thought that a person of such inferior birth could be a danger to her precious niece was preposterous. To Martha, Margaret was as safe in Frank's company as she was in the company of Jacques the cook, Peter the footman or Sternes the butler.

Frank met Margaret's look squarely.

"Shall I continue?" he inquired.

"Certainly," she said uncomfortably. To retreat would be an admission of her confusion. She thought

186

she would listen for a little while, then, when the awkwardness of Martha's departure had worn off, she would make her excuses gracefully and retire.

Before long, Frank's soothing voice had sunk her into a pleasant half-doze. She really would get up any minute, but the fire was so warm and the sound of Frank's voice so soothing. Then, sudden comprehension of the words he was intoning burst upon her.

"While Emily kept her eyes fixed on the spot, she saw the door move, and then slowly open, and perceived something enter the room, but the extreme duskiness prevented her from distinguishing what it was. Almost fainting with terror, she had yet sufficient command over herself, to check the shriek, that was escaping from her lips, and, letting the curtain drop from her hand, continued to observe in silence the motions of the mysterious form she saw —"

Margaret, her face mirroring her indignation, jumped up quickly and approached the culprit with her hand outstretched. A smile quirking the corners of his mouth, he pretended to be ignorant of her intention and continued reading.

"It seemed to glide along the remote obscurity of the apartment, then paused, and, as it approached the hearth, she perceived, in the stronger light, what appeared to be a human figure. Certain remembrances now struck up on her heart, and almost subdued the feeble remains of her spirits; she continued, however, to watch the figure, which remained for some time motionless, but then, advancing slowly towards the bed, stood silently at the feet, where the curtains, being a little open, allowed her to see it; terror, however, had now deprived her of the power of discrimination, as well as that of utterance . . ."

At this point, Margaret gave an unladylike snarl of outrage and snatched at the book he had in his hand.

187

Perceiving her intention, he stood and held the book, which she recognized as her copy of *The Mysteries of the Udolpho* by Ann Radcliffe, out of her reach.

"Mr. Watson," she exclaimed. "How dare you make free of my property!"

"Persons who leave said property open on the library table," he said virtuously, dodging her attempts to snatch the book from him, "should not complain when other persons appropriate said property for their own base ends. Besides, you recommended the book yourself at our first meeting. When I saw it so close to hand, I could not resist the impulse to examine it. I now see why you imagined horrors in the Verelst family chapel. I'm only amazed you didn't run shrieking at the sight of me."

A reluctant smile crossed her face.

"Mr. Watson," she said quietly, "please give me the book."

"But Miss Willoughby, don't you want me to read the part in which she finds the trail of blood on the stair?"

"No, I do not," she said in deceptively calm accents.

He relaxed and she made her move. One hand on his shoulder for support, she leaped for the book and, laughing down into her upturned face, he grasped her around the waist to keep her from reaching it.

Her sharp intake of breath recalled him to his position. The laughter died from his eyes and he released her slowly, as if reluctant to do so. She averted her face in embarrassment.

"I should have surrendered this at once," he said quietly. "Please forgive me."

"Of course," said Margaret, taking the book. "It is quite late. I will bid you good night, Mr. Watson."

"Miss Willoughby," he said with his subservient bow.

It was long before Margaret slept, and when she woke she found her bed linens twisted and disheveled by her disturbing dreams.

She remembered how it had felt to be crushed to Frank's chest for that one, mad instant. She realized that if he had attempted to take advantage of the situation, in her weakness she would not have protested.

In her dreams, she watched the beloved shade of Jeremy Verelst stare at her with alien eyes, then walk away into the mist as she pleaded with it to return.

It was then that she realized the full enormity of what had happened that night. She could let the shade of Jeremy Verelst rest now, but the price of her release was agonizingly high.

The rich, the independent, the Unattainable Miss Willoughby had committed the only true sin of her class, that of falling in love with a person of inferior birth. The future could hold only despair for her unless she could exorcise Frank Watson from her mind and heart, for heartache and alienation from all that was familiar to her could be the only logical result of so shocking a misalliance.

Was she strong enough to remove temptation by expelling him from her household? She realized that she was not, and she was doomed to endure the torture of having him near while being forced to keep him at a distance.

Chapter Eight

"I might have known," said Edward melodramatically as he bent a stormy gaze upon Margaret and Frank, surprised in the very act of drinking coffee over the broken meats of their breakfast.

"What *is* the matter with you, Edward?" asked Margaret in a voice of long-suffering. "I won't stand for Cheltenham tragedies before I've barely swallowed my coffee, and so I warn you."

"What is *he* doing here?" Edward said accusingly as Frank made as if to pass him a plate of buttered toast.

"I'm eating my breakfast," said Frank.

"I *know* that," said Edward, goaded. "And, worse, the two of you are having it alone. Have you *no* shame?"

"None whatsoever," said Frank, unperturbed.

"Stop that, both of you," Margaret demanded. "I won't tolerate this sort of thing over the breakfast cups. It isn't civilized. And we weren't having breakfast alone, not that it's any of *your* business, Edward. Aunt Martha was here until just a few minutes ago."

"A likely story," said Edward accusingly.

Frank stood up.

"I think Mr. Willoughby and I should continue this discussion elsewhere," he said in a voice of steely calm.

"Stop it, I said!" Margaret shouted. "Edward, it is

none of your business who I have staying in my house. Mr. Watson is here at my request because I have some commissions for him to perform before he returns to Yorkshire, not that I should have to explain myself to you. And, Mr. Watson, I will thank you not to encourage my cousin to make a cake of himself."

Frank sat down and calmly began munching on a piece of toast.

"Sure you won't have some, Willoughby? It's very hot," said Frank provocatively.

"Mr. Watson," said Margaret dangerously.

"Yes, ma'am," said Frank, a smile lurking in his eyes. "I'm certain you would prefer to continue your discussion in private, so I'll just go along to the library, shall I? I'll be close at hand if anyone wishes to call me out."

He left with a bow in their general direction.

"It's beyond me how you tolerate that fellow's presumption," said Edward. "If he weren't unworthy of a gentleman's steel, I'd—"

"Edward," said Margaret sweetly. "I'm sure you didn't come here at this uncivilized hour to exchange insults with my steward. Did you want something?"

"Oh, yes," he said sheepishly. "I wanted to apologize for last night."

Margaret burst into laughter.

"Well, that's a peculiar way of making an apology," she said. "First you rather rudely force your way past my butler. Then you have the impertinence to make wild accusations (although I'm still not certain what it is I am being accused of) about some wholly imaginary relationship between my steward and myself. Then you make veiled threats against a man who has never done you harm."

"I'm sorry, Margaret," said Edward. "That fellow makes me so angry, I lose all reason."

"Well, try to control yourself," said Margaret.

"I will," he promised. "I don't know what came over me last night to lecture you on the dance floor. Of course I don't believe you would disparage your birth and position by conducting yourself in an improper manner with Watson. I was jealous. I'm jealous of any man who enjoys your regard, even though I know you can only think of him as an employee."

"Oh, come now," said Margaret. "Do you really expect me to believe you are jealous?"

"Yes," he said simply.

"Well, I don't," she said with spirit. "You know as well as I that any affection you have for me is purely cream-pot love. It would gratify your father if you could regain the ancestral acres, and you'd love being the lord of the manor. You've never liked me above half, and you know it."

"I love you, Margaret. I told you so last summer," he protested.

"My dear cousin, it would make me very sad to hear it if I believed a word of it, for I will never have any feeling for you except proper family affection," said Margaret, laying a hand on his arm. "You are very handsome, and you can be kind on occasion. You can even be pleasant company when you aren't carrying on like the patriarch in a bad comedy about my precious reputation and the danger of contamination with inferior persons. But you are not for me. I'm sorry. I wish it were otherwise, because it would be so suitable."

"I hope you don't regret this day's work," said Edward, looking sulky.

"That's just what I mean! Everything that comes out of your mouth sounds like a threat of some sort. I could never love someone who so strongly disapproves of me. And I won't be bullied. With my wealth, I don't have to be."

"I wish you would not bring up your wealth every two

192

minutes," Edward complained. "It smacks of vulgarity."

"Hmmmph. You and your family aspire to my sort of vulgarity. You are forgiven for helping your parents ambush me at the ball last night. You are even forgiven for lecturing me as if I were a naughty child in a crowded ballroom. Let's shake hands and cry friends."

He took her outstretched hand and pulled her close to him until she was in the circle of his arms. She gave a surprised squeak. He put his lips close to her ear.

"Are you very, very sure, Margaret?" he asked softly.

"Quite," said Margaret, laughing.

He pulled her closer.

"Do you mean to tell me you feel nothing at this very moment? Can you look me in the eye and say that?"

Margaret looked up into his eyes.

"Yes, Edward. I can. The strongest emotion I can conjure up at this moment is mild pleasure, and that's if I really concentrate."

Edward released her reluctantly.

"You mean it," he said, astonished.

"Yes, dear. I'm afraid so," she said apologetically.

"If that doesn't beat all," he said in a dejected tone. "When you were a plump, spotty child, you followed me about with adoration in your eyes for three solid years. I actually tied you to a tree once to keep you from following me and getting in my way. Now that you've turned into a beauty, you don't want any part of me."

"Perhaps you should have been kinder to that unattractive child," she said.

Then, after an infinitesimal pause, she added in order to change the subject, "Is Anne getting excited about the ball?"

"Yes. Very," said Edward unenthusiastically. Margaret bent an exasperated look on him, so he tried again.

"She can talk of nothing but the clothes you bought for her. It is too generous of you, Cousin."

"It is a pleasure to take such a pretty girl around to the shops," said Margaret. "Even in her most unattractive stage, Anne was neither spotty nor stout. I am determined she will be a sensation."

"Anne? Hardly. But she is a pretty girl and she will enjoy the remainder of the season. I just hope we can get her married off before the summer."

"Why?" asked Margaret. "She's only sixteen. There's plenty of time for her to be thinking of marriage."

Edward shifted his weight uncomfortably.

"Tell me," Margaret commanded him.

"My parents are in debt again."

"I settled all of their debts last year!"

"I know. And I settled some of them, too, but I cannot allow myself to be beggared, particularly since you're being so stubborn about not marrying me."

"But I don't understand! How can anyone manage to spend so much?"

"It's Mother. She cannot say no to anything that catches her eye. And Father. He has turned to gambling. And women."

Edward looked so embarrassed that Margaret laid a comforting hand on his arm. He closed his hand over it and brought it to his lips.

At that moment, Frank appeared in the doorway.

"Excuse me," he said, clearing his throat.

"What do *you* want?" demanded Edward, forgetting himself.

"What is it, Mr. Watson?" asked Margaret in a milder tone.

"You asked the florist to wait on you today, ma'am, and he is here."

"I see. I will be with you directly. Show him to the library, if you please."

"Yes, ma'am," said Frank, leaving the room.

"And if you say one word," Margaret cautioned

194

Edward, who was about to give voice to an acid remark about Frank, "I shall scream."

"Yes, Margaret."

"I don't know what is to be done about your parents. I cannot continue pulling them out of River Tick. They have already begun to make inroads into even my fortune. Forgive me for sounding heartless, but they are not my responsibility. They must learn to live within their means."

"I know. Believe me, I have told them that."

"And?"

"They tell me if I'd make more of a push to attach you, there wouldn't be a problem. Part of the mischief is when they left your household, some of their creditors started dunning them. In order to quiet them, they ordered more and more."

"Oh, so it's *my* fault, is it?" said Margaret indignantly.

"And mine for letting your beauteous person and fortune slip through my careless fingers."

"Everyone's fault but their own."

"Exactly."

"So Anne will be the sufferer. I don't suppose it occurred to my uncle to reduce the state of his own household instead of depriving his only daughter of the opportunity to take her rightful place in society?"

"The way he sees it is, if she fails to exert herself enough to marry an eligible man this season, then it's her own fault if she is deprived of another. In fact, if she had an ounce of family feeling, she would immediately marry the richest man she could find and repair the family fortunes. I shudder for Anne if a rich dotard should offer for her. My father wouldn't think twice about selling her into marriage."

"That's despicable!"

"I agree."

"Well, *do* something."

"I shall. If they try to compel her to accept an unequal marriage for the sake of the settlements she'll bring them, I shall rent a house and install her in it."

"Would you do that, Edward?" asked Margaret, her expression softening.

"Yes. I'm very fond of Anne. I won't let them do to her what our grandparents did to Aunt Martha. She was shy, too, but she had enough courage to refuse to marry a wealthy cit at their command. Our grandfather, like my father, was very expensive. He was spiteful enough to leave Aunt Martha nothing when he died."

"I didn't know that was the reason!" exclaimed Margaret. "Poor Aunt Martha."

"Yes. My father told me this but not, as you would suppose, in a tone of regret for the injustice done her. When I was younger, I was naive enough to ask him once why Martha was your dependent and not his. Logically, you would think her brother would provide for her, not her niece. And that was his explanation. She had defied her father, and she deserved her poverty. As her father's heir, my father felt no obligation to provide for her or, at least, he considered his father's grudge a good excuse not to."

"Poor Anne," said Margaret. "I am glad she has you to protect her. It would cause no remark for her to leave her parents' home to keep house for her brother as it would if she would come to live with me. But I would find a way to rescue her if you did not."

"I know you would," said Edward. "But that, at least, shall not be left to your charge. I must go."

He took her in his arms again.

"Are you sure — ?"

"Quite sure," said Margaret, laughingly disengaging herself. He left her with an exaggerated sigh and a jaunty wave of his hand.

She entered the library to find Frank in deep conference with the florist. They had decided on how many floral arrangements would be needed to festoon the ballroom, and how many flowers would be needed to grace the supper table. It was left to Margaret to choose the color and style of the arrangements.

This done, Frank asked leave to return to Yorkshire. Margaret was plainly dissatisfied, but she agreed.

He arrived at the little brick house late at night to find Fanny Watson up and about. Mathilde had gone for the day and Fanny eyed him speculatively as she prepared a cold meal for him.

"You shouldn't be doing that," said Frank, trying to persuade her to return to bed. "I can do it."

"No," she said quietly. "I have to get used to it sometime. Now you sit down and tell me about London."

"London? Well, it's very large and very noisy and very exciting," he said. "I've brought you something."

He fished around in his bag and came up with a white handkerchief edged in lace and a soft wool shawl.

"You shouldn't have gone and done that," she said, embarrassed.

"Why not?" he asked in surprise.

"Oh, no reason," she said, averting her eyes from his.

"This is very good," Frank said, eating the cold meal she had put before him. "I didn't have time to eat anything on the road because I wanted to make it home in one day. I have to keep an eye on Miss Willoughby's bailiff because she doesn't quite trust him. Then there are all the accounts —"

"Will you do something for me?" asked Fanny.

"Certainly," said Frank. "What is it?"

"Read this."

She gave him one of his own books. Puzzled, he started reading the paragraph she pointed out.

"That's enough," she said.

He saw there were tears in her eyes and, alarmed, he

stood up and put a strong arm around her shaking shoulders.

"Who are you?" she asked.

"What do you mean?"

"I mean, who are you, really? You're not my Frank."

He remained silent, appalled by her tears and the conviction in her voice.

"Frank hated to read," she said. "He took lessons with the vicar, but they didn't do him no good. He could make out some of the words, and he could write after a fashion. But he didn't like to do either one and didn't, if he could avoid it. Another thing about Frank. He couldn't do figures. He couldn't cipher to save his life. But ever since you've come, all I've heard from Mathilde and from the servants at the manor is what a hand you are with numbers."

"Many young men ignore their studies only to apply themselves later," he suggested.

"Not my Frank," said Fanny. "You're *him,* aren't you?"

"Who?"

"Mr. Verelst. You can't be anyone else. You always did look alike. Ever since you were nipperkins. My son is dead, isn't he?"

"Yes," said Jeremy. "I'm so sorry—"

"He's buried in your place."

It was a statement, not a question.

"Yes."

"What happened that night in Hampshire?"

"I was out riding. I had just seen Frank in the stable. When I returned, Frank and some of the others from the village were watching the hunting box go up in flames. I ran in to save my father. Frank ran in after me."

"So they thought Frank was you."

"Yes. The last thing I remember was climbing the staircase to my father's room. Frank must have found me and carried me out of the house, then he must have gone back in to find my father. I was overcome by smoke and out of my senses. Molly, a girl from the village who was acquainted with Frank, found me lying in the dark. She had me carried to her brother's house because Frank had been staying with them."

"Surely someone must of known—"

"No. The witnesses saw Frank and me run into the house. They found two bodies inside. By that time Molly had had me carried away, ready to swear I was Frank."

"I see."

"She nursed me day and night until I regained consciousness. She refused to let me die. It was a bitter culmination to all of her care to find that I was not the man she loved."

"Didn't she *tell* anyone who you are?"

"She did. But she was not believed. Especially when I was forcibly put on board the ship upon which Frank had signed as a crew member. My protests were ignored. My claims were dismissed as delirium from my injuries. I recognized some of the men who took me aboard. They were from Crossley."

"So the present lord—"

"Yes. Convinced, no doubt, that I was a charlatan about to perpetrate a cruel hoax on his family and deprive him of his estate, he decided to remove the threat I posed to him. I can't say that I blame him. He's the best of good fellows, is Mark. If he'd had any inkling that I was his brother-in-law, he would have welcomed me home with open arms. I will never believe that Mark deliberately would have done me such an evil turn if he'd known I had survived. I've had a lot of time to think about it, and I think he was afraid that my sisters and my mother would claim the impostor as the heir in their grief. Of course, Frank would never have done such a thing."

"I know," said Fanny. "He was not the steadiest person, but he was a good boy."

She burst into tears.

"Forgive me," she said, sobbing. "I knew he was dead all along. Frankie could not have been alive without my knowing about it. He didn't write, but he always sent me money when he was in the way of earning it. He would have found a way to send me word."

"I am so sorry," Jeremy said again.

"You've been decent," said Fanny. "I was so sick, and there you were. I thought you was Frankie come back. I believed in the miracle, because I was too sick to know better. Then I got better and realized you couldn't be Frank, because of the writing and the reading."

She burst into tears again.

"So now he's lying in a grave with somebody else's name on it, and the last of my blood is dead," she sobbed. "Some might say a bastard brat is no loss, but he was all I had, and I loved him."

In that moment, Jeremy made a decision and hoped it was the right one.

"There is a child," he said.

Fanny looked up, disbelief on her face.

"A girl named Becky. She's three years old."

"His?"

"Yes. The child's mother is Molly Harnish, the girl from Hampshire I told you about. She lives in London, in a house I rented for her and the child."

"Why?" she asked suspiciously.

"Not because I have any designs on her, if that's what you're thinking. Frank saved my life. I owe it to him to make sure Molly and his child are taken care of. It isn't easy for a young woman to raise a child alone."

"No," said Fanny, hope in her eyes. "I reckon I know *that*, right enough. But maybe a young woman and an old woman together might make a good job of it. When

200

can I see them?"

"When you are well enough to travel. I'll take you to London myself."

"Thank you, sir! Oh, thank you," she said joyfully. "To think of Frank's child."

"Mrs. Watson, I must ask a favor of you."

"Anything," she said simply.

"My identity must remain a secret. No one knows except you and Molly. And that's the way it has to be until the Verelsts return from the Continent."

"Why? I don't understand."

"For one thing, because I want to convince Mark Verelst that I am truly his brother-in-law by confronting him face to face. I don't want news of my 'miraculous' survival to reach him before I do. I don't think he would resort to violence, but if he put me aboard a ship once, he might find an equally effective way of ridding himself of my presence again."

"This means my son's body has to stay where it is."

"Yes. I'm sorry. I don't like it, either. I'll have him moved to a grave of his own as soon as this is over."

"To think of Frank in the chapel with all the Quality," said Fanny. "It ain't fitting for a body to be in a dark, heathen place like that, just thrown under the floor for people to walk over. He should be buried in the earth, with the sky over his head."

"He will be. I promise," said Jeremy, touched.

"But what about your Miss Willoughby?"

"What about her?"

"She was going to marry him, er, you. Have you told her? Is that why she made you her steward?"

"No. She doesn't have any idea. I won't tell her until my family returns, if then. I came here with the intention of revealing myself to my sister and her husband. Instead, Pastor Wilkins spotted me in the village and insisted upon bringing me to your bedside."

201

"I might of died if you hadn't moved me to a house and taken care of me," Fanny said.

"Possibly. Possibly not. At any rate, I felt obligated to take care of you for what I owed Frank. So I did. Between taking care of you and taking care of Molly and the child, the funds I had saved at sea were dwindling. I decided to find work. So, Mrs. Purdy watched you for me while I went to the village and tried to hire myself out as a clerk. By then I'd learned my family had gone to the Continent. I couldn't very well follow them there, and I couldn't establish my claim without them. Meanwhile, my former valet managed to contact me, thinking I was Frank, with the idea, if you please, of having me impersonate Jeremy Verelst and cut him into the profits to be made from the deception."

"No," said Fanny, awed.

"Yes. I had to get rid of him, so I pretended to go along with his scheme. I persuaded him that I should come to the country and establish my claim, then he could come along and be my star witness. It was the best I could do."

"What happened to him?"

"To my knowledge, he's still in London, and I hope he stays there. Anyway, the day I went to look for work, I was drawn irresistibly to Crossley. I was born there, you know. I'd known all along Frank had been mistaken for me, so I knew he would be buried in the family chapel. It was there that I met Miss Willoughby. We talked, and she offered me the job as her steward. When she told me the position came with a house, I accepted and made arrangements to move you into it."

"The house!" exclaimed Fanny. "Does this mean I have to go back to the village?"

"No," said Jeremy soothingly. "You may stay here as long as I do."

"That's all right, then," said Fanny contentedly. "Now tell me about my granddaughter."

Chapter Nine

While Fanny Watson was listening hungrily to Jeremy's description of her angelically fair, blond granddaughter, Becky herself was inventing a new game.

One of the child's favorite activities was walking in the park with her mother on fine afternoons. Without Jeremy's escort, Molly didn't dare inhabit Hyde Park at the fashionable hour of the promenade. But she didn't see any harm in taking Becky at an earlier hour with one of her neighbors, a vivacious young widow with the good fortune to have been briefly married to an elderly gentleman who had, as the expression went, cut up warm.

While Molly and Maria were engaged in conversation, Becky liked to steal away. Before long, both of her keepers were frantically searching for her. Becky, who had been used to the exclusive attention of first her grandmother and then her mother, didn't like it when Molly devoted herself to adult companions. The clever child quickly learned that the easiest and most effective way of turning her mother's attention back to herself was simply to disappear.

It was amusing to watch the two older women importune passersby for news of her. She usually found a hiding place behind a bush where she could watch the fun. Sometimes strangers saw her and told Molly where she was hiding. She usually shook her head "no" to try to prevent them from doing so, but they always told her mother, anyway. She couldn't understand why none of the grownups she met had any sense of humor.

On this occasion, Becky was standing behind a bush exactly her own size, watching with bright, sparkling eyes while Molly frantically ran down the path looking for her, when she felt herself scooped up in a pair of powerful arms.

She frowned at the gentleman, who was smiling at her. She didn't like his smile. It wasn't like nice Mr. Watson's. Mr. Watson always brought her things when he came to visit, and he never pinched her cheek or called her sweetheart. This man had kind of a mean smile. He also had dark hair and he wore a black cape. And he smelled of liquor and tobacco, just like her Uncle Tom, who used to tease her until she cried.

"What have we here?" the gentleman asked, turning her face up so he could look at her. She frowned harder.

"My baby!" came her mother's voice from the path. "Oh, sir! You've found her!"

Edward Willoughby's smile grew wolfish as he regarded the pretty, flaxen-haired woman standing before him. Molly was dressed modestly but becomingly in a green gown and a white hat decorated with pink roses. As Molly reached for the child, he turned to elude her.

"Ah, but you haven't asked what ransom I'm asking for her," he said. "I think a kiss would be appropriate."

Molly regarded him with indignation. She was about to give him her opinion of so-called gentlemen who would tamper with a mother's anxiety when Becky took matters into her own hands and poked Edward in the eye.

He might have dropped her if Molly hadn't snatched her child to her bosom.

When he had rubbed his eye and ascertained that he

204

could see out of it, he watched Molly's attractively rounded bottom disappear from view. Grinning, he went in pursuit only to find that she had been joined by another female. This didn't particularly bother him. He prided himself on his success with the fair sex.

The girl was exquisite. And she had spirit. Edward liked women with a bit of spirit. A woman who didn't melt in his presence was a novelty, and he didn't expect her resistance to last too long.

"Here he comes," whispered Molly's companion loudly enough for Edward to hear. "God, he's handsome as—"

"I didn't notice," Molly said indifferently.

"Pardon me, ma'am," said Edward, overtaking them and bowing graciously. Molly had the distinct feeling that he was making fun of her with this courteous display of affability, and she frowned at him, reminding him forcibly of her ill-natured child.

"You are blocking our path," Molly pointed out. "I will thank you to let us pass."

"I wish to apologize."

"Your apology is accepted. Now if you'll allow us to pass—"

"Not until—"

"Very well," said Molly calmly. With that she turned around and walked away from him!

In a different humor, Edward would have consigned her to the devil. After all, pretty women were hardly a rarity. But he chose, instead, to be piqued by her pretense of indifference. The fact that it might not be a pretense didn't occur to him.

"Molly!" exclaimed Maria. "Such a beautiful man! Rich, too, by the look of his clothes."

"I don't like his looks."

"Are you daft? He's the most handsome man I've ever seen."

"Me, too. That's what I don't like. Men like that aren't for women like us. They may make up to a body for a while, but when I decide to get friendly with a man, it's going to be someone who wants a wife and a child and a home of his own, not some rooster on the strut."

"If I didn't know better, I'd think you didn't like men."

"Oh, I like men all right. Just not that kind," said Molly frankly. "The only thing a man like that could ever give the likes of me is a babe in the belly before he runs off to marry some high-born lady with her nose in the air."

"Molly! You shouldn't say things like that. It ain't genteel! Anyone would think you—"

"I knew someone who was taken in like that once," said Molly, angry with herself for forgetting that she was supposed to be a young widow whose husband had been killed in a carriage accident right after her child's birth.

Maria, who had a lover, nevertheless was obsessed with propriety and would have dropped Molly's acquaintance like a scalding brand before she'd associate with a Fallen Woman.

"Of course, I'm forgetting you don't need any beaux with that heavenly man we've all seen visiting you at all hours," said Maria.

Molly realized immediately that she was talking about Jeremy, and opened her mouth to explain that he was not interested in her in That Way, but thought better of it.

She lived alone and unprotected in the house, and more than once she had had to turn gentlemen interested in flirtation or Worse from her door. It would do no harm for the neighborhood to think she had a protector, and she didn't think Jeremy would mind. After all, he moved in circles high above hers. She was flattered that her neighbors thought such an obviously refined man might be interested in her charms. If only it were true, she thought wistfully.

Meanwhile, Edward had been embarrassed to encounter his crony, Anthony Marsdon, who obviously had seen the whole exchange.

"Pretty little ladybird, ain't she?" Anthony drawled. "See you met the same fate as the rest of us."

"You mean she's a—," began Edward, annoyed that a lightskirt had had the effrontery to reject him.

"No, not really," said Anthony regretfully. "That's the trouble. The girl doesn't respond to any of the lures sent out to her. I bet she'd make a cozy armful. It makes me feel better that she didn't fall for your handsome face, either."

"Well, she hasn't seen the last of me," said Edward stubbornly. It was bad enough that Anthony had witnessed his defeat. He'd be darned if a girl who didn't look more than eighteen was going to best him.

"Then you'd best enter your name with the rest of them," said Anthony.

"What do you mean?"

"The betting books, of course. Half the men in town are betting they can bring about the widow's downfall."

"A widow, is she?" said Edward thoughtfully. He was pleased to hear she didn't have a jealous husband. He had qualms about trespassing on another man's property. "I'd better make it official, then."

The next day when Molly and Maria appeared with Becky at the park, Edward was ready for them. Driving an open carriage, he pulled over to the side and offered the ladies a turn about the park under his escort.

"No, thank you," said Molly in icy accents.

"Don't want to," said Becky, her tiny face set in a mulish expression.

But Maria looked so disappointed that Molly capitulated. She was careful, however, to seat herself and her daughter in the back, leaving the seat beside Edward to

207

Maria, who took it with alacrity.

Although Maria was pretty, with red-gold hair and a twinkle in her merry hazel eyes, Edward responded to her conversational gambits with indifference. He caught sight of some of his friends and scowled, because he had intended to display Molly in triumph during this ride.

"Thank you for the ride," said Molly politely but firmly when they had gone around the park twice. "Now we must go home. Becky is sleepy."

Infernal brat, thought Edward, eyeing the child with dislike. Becky returned the look in kind.

"I don't even know your name," he said earnestly to Molly as he hurried to hand her out of the carriage.

"I know," she said sweetly, jumping lightly to the pavement without assistance. She ignored the hand Edward held out to her. "Come, sweetheart," she added to Becky, who jumped into her arms and glared at Edward as if daring him to touch her.

He had thought of patting the child's head, strictly by way of ingratiating himself with the mother, but thought better of it. The brat looked capable of biting him. What a hellcat *that* one would grow up to be.

"My name is Maria Slaide," said Molly's companion. "And this is Molly Harnish and her daughter Becky. We are both widows."

"I'm delighted to meet you," he said, bowing over Maria's hand gracefully in gratitude for the introduction. "And I am Edward Willoughby."

"Come, Maria," said Molly firmly. "We must be going. Becky wants her nap."

"All right," said Maria, leaving Edward with a languishing look.

"How can you be so rude to such a pretty-behaved gentleman," said Maria when they were out of earshot.

"I don't call it pretty-behaved to scowl at a three-year-old child."

"Maybe he isn't fond of children."

"Anyone who doesn't like Becky isn't worth knowing," said Molly with a toss of her head.

Unknown to them, Edward had his tiger follow Molly home and report her address to him. He had flowers delivered to her door every day for the next week.

On the eighth day, he delivered his bouquet in person. By this time, Molly was weakening. She adored flowers. When she opened the door, the house was full of them.

"Their beauty pales before yours," he said unoriginally.

"Don't like him," said Becky, standing behind her mother with her small fists upon her hips and scowling hideously.

"Becky," said Molly reprovingly as she took the flowers.

"Thank you for your flowers, sir," said Molly, "but please don't send any more."

"Don't you like them?" he asked, moving close and looming down at her with desire plainly written in his eyes.

She stepped backwards, feeling a trifle dizzy. She was, after all, a healthy young woman, and he was a very handsome man.

"I like them very much," she said, "but —".

"But what?"

"But I don't want to feel obligated to you —"

"Then discharge your obligation," he said silkily. "One kiss and —"

"Don't like him," Becky repeated belligerently.

He smiled ingratiatingly at Becky.

"Sweet child," he murmured, raising a hand as if to pat her golden head.

"No," said Becky, dodging his touch. "Go away."

Edward returned Becky's glare impassively.

"I wonder, Mrs. Harnish. Are you fond of the opera?" he asked.

"I've never been—that is, yes. I am," said Molly.

"Then perhaps you will accompany me—"

"No. That is impossible. Thank you for your flowers, sir, but please believe—"

"Go away!" said Becky again.

"I see," said Edward, comprehending that as long as Becky was present to distract her mother from his charms he might as well leave the field to renew the battle another day. "Then I'll bid you good day, ma' am."

He bowed and sauntered down the street.

"Well," said Molly. "What do you make of that?"

"Don't like him," said Becky.

Later that week, Edward began cultivating Maria Slaide. At first Maria was disappointed that Edward was so obsessed with her friend that he was immune to her own considerable charms. But, being a good-natured young woman who was not averse to indulging in a little harmless matchmaking, she was quite content to answer Edward's questions about Molly and enjoy the distinction of riding with him in his carriage. To her delight, several of her friends spotted her instantly, and she couldn't resist the impulse to smile and wave persistently at the others until they did, too.

"You say she lives all alone with her daughter," said Edward thoughtfully, wondering that Molly had no servants.

"Yes, although it isn't for want of opportunity, if you know what I mean," said Maria with a smirk.

"I think I do," he said encouragingly.

"She's unaccountably loyal to her gentleman friend that visits her now and again, although I'm at a loss to understand why. He hasn't visited now for some weeks, and he only took her out once, and the child with them. Usually he just visits her for an hour or so and leaves.

Sometimes he brings flowers or small gifts for Becky, but I've never seen Molly wear jewels. She has no servants at all. He isn't much of a prize if you ask me."

Edward did ask her, and he was delighted with her answers.

It appeared to him as if Molly's lover had defected since he hadn't visited her lately. He certainly didn't appear overly generous. Most men who took women under their protection indulged them with pretty clothes, carriages, horses, jewels, and servants. Although it was immaculately clean, Edward didn't think much of Molly's love nest if, indeed, that's what it was. It looked to him like the pokey kind of house any respectable widow would inhabit with her daughter.

"Is the child always there?" Edward asked.

"Always. Molly rarely leaves her, although occasionally the child visits with another family in the neighborhood with a child the same age. But Molly is very devoted to her child. Almost *too* devoted. It's a pity to see a pretty young woman like Molly spurn male companionship, but that she does. Her 'friend' is the only one I've seen visit her."

"Hmm. It's plain the man is too sure of himself and would profit by a little competition," said Edward.

"I think so, too," said Maria, delighted for her friend's good fortune. She could think of no felicity greater than to have two handsome men vying for her attention.

Knowing that Molly was already involved with a man relieved Edward of whatever qualms he might have had in seducing the widow. Virtuous women, he had found, were more trouble than they were worth. He became all the more determined in his pursuit when he encountered Anthony Marsdon in Bond Street one afternoon.

"How prospers the hunt?" asked Anthony jovially.

"It's progressing very well," Edward lied.

"I can see that," his companion said sardonically.

"The odds in your favor are being reached, did you know that?"

"No, I did not," said Edward, incensed. "But it is a matter of indifference to me."

Edward was desperate. He imagined that there was a sly look on the face of every one of his cronies. He began avoiding the club, and one day he hit upon the perfect scheme to soften the widow's resistance.

"Good day, sir," said Molly gravely as she opened the door to him.

"Good morning, Mrs. Harnish," he said. "May I come in?"

"There would be no point. I'm sorry, sir."

"I'm not going to have to put my foot in the door, am I? It would be too ridiculous. May I come in?" he asked with a conspiratorial smile.

"I suppose," she said grudgingly.

"Go away," said Becky when he walked into the parlor. She had been playing on the floor with her dolls spread out around her.

"Hello, my dear," said Edward, making a last-ditch effort to make up to the child. "What a pretty doll."

Becky gave him a cold stare unnerving to see on one so young.

"Becky, love," said Molly. "Do play in the bedchamber for a little while so the gentleman and I may talk."

"Yes, Mama," said Becky reproachfully. The child took her time gathering her toys and moving away.

"Good-bye, sweetheart," said Edward with a forced smile on his face.

Becky gave him the look of contempt this insincere endearment deserved and left the room with her tiny turned-up nose in the air.

"What did you wish to say to me, sir?" asked Molly. "I hope you are not come to bother me with more invitations. I thought I made plain—"

"Well, actually, I had hoped to persuade you to go to the opera with me, after all," he admitted.

"I am afraid that is impossible," said Molly in a tone of unmistakable dismissal. She rose from her chair as if to end to the interview. "If that is all —"

"No, it isn't," said Edward. "I haven't been honest with you, and I've come to make a clean breast of it."

"Whatever you have to say won't matter."

"Perhaps not, but I hope you will grant me the indulgence of a hearing."

Molly shrugged and resumed her seat.

"Very well, sir," she said.

"What I have to tell you is extremely painful for me," he said. "I haven't told a living soul. I am telling you because I hope it will make you take pity on me and grant me the little happiness that is possible for one of my condition."

"Sir?"

"I assume your refusal to accept my invitation to the opera has its basis in the fact that you are not interested in initiating a personal relationship with me."

"I have a child and my good name to think of," said Molly.

Little hypocrite, Edward thought. Virtuous words for a woman who has a lover visiting her in secret.

"Well, I think you should know that my invitation was exactly what I said. An invitation to the opera. Nothing more. You see, I am incapable of enjoying the kind of relationship with a woman that you are anxious to avoid."

There. That was about as delicately as he could put it.

"You mean you can't —" She broke off in embarrassment. Her look of pity elated him, although he did his best to look cast down.

"I mean that I am physically incapable of such a relationship. It is the result of a fall from a horse when I was

213

in my teens. Fortunately, my full growth was in, and it didn't affect my physical development in other ways. But I have the private anguish of knowing that I can never experience the pleasure of having an intimate relationship with a woman, nor can I ever father a child."

"Oh, Mr. Willoughby. I am so sorry," said Molly, tears of sympathy forming in her eyes.

"All I wish from you, my dear, is your companionship. Believe me, I am no threat to your virtue. I want to take a pretty woman to the opera. That is all. I must choose a woman who is not interested in that, er, aspect of a friendship. If I choose a woman who expects something more, my secret will be out because I cannot, er, perform. Then I will be held up to the ridicule of my peers.

"So will you go with me to the opera?" he concluded with a look of such tragic appeal in his fine brown eyes that she nearly melted.

"Yes. Yes, I will," she said.

"Good. It would give me great pleasure to give you a gown for the occasion. I have a fancy to see you—"

"No, no," said Molly. "That would be—"

Her cheeks had flushed crimson. She reluctantly had accepted money from Jeremy for new clothes, but that was different. Respectable girls didn't allow gentlemen to buy clothes for them. She would feel just like a well, never mind what she would feel like. She couldn't do it.

Yet the poor gentleman looked so disappointed. It was true Molly didn't have anything suitable to wear. She had thought she would try to borrow something from Maria, who was about the same size and generous to a fault. Even so, Molly was only human, and the chance to appear at the opera on the arm of a handsome gentleman and clad in a beautiful evening gown of her own instead of borrowed finery was irresistible.

She consented.

"You've made me very happy," he said gravely. "Would you like to visit the shops now?"

Molly's face lit up, but she didn't wish to appear too anxious.

"What shall I do about Becky? You will hardly want to take her with us, and she is too young to be left alone."

Edward agreed with alacrity that he did not wish to take that hostile child with him to an establishment where he was quite so well known as the one he had intended to patronize on this, as on similar occasions.

"Perhaps your friend, Mrs. Slaide, would watch her for a little while?" he suggested.

"Of course! Maria loves Becky. If you will wait here, I will take Becky to Maria's house at once and see if she would mind keeping her."

Becky looked at him accusingly as her mother bundled her into her pelisse and tied a bonnet on her head, but she went obediently enough. Soon Molly was back, her cheeks flushed with the exertion of practically running back to her house.

Edward handed her into his carriage and took the long way to Bond Street in order to ensure that as many of his acquaintances as possible had the opportunity to see his charming passenger.

Margaret and her aunt, who were shopping for some new ribbons to go with Margaret's lilac promenade gown, saw him pass by but gave no sign. They didn't know his passenger, but they had an idea what significance she played in his life. A lady of breeding had very selective powers of observation and would go naked in the street before she would acknowledge the presence of an acquaintance in company with a person who was of the muslin company.

Edward saw them but gave no sign. He, too, knew the rules.

"If ever I saw so many beautiful things!" exclaimed

215

Molly in awed tones when Edward took her into the shop of his choice.

"Mr. Willoughby," said the neat lady who greeted them. "It is always a pleasure to see you. And how may we serve you today?"

"My companion would like to see an evening gown."

"How charming! If you will be seated. May I offer you some refreshment?"

Molly remained silent, feeling very timid in so fashionable a shop. It was obvious that the question was not addressed to her, and that if she had been alone, the lady's cordial tones would have turned icy with contempt.

"No, I thank you," said Edward. It didn't occur to him to consult Molly's wishes.

Molly soon forgot her self-consciousness as she tried on one stunning gown after another. She fell quite in love with a primrose gauze, but Edward's choice was a sophisticated, low-cut ivory silk that clung to every curve of her lovely body.

Molly's shoulders slumped in disappointment. It would be impossible to wear so much as a chemise under it, and if she didn't fall out of the top by the end of the evening it would be a miracle. Moreover, its pale, luminous color suggested something vaguely loathsome to her, like the underbelly of a fish.

"It is perfection," said the shopkeeper in congratulatory tones. "We will perhaps take it in a bit at the waist because Madam is *so* tiny there. And perhaps the bodice can be cut just a *little* lower because Madam is so lovely."

It was clear to Molly, who had not once been directly addressed by either one of them, that the compliment was not intended to gratify her, but to oblige her companion.

"Yes," said Edward. "You are a genius, Madam Celeste. I put complete confidence in your judgment."

Molly was too much overawed to debate his choice, so

216

she watched meekly as the overpowering lady put the gown to the side and suggested that perhaps Madam would need a wrap.

Edward, not bothering with the formality of consulting Molly, selected a swansdown tippet and completed the transaction by making arrangements for the gown to be altered and delivered without fail to Molly's house the following day.

Molly was very quiet on the way home, perhaps because she was forced to endure the open stares of so many young men who looked as if they were savoring a joke she didn't understand. She looked questioningly at Edward, and saw that he was returning some of these looks with a jaunty wave of the hand. She felt she was being humiliated in some subtle way.

When she returned to her home, she went to fetch Becky and found Maria waiting with bated breath for an account of her excursion.

Molly reluctantly admitted that Edward had bought her an evening gown.

"You will need jewels," said Maria. "I don't suppose you have—"

She broke off in embarrassment.

"No, I don't," said Molly. "How kind of you to think of it."

Maria looked uncertain. Molly didn't seem very happy about her good fortune, and Maria could have kicked herself for her insensitivity in mentioning Molly's comparative poverty.

She offered her the loan of several lovely necklaces and bracelets, and Molly, quite at random, chose a garnet set. The ladies parted with expressions of mutual esteem, and Molly went so far as to invite Maria to call late the following afternoon before it was time for her to dress in order to view the new gown.

"And I'll keep Becky for you tomorrow night," said

Maria generously.

Her enjoyment thus assured, Molly felt strangely downcast. She wished Jeremy wasn't in Yorkshire just then. If he had been in London, she would have confessed all to him and abided by his decision if he told her not to see Edward. There was something about Edward she didn't trust, and she didn't like the proprietary way he treated her. She hadn't missed the significance of the fact that his surname was Willoughby. Was he related to Jeremy's employer? Did Jeremy know him?

On the night Edward was to take her to the opera, Molly dressed far too early and sat nervously in her parlor waiting for him to collect her.

Maria's jewels felt cold against her throat.

"You look lovely, my dear," said Edward when she opened the door to him. "We must leave immediately."

He said that as if she had been keeping him waiting, when it was he who had arrived later than the appointed hour, she thought resentfully. She pulled the tippet closely around her and allowed him to hand her into his carriage.

Edward kept up a barrage of inconsequential conversation on the way to the opera house, exchanging greetings with more of his friends, who were openly leering at her. He didn't introduce Molly to anyone.

She forgot her insecurity for a moment when they entered the opera house, which was a blaze of light and color reflecting from scores of crystal chandeliers. The jewellike dresses of the other ladies intoxicated her, and she noticed with self-consciousness that hers was cut lower than most of them.

An exquisite young lady with brown hair and gray eyes was surprised by Molly in the act of gazing thoughtfully at Edward. Edward returned her regard with a barely perceptible nod. The lady, who Molly thought was quite lovely, lifted one eyebrow and turned away.

218

"Who is she?" whispered Molly. Edward looked down at her as if he had forgotten her presence.

"My cousin, Miss Margaret Willoughby," said Edward.

"She didn't look surprised to see you."

"No."

He hadn't meant to snub Molly. He was just preoccupied with his cousin. He still would have married Margaret if it were possible. She looked like an ice maiden tonight. Edward strained to see who was squiring her and saw she was accompanied only by his sister Anne and their aunt. Anne spotted him and, although her eyes widened, she gave no other sign. She, too, knew the rules.

Then the opera began and Molly was lost in wonder. She had never heard such singing in her life. Edward was amused by her absorption and promised he would take her again on another night. She was so enthralled by the activity on stage that she shushed him. He laughed indulgently.

When they returned to her house, Molly would have said goodnight to him at the door, but he asked if he could come in and talk with her for a few minutes.

"It is rare that we have a chance to converse alone," he said. "Your daughter doesn't like me."

"She is very young," said Molly excusingly.

"Yes," said Edward, seating himself on a sofa and patting the cushion beside him suggestively. "She has not yet learned to be civil to those whom she dislikes."

"No."

He put his arm around her and drew her close.

"Have I told you yet that you were the most exquisite woman there tonight?"

"No," said Molly gravely. "And if you had, I wouldn't have believed you."

"You are much too modest, my dear," he said, kissing

her deeply.

She drew back.

"No," she said.

"Is that all you can say? 'No'?"

"Yes."

He smiled and gathered her close to him again. He thought her obvious nervousness in his presence was enchanting. His intention at the beginning of their acquaintance was only to amuse himself for a short time at her expense while his fleeting infatuation persisted, but now he considered the possibility of putting her under his own protection. It would be expensive, but she would be worth it.

He caressed her bare shoulder, a touch so intimate that she would have jumped from the sofa if he had not held her firmly.

"Don't do that," she whispered, trembling.

"No?" Smiling, he kissed her again, and felt the satisfaction of hearing her sigh voluptuously. He could feel her heart beating through the thin gown, which was so revealing that she might as well have been naked. As he kissed her again, he caressed the rounded part of her breast that appeared above the bodice.

"No! You must not," she said, struggling.

"There it is again. 'No.' I can't harm you, sweetheart."

"Don't call me that."

"As you wish."

He kissed her again, this time pushing her backward on the sofa so that they were both half-reclining. Again he ran his hand over her breast, and she gasped.

"You like that, don't you?" he said with satisfaction. "You're a very passionate woman, Molly. Don't be cruel, fair one. Allow me the indulgence of enjoying your beautiful body."

"Isn't it cruel to lead you on when nothing can come of it?" she asked breathlessly.

"No, my dear. It is not cruelty but kindness to give me the only pleasure I can have with a woman."

"It is cruel to me, then," she said, struggling to sit up. He pinioned her arms above her head on the sofa and his kiss nearly robbed her of her senses. She was breathing in ragged gasps when he pulled down her bodice and freed her breasts.

"You are beautiful, Molly," he said softly.

She was really frightened now. Because of the closeness of their bodies it soon became obvious that there was nothing wrong whatsoever with *that* aspect of Edward's anatomy. She looked into his eyes and saw no mercy there. Frantically, she tried to push him away, but he was too strong for her. Her gown was practically stripped from her now. He was kissing her again as his hands roved her body, and she was lost. His kisses were no longer sensual and exploratory. They were hard and demanding and vaguely insulting. She felt soiled.

It was so different from that time four years ago when Frank Watson had awakened her passion with gentle, almost reverent caresses. There had been beauty and dignity in the act of love that resulted in Becky's birth.

Now her tender lover was dead, and she was being devoured by a ruthless, insatiable beast.

"Have pity—" she whispered.

"Pity?" he said, laughing deep in his throat. "My love, I seek only pleasure."

"Does it give you pleasure to take a woman against her will?" she said, breaking into loud, wrenching sobs.

He froze and went down on one knee beside the sofa as she struggled to sit up. He turned her to face the light of the single candle burning on the table and touched one of the tears streaming down her face with a tentative forefinger.

"You're weeping," he said in amazement. He had felt her trembling, but in his vanity he had assumed it

221

stemmed from passion. "Why? You can't be frightened by *me*. My darling, I would never hurt you—"

"You *are* hurting me!" she said indignantly, touching her swollen mouth. "You've practically raped me."

"Rape!" He flinched at the ugly word. "I have never forced a woman in my life. I've never had to! I would be willing to swear you enjoyed it—"

"I reckon that was the way it seemed to you," said Molly, making a move as if to rise from the sofa. He caught her wrist to prevent her from doing so, and she glared at him so fiercely that he let go of her with a look of apology in his eyes. She turned her back to him and adjusted her gown more modestly.

"You lied to me," she said, facing him. "I feel like a fool for being taken in by your tragic tale. How you must have laughed at my stupidity behind my back."

"Molly, I—" He reached for her, and she sidestepped him.

"I want you to leave my house," she said, "or I am going to open the door and scream so loudly that everyone on this street is going to hear me. I may be dirt beneath your feet, but the laws in this land allow a woman some protection in her own home."

"No, don't do that!" He regarded with horror the melee that would result from her screams in a respectable neighborhood. He would be made a laughingstock.

She looked so miserable with her tear-stained face and swollen lips that he longed to take her in his arms again, but he knew it would be a mistake to do so. He had wronged her. Hers had not been the response of a wanton. If she were not the mother of that appalling child, he would have thought her totally inexperienced in the act of lovemaking. His ardor had frightened her. He cursed himself for his clumsiness. Whatever she was doing with the "gentleman" who visited her, he realized, it was not this.

"My dear, I am so sorry—"

"I don't care about your feelings, Mr. Willoughby," she said coldly. "Please leave my house."

He bit his lip, then turned and left. It was obvious that Molly was not going to listen to reason in her present humor, yet he was not without hope that he might yet manage to appease her. She was exquisite. He wouldn't rest until she was his.

The next day he went to Madam Celeste's establishment to find that Molly had been there before him. He had gone with the idea of purchasing a peace offering. Instead, he was greeted by the intelligence that the young person had arrived on Celeste's doorstep early that morning with her child in tow and the box containing the ivory gown in her arms. She simply handed it to Madam, turned on her heel and left, despite the shopkeeper's attempts to detain her.

"I do not understand," said the confused modiste. "Did she not like the gown?"

"No," said Edward. "I don't think she did."

The modiste remembered that the young lady had seemed to like the primrose gauze gown, so he bought it. He sent it with a servant to her home, and enjoyed a pleasant daydream of being Molly's escort when she wore it to the opera. He would buy her a diamond necklace to go with it, he decided.

The dress was back in less than an hour. He dispatched flowers. The astonished servant no sooner turned from Molly's door after delivering them when the door opened again and the bouquet sailed over his head and into the path at his feet.

Still, Edward was confident that Molly was indulging in a fit of pique over his insensitivity and would soon come around.

He persisted in this delusion for almost a week.

Chapter Ten

While he was in Yorkshire, Jeremy had gone over every inch of Margaret's manor and found, as he feared, that someone had laid subtle traps all over it. Whoever set the traps knew Margaret's habits well. They appeared only in those parts of the house she would use.

No one could point openly to treachery if a fatal accident would befall her. The author of this perfidy was cold-bloodedly clever. The tragedy, when it happened, would be blamed on faulty workmanship or imperfect repairs.

Jeremy embarked upon an orgy of refurbishment, personally overseeing every one of the trivial repairs to be made. He didn't trust any of the servants to remedy them without supervision. It was clear to him that whoever wished Margaret harm had an accomplice in the house. And he feared that as soon as he finished his work, the villain's henchman would undo it. Still, he had to do what he could to protect her or he would go mad.

To his knowledge, nothing had yet befallen Margaret in London, which indicated that she probably was safe in the city. Even so, he lived in a state of uneasiness until the letter that would summon him to London arrived. He lost no time in riding to Margaret's side.

Fanny Watson greeted his defection with relief. She had watched his restless discontent with vague sympathy and wished she could do something to help him. She didn't dare offer maternal comfort. After all, he was not her son. He was merely a stranger who, out of gratitude for her son's bravery, had made himself responsible for her. It was all she could do to keep the secret of his identity from the garrulous Mathilde. But she managed to do so.

Jeremy arrived at Margaret's town house late one evening to find her gone to a ball. Her aunt greeted him with acclaim.

"Mr. Watson," the good lady said. "How providential that you would come tonight. Margaret and I have just received a book of poems in the post."

He smiled affectionately at her and, begging leave to wash the dust of travel from his person before joining her in the parlor, went to the room he had slept in before he went to Yorkshire since Martha plainly expected him to stay in the town house. He had, at first, intended to go to the inn for the sake of Margaret's reputation, but it occurred to him that if Margaret were in danger from some unknown enemy, he had better be close at hand, and hang the gossips.

As it turned out, the villain would strike that very night while Jeremy was occupied in reading some sickeningly sentimental verse to Margaret's aunt.

The tea tray had just arrived when Sternes burst into the room. Martha stared disapprovingly at his undignified entrance.

"Miss Willoughby," said Sternes, clearly enjoying his dramatic moment. "Miss Margaret has met with an accident."

Their reaction was all he could have wished. Both Martha and Jeremy leaped up, but Jeremy soon outdistanced her as they ran to the front hall. There Jeremy was shocked to see that Margaret was being supported by a handsome man. Anne, her eyes huge with fright, was on their heels.

"Oh, my love!" exclaimed Martha, pushing past Jeremy, who had checked in the doorway. "What has happened to you?"

"It is nothing, Aunt," said Margaret faintly.

"Oh, Aunt Martha," said Anne. "Mr. Crawford *saved* Margaret from being crushed to death! He was truly *splendid—*"

"Hush, my dear, you are alarming your aunt," said Mr. Crawford, who Jeremy saw with jealous eyes was not to be classed with Margaret's other suitors. He was tall and distinguished, if a bit older than the men who formed her usual court. He had dark hair and, although his dress had none of the excesses of fashion, its cut and style pronounced it to be unexceptional.

Jeremy was appalled by Margaret's appearance. Her gown was soiled, and she had a smudge of mud on her cheek which her aunt wiped off with her handkerchief.

"Perhaps I had better carry you to your room," said Mr. Crawford to Margaret.

"No, that will not be necessary," said Margaret, pulling herself together. "I think if I can sit down for a few minutes I will feel much more the thing. I wasn't hurt, only frightened."

Mr. Crawford regarded her doubtfully, but lent

her his arm as the party moved to the parlor. He settled her tenderly in a chair by the fire and watched her face anxiously for signs of impending collapse.

"For heaven's sake, Beverly," said Margaret, laughing shakily. "There is nothing whatever the matter with me."

"Perhaps some brandy—," suggested Martha.

"No," said Margaret, "but a cup of tea—"

Anne moved toward the tea table as if to grant this request, but suddenly stopped stock still in the middle of the room and burst into tears.

"My child," said Martha, appalled.

Jeremy reached Anne first, and gently pressed her into a chair. He went to the far side of the room and returned with a glass of brandy in his hands, which he held to her lips. She took a few sips, coughed, and said she was better.

"It was so *horrid!*" she said, her pretty face crumpled in distress. "We were leaving the ball, because it was such an insipid party. Margaret had started across the street because her carriage was on the other side, and Mr. Crawford had kindly offered to escort us, when this other carriage came down the street, and so *fast*. It sounded like thunder, and Margaret was in its path. I tried to scream, but I couldn't—"

She gulped convulsively.

"Don't, child," said Martha, putting maternal arms around Anne, who had turned pale and looked as if she might faint. "You're upsetting yourself. Mr. Crawford, perhaps you had better tell us what happened."

Mr. Crawford, who had been looking anxiously at Anne, seemed unwilling to do so. Margaret took up the tale.

"It *was* frightening," she said, shuddering. "Lord, I must look a sight."

"Never mind that," said Jeremy sharply. Martha and Mr. Crawford both looked at him as if a chair had spoken. It was obvious they had forgotten he was in the room. But Margaret laughed.

"Mr. Watson," she said as if noticing him for the first time. "I am glad to see you restored to us. There is so much to do before Anne's ball—"

"Yes, yes. And it shall all be done," he said impatiently. "But *what happened?*"

"Oh, well, it was over in a second, I dare say, but it seemed like hours at the time," she said. "I was in the street, and I heard hooves. I looked up and the carriage was bearing down on me. It must have been a runaway. Certainly it was going much too fast for a city street. I tried to run, but I found my limbs wouldn't move. I thought I would be killed for certain, but Beverly, Mr. Crawford, I mean, pushed me out of the way and threw his body over mine to protect me."

"It was the most *heroic* thing," said Anne, regarding Mr. Crawford with a worshipful light in her eyes, even though she still looked shaky.

"You, my dear, are going straight up to bed," said Margaret uncompromisingly to Anne. "You shall stay in the blue room. I will just have a word with—" She made as if to rise.

"You will do nothing of the sort," said Martha. "I will see that it is made ready. You are going to relax and drink your tea. Mr. Crawford, you have our gratitude."

"It was nothing," he said modestly.

"Hardly that," said Margaret. "I am persuaded

you were more hurt than I, but what must I do but lie there whimpering like a ninny—"

"You had suffered a severe shock, ma'am," said Mr. Crawford. "If you are sure you are recovered—"

"Perfectly, I thank you," said Margaret.

"Excellent. Then I must leave you." He stood and shook hands with Jeremy.

"Oh, where have my wits gone begging?" exclaimed Margaret. "Mr. Beverly Crawford, this is my steward, Mr. Frank Watson."

"Delighted to meet you, sir," said Beverly, unsmiling.

"I'll see you out, shall I?" said Jeremy.

"Thank you," said Beverly. He moved toward Margaret and, going down on one knee beside her chair, took her hand and kissed it. It was prettily done, and Jeremy involuntarily clenched his jaw. "Until tomorrow, ma'am," Beverly said.

"I shall look forward to it," she said. "And thank you—"

"Pray don't mention it, ma'am. I was happy to be of service."

He left the room with Jeremy.

"Tell me, Mr. Crawford," said Jeremy when they were out of earshot. "Did you notice anything special about the runaway coach?"

"Only that it was traveling very, very fast," he said ruefully.

"No distinguishing marks? A crest, perhaps?"

"No. Nothing. Why do you ask? Surely you aren't suggesting it was deliberate—"

"No. Of course not," said Jeremy. "Good evening."

"Good evening," said Beverly.

Jeremy returned to the parlor and stood before

Margaret, looking down at her gravely.

"I'll have that brandy now, if you don't mind," she said.

He went to the other side of the room and returned with another glass of the wine.

"Shall I hold it for you, or can you manage?" he asked.

"I can manage," she said, reaching for it. She took a sip, then regarded him over the rim. "I would be obliged to you if you would sit down and stop looking at me as if you expect me to expire any instant."

"I'm sorry."

He seated himself opposite her and waited expectantly.

"You know, don't you?" she asked. He could see from the way her hand was shaking that she was much more distressed than she had allowed the others to see. It disarmed him that she could let down her guard in his presence.

"I beg your pardon?"

"That someone is trying to kill me, of course." She closed her eyes for a moment. "I didn't believe it until tonight. But you knew. That was why you asked me that night in Yorkshire who would inherit my fortune if I were dead. All those 'accidents.' The balcony, my fall from Mirabel, the loose runner on the stairs. Even the tainted fish that made Aunt Martha and me sick. They were deliberate."

"Yes. I wasn't sure at that point. I had hoped I was wrong."

"But now you know. So why were you so anxious to leave London? Pretty behavior to run off to the country without even trying to warn me."

"I wasn't certain then, and I knew you would

only laugh at me. You weren't receptive to my hints. I wanted to go to your house in Yorkshire and look around."

"And?"

"I found traps. Dozens of them. All concentrated in the rooms you use. Whoever set them knows you intimately. One of them was in the old schoolroom library. One of the heavy shelves above the bookcase where you keep your favorite books was secured with only two nails. It nearly fell on me when I gave the bookcase a gentle shove, but I managed to jump out of the way because I was expecting it. You, suspecting nothing, would have been crushed. The thing must weigh at least a hundred pounds, and there was a bronze bust on it."

"That has been there forever."

"All the better. Who would suspect treachery if it fell on you after all those years? The nails must have been removed only recently, or the shelf wouldn't have been there all this time. And there was no sign of the nails themselves. Where were they if it had happened accidentally? It is of a piece with the loosened runner on the stairs used only by you. Whoever set that trap didn't know that on the day you tripped on it, I would be following you up the stair. The thought of someone cold-bloodedly setting traps for you as if you were an animal, and then sitting back and waiting for you to fall into one, makes my blood run cold. I spent all week going over your rooms and securing them. I have no guarantee that the person who wishes you harm won't go through and undo my handiwork. I can only speculate upon what he may try next. You must be very careful."

"You think it is some member of my family,

don't you?"

"It seems logical. Sir Robert and his lady, your Aunt Martha and your cousins are the only ones who will benefit significantly by your demise. None of the traps required great physical strength to set, only a vicious mind."

"Do you know what it's like to face the possibility that your nearest relatives may be plotting in your death?"

She looked so desolate that it took all of his self-control not to gather her into his arms and vow to protect her with his dying breath. Instead, he forced his tone to be cool.

"It occurred to me that it might be one of your suitors, crazed by passion and unrequited love—"

"How ridiculous," said Margaret, laughing reluctantly. "The only thing likely to craze my suitors is the thought of my fortune being captured by another of their number. Murdering me would hardly do them any good."

"Sometimes crazed people are not particularly logical. And there is no reason why one or two of them might not be as enamored of your, er, person as of your fortune, and in a passion of jealousy—"

"Highly unlikely. I thank you for trying to divert me, but this is no time to be funning. The runaway coach was a desperate act," said Margaret. "Nothing that risky has been tried before. If I had been killed, surely the driver of the coach would have been discovered."

"I've thought of that," said Jeremy. "Frankly, I had not wanted to suggest it to you quite yet."

"Such delicacy! Do you think me a coward? Well, I suppose I deserve that, sitting here shaking like a leaf and tippling brandy. It appears that my ill-

232

wisher is getting more careless, or more desperate to put a period to my existence."

"So it appears," he agreed.

"Mr. Watson, you are such a comfort to me," said Margaret warmly. "How I need your cool, logical common sense right now. At least your reason is not clouded by emotion—"

She broke off in dismay. Jeremy had looked startled, and then angry.

"What have I said?" she asked, confused. "Have I offended you? I surely didn't mean—"

"Oh, no," he said furiously. "You haven't offended me. What would you have me do, Miss Willoughby? Burst into tears like your ninnyhammer of a cousin? Or make you pretty speeches like your precious Mr. Crawford?"

Margaret's mouth gaped open in astonishment.

"I am still very much alive, you know," she said gently when she found her voice. "And I don't intend to die just yet. You're the only one I can trust. Everyone else I care about is a suspect. That is, *you* aren't trying to do away with me, are you, Frank?"

He smiled involuntarily. He might have been angry if it hadn't been for the use of what she thought was his Christian name and her unconscious slip of the tongue. Everyone *else* she cares about, she had said. Her face was flushed, although he couldn't tell whether it was from a realization of what she had given away, or the effects of the brandy.

"It seems like every time we see one another, one of us is bruised or bleeding," she said into the uncomfortable silence with an attempt at lightness. "I have consumed more brandy for medicinal purposes in the past few weeks than I have in my entire life prior to that."

"Yes," he said grimly. "And I don't like it."

"Perhaps I'm becoming clumsy in my dotage," she suggested hopefully, taking another sip of the liquor, "and there is no murderer after all."

"You don't believe that."

"No," she admitted, "but I wish I could."

"Do you remember anything else about that coach? Anything at all?"

"How can I? It was over in a second. I had barely seen the thing bearing down on me and the next thing I knew I was thrown to the ground and Beverly had thrown himself on top of me. I don't even remember the ride home. Between them, Beverly and Anne must have bundled me into the carriage, although I don't remember it. My teeth didn't stop clattering until we were in the hall."

"No wonder," he said. "Shouldn't you retire?"

"Probably. I cannot sleep, though. I wonder if Miss Poole has gone to bed. I hope so. She'll *die* when she sees this gown. Not all of her arts will be able to restore it, I'm afraid."

She rose.

"Perhaps I should accompany you—"

She smiled at him ruefully.

"Mr. Watson, I don't think our unknown 'friend,' or perhaps I should say 'fiend,' is any threat to me tonight. We must be rational or I shall go mad, seeing daggers and assassins behind every curtain."

So he was "Mr. Watson" again.

"You're right, of course," he said meekly. He lit a candle for her and their hands touched briefly as he gave it to her. "Good night, Miss Willoughby."

"Good night, Mr. Watson. Have I said I am happy to have you restored to us?"

"Yes. You have."

234

She left the room, and he stared after her for some minutes before he went in search of the rest he knew he would not find that night.

Margaret herself stared at the ceiling for a long time. What she didn't tell Jeremy was that she had left the ball early because her aunt and uncle, masquerading as affectionate relatives, had rendered her evening hideous by holding a small court in the corner of the ballroom and lamenting to anyone willing to listen that their beloved niece was about to become the victim of a dastardly adventurer presently installed in her household.

The gossip Chloe had engendered had died down, but for some reason her aunt and uncle were trying to keep it alive. This, despite the fact that most of their more informed acquaintance attributed their maliciousness to the fact that they could no longer enjoy the accommodations of Margaret's town house and country estate and were now forced to live at their own expense.

Margaret was certain they could not seriously believe that she would be so dead to propriety as to become intimate with her steward, even if they suspected her true feelings for him.

She detected the hand of malice in this attempt to discredit her with the ton, and only wondered that they would do so before the ball that she would give to launch their daughter into society.

Mere gratitude should have made them rally to their niece's support, or, on the other hand, perhaps their very obligation to her was what rankled so much that they would gratify the gossipmongers with their poison.

She could believe they wished her ill. She had sensed their resentment of her from the time she was a child. But would they be willing to kill her, even for a fortune?

And, if not, would Edward?

Margaret considered her handsome cousin for a moment, and realized that he was cold-blooded enough to do the deed. No one ever knew what Edward was thinking, not really. She could see him in the role quite well. Tonight's attempt to run her down with a coach was dramatic and violent enough to suit his nature, but she had to admit the nasty little traps set for her at her country house were not in his line.

Whose then? Anne's? Or Aunt Martha's?

Both of them would benefit by her death. This line of reasoning was so painful she couldn't pursue it. She loved them the most of all of her relatives.

Then there was Frank Watson. Could he really be a fortune hunter, her supposedly cool, competent, reasonable, vaguely disapproving steward? She refused to believe it, nor could she believe that he was using his resemblance to Jeremy Verelst to ingratiate himself with her as the gossips suggested.

There was no mistaking his fear for her tonight, for all that he had tried to hide it after she made her unfortunate remark about his cool, unemotional logic. He obviously was more attached to her than she had thought, and she was horrified by her own elation at this new evidence.

But if she had learned something of his true feelings for her, then he had learned something, too.

She was well aware that her unruly tongue had let the disastrous truth slip out, and that he had recognized the significance of her careless words. He had preserved the delicate balance of the employer-employee relationship to which they both clung so desperately by pretending that he had missed her meaning. But now he knew the truth, if he hadn't suspected it already.

The next day, Jeremy came down to breakfast just in time to greet Mr. Crawford as he called to collect Margaret and Anne for an early morning ride. Anne looked enchanting in one of Margaret's riding habits which was a little too large for her. It made her look even tinier and younger than she actually was, because it appeared as if she were wearing an older sister's clothes. She gazed with worshipful eyes at Mr. Crawford, who smiled tolerantly at her prattling.

"Margaret, are you sure you are not too fatigued after last night?" Beverly suggested solicitously.

"Certainly not, if you aren't," said Margaret, who was ravishing in a green habit à la hussar. She was in the act of pulling on a servicable pair of leather riding gloves, and so did not notice Jeremy at first. Anne apparently had eyes for no one but Mr. Crawford, whom she regarded in the light of a heavenly being sent by providence to save her cousin from a hideous fate.

"Ah. Good morning, Mr. Watson," said Beverly politely, catching sight of Jeremy.

"Mr. Crawford," said Jeremy with a nod that might have been perceived as a bit too casual for a mere employee if anyone had been paying attention to him, which no one was.

"Mr. Watson," said Margaret, turning and smiling at him. "I shall be home later this morning. I wish to discuss the ball with you."

"I am at your service, ma'am," said Jeremy

gravely.

He made his subservient bow and joined Martha in the breakfast parlor.

"Mr. Watson! Do have some of these delicious muffins!" she said.

"Thank you, ma'am," he said, seating himself.

"Coffee?"

"Please. You are certainly in fine spirits today," he said, forcing a smile to his stiff lips.

"Yes. I am so delighted to see Mr. Crawford back in town," she replied. She lowered her voice confidentially. "Such a charming man, and so distinguished! I have always thought him perfect for dear Margaret. Imagine his saving her life last night! It is so romantic!"

"Yes," said Jeremy, stony-eyed. Martha didn't notice his lack of enthusiasm.

"I have always thought that of all Margaret's suitors he was the most promising."

"Has she known him long?" asked Jeremy.

"Oh, dear me, yes," said Martha. "He offered for her in her *third* season. He has an estate in Yorkshire as well, you know, and his fortune is quite good. It would have been so suitable. The Willoughbys have known the Crawfords forever."

"Then why did he not offer for her in her *first* season?"

"Why, he could not have done so on account of he was betrothed to one of Margaret's school friends. Such a tragic loss for both of them when Cynthia died. She and Margaret were very close, and everyone said they looked like sisters. Both had light brown hair and gray eyes, and they had similar figures and bought their clothes in the same shops."

"I see."

"Mr. Crawford was so heartbroken when dear Cynthia died that his friends feared for his reason. Then he offered for Margaret, but Margaret said she had never thought of him in That Way, which was quite true. Margaret was Cynthia's bridesmaid at their marriage. Margaret believed he only wanted to marry her because they both had loved Cynthia, and because Margaret resembled her. He was so despondent in those days that it quite broke one's heart to look at him."

"I quite see," said Jeremy. "How wise of Miss Willoughby to realize it would not have done."

"Yes, I see that now, although I was quite cross with her at the time because it would have been so suitable and it wasn't as if she *disliked* him—"

"I know. What did Sir Robert think of the match?"

"He didn't care for it, and was inclined to agree with Margaret that the man was offering for her in a fit of dejection because of the loss of his wife, and his regard for Margaret wouldn't prove to be lasting and that Mr. Crawford would make her *dreadfully* unhappy."

"But now you think Mr. Crawford is renewing his suit."

"Well, yes. He has been quite attentive since he came to town last week. He has squired Margaret and Anne everywhere. He has quite gotten over his wife. She died *years* ago, you know. They had no children, so naturally he must be thinking of marrying again."

"Naturally," echoed Jeremy thoughtfully.

"It would be such a wonderful thing for Margaret to marry someone worthy of her. She loves children. And she would be such an excessively beautiful

239

bride!"

Unbidden, a picture of Margaret dressed as a bride flashed into Jeremy's mind and it was all he could do to restrain from grinding his teeth. He had never, to his knowledge, ever done so before, thinking that only villains in romantic novels were capable of grinding their teeth and it was, in fact, quite anatomically impossible for real people. But now, as he repressed the thought of Margaret's marrying Beverly Crawford and having his children, he was quite certain that he could grind his teeth with no difficulty.

"Mr. Watson?" said Martha hesitantly, not liking the set look on his face.

"I beg your pardon, Miss Willoughby," said Jeremy, pulling himself together. "My mind was wandering, I'm afraid."

"No, I should beg *your* pardon," she said with a rueful twinkle in her eye. "I should know that there is nothing so calculated to put a gentleman to sleep than the mere mention of a bridal."

"Not at all," said Jeremy politely. "I would assume that I am at liberty for a few hours, am I not?"

Martha blinked at him. No one ever came to *her* for orders, and she didn't quite know what to say.

"I would not want to put Miss Willoughby to any inconvenience, but I do have some personal business to discharge," he said. "I want to visit my bank and look in on a friend while I'm in the city. The ball is only a few days away, and I imagine I will be so much occupied with it that I won't be able to get away later."

"Probably not," said Martha enthusiastically. "Won't our Anne be a *ravishing* debutante?"

240

"Yes," said Jeremy, wondering why any man would look twice at such an insipid creature as Anne Willoughby with Margaret in the same room.

"I should think Margaret will be gone until at least eleven o'clock," said Martha. "I imagine it would be safe for you to go if you can discharge your business by then."

"I am sure I can," said Jeremy. "She has left no orders, and it seems ridiculous to squander the morning."

"Quite right," said Martha. "I will see you later."

"Good-bye, ma'am," said Jeremy.

It was a little after nine o'clock when he arrived at Molly's house. She saw him coming up the walk and opened the door with a smile of welcome on her face. As she did so, little Becky came bounding down the stairs and threw herself into his arms. He kissed her and put her up on his shoulder as she squealed with excitement.

"Good morning, sir," said Molly. "Becky, love. You mustn't tire our kind visitor."

"She's not tiring me, Molly," said Jeremy.

"Very well," said Molly, "but you may be sorry later."

As it turned out, she was right. Nothing would do but for Becky to sit in his lap for a little while, and then to beg for a ride on his shoulders after the first few minutes. Then he was compelled by the cajoling look in Becky's blue eyes to see all of her dolls. It was with great difficulty that Molly persuaded her daughter to play quietly in another room while the adults talked.

"She's a beautiful child," said Jeremy. "Molly, I've done something you might not like."

"What is that?" she asked curiously.

241

"I have told Frank's mother about the child."

There was a short silence.

"So she also knows that you are not her son."

"Yes. She's almost recovered. I'm afraid I had underestimated her. She recognized me as an impostor when I went back to Yorkshire this time. She has made me a promise not to reveal my secret, but I don't know how long she can keep it."

"What did she say about Becky?"

"She wants to meet her. Molly, I had to tell her. She was so crushed when I admitted that I am not her son. He was all she had. The only thing that comforted her was the knowledge that his child lived. Will you agree to let her see Becky?"

Molly nodded.

"Now that I'm a mother I reckon I know how she feels," she said. "I can't be mean enough to keep Becky from her. But understand, Becky is my baby. I won't give her up to Frank's mother."

"I understand. Believe me, it won't come to that."

"When will you bring her to see us?"

"As soon as she is well enough to stand the journey."

"Will she like me?" Molly asked softly.

"She will love you," said Jeremy. "No one could help it."

"You can."

"That's different, my dear. You are not for me."

"I know," she said.

"Molly, listen to me," he said tilting her face up to his. "I am not Frank Watson. I look like him, but I am not he. You don't love me. You don't know me."

"I'm not good enough for you, not even good enough to be your mistress. And if I were," she

242

added, bursting into tears, "I wouldn't want to be. No one will ever want to marry me because I'm a fallen woman! And I don't know what will happen to me because I want to die before I'll be any man's mistress."

Appalled, he took her into his arms and stroked her hair.

"Molly, what has happened?" he asked. "Has someone insulted you?"

"Yes," she said. "It was so awful. I felt like a piece of goods in a shop. He took me to the opera and everyone stared at me."

"Because you are beautiful," Jeremy suggested soothingly.

"Because I looked like a cheap hussy. And when he brought me home he—"

She broke down again.

"Molly, answer me," said Jeremy, his voice hard. "Did this man force you?"

"No. No, he didn't," she said, "but he tried. I fought him, but he was stronger than me. But he let me go, because I started crying, and I couldn't stop."

"Well, thank God for that," said Jeremy in relief. "My poor dear."

"I'm afraid," she said. "I'm afraid every time a man looks at me now. I'll be alone for the rest of my life. And Frank's mother will hate me, because I'm a fallen woman."

"My dear, don't you realize she was never married, either?"

"All the more reason why she probably wanted her son to marry a respectable woman and give her grandchildren with his name," she sniffed.

"No, Molly. She won't blame you. You were only

fifteen when Frank made love to you. Only a child. If anyone is to blame, it is Frank for taking advantage of you."

"I wanted him," said Molly. "I wouldn't let him alone until he—I didn't know what I wanted. I wanted *him*. That night in the stable, the night he died—"

Sobbing, she leaned against Jeremy's shoulder. He was helpless in the face of her pain.

"It's over now, Molly," said Jeremy. "You have Becky. And I will make sure you have a house and enough for your keep as long as I am alive. I swear it."

"But what about you?" she asked. "Are you going to tell them who you are? The family, I mean?"

"I haven't decided," he said. "My sister and her husband will lose Crossley. They'll have to give it back to me. And there's always the chance that no one will believe me. I've used Frank's name for four years because I was afraid not to. Would you believe me if you didn't know who I am?"

"Yes," she said unhesitatingly. "I would."

Jeremy laughed.

"I am much obliged to you, my dear," he said. "I have brought your allowance for next quarter. If an emergency comes up and you need more, let me know. Send word to Miss Willoughby's house."

"I will," she said, smiling mistily. "But we won't need anything. Thank you, sir."

"You are welcome. Molly, if you ever are frightened again, or if anyone bothers you, you have only to send word to me."

"Thank you. I will," she said.

Jeremy left the house with a thoughtful pucker between his brow. He wondered if Molly had told him the whole truth about the ugly incident that had so upset her. He wasn't in love with Molly, and if anyone had asked him about her a week ago, he would have said that he had no interest in her beyond seeing that she had the means to rear her child in decency because of the great debt he owed Becky's father.

Now he realized that he was much more interested in her future than that. He could never love her, true, and because of his devotion to Margaret his conscience would never allow him to have one of those convenient arrangements with Molly that even the most respectable men of his class were expected by society to enjoy. But he knew that if he ever found out who had frightened her, he would do his best to punish him.

Unknown to him, the object of his violent musings was standing unobserved behind a tree, having the same murderous thoughts about Jeremy.

"Damn him," said Edward Willoughby, realizing that Molly's "protector" was none other than his cousin's steward. He was so angry at the thought of being bested by that scoundrel for the delectable Molly that he actually took off in pursuit of him, only to be brought up short by the sight of Molly's friend approaching him.

"Why, good morning, Mr. Willoughby," said Maria Slaide with a pretty start of surprise. "How delightful to see you. Have you been visiting Molly?"

"No, I have not," he said in high dudgeon. He felt like the lowest of creatures, and he didn't relish the thought of explaining himself to Molly's friend. Molly had slammed the door in his face, returned his gifts, and generally made it plain she wanted none of him. When he offered to set her up in a better establishment than the one she now inhabited, she made a horrible grimace and called him a pig-headed clod. Then she told him she wouldn't be his mistress if he set her up in a marble castle and bought her a solid gold carriage.

Not accustomed to being addressed as a pig-headed clod by beautiful young ladies, Edward had been quite speechless. Molly slammed the door so violently that he had limped for a full day on the foot he had been so unwise as to insert in the door.

To make matters worse, his cronies who had seen him with Molly at the opera congratulated him with many warm jests upon his good fortune in capturing the lovely widow. He had been the object of ribald toasts at the Daffy Club, and a few of his friends had offered to take her off his hands when he tired of her. Plainly they expected to see her on his arm again. How they would laugh if they knew he had never brought her to bed, and that she hated the sight of him.

He was desperate to make peace with her. He wanted her so badly he could hardly stand it. He had even managed to convince himself that he would never be happy again in this life unless she reciprocated his passion.

"She's obviously taken a pet against you," said Maria comfortingly, accepting Edward's arm although he had not offered it. She paused expectantly, plainly hoping he would elaborate on his relationship with her friend. Molly, despite her gentle probing, had told her nothing.

"A misunderstanding," he murmured. He considered, then rejected, the possibility of embarking upon some idle dalliance with Maria. She was pretty enough, but he didn't trust her not to spill the whole to Molly and effectively ruin any slim chance he would have of animating her affection toward him.

He had one comfort as Molly continued to look at him as if he were a dead toad whenever her eyes lighted on him.

He regarded with relish the delightful task of informing his cousin Margaret that her steward had a mistress in keeping, and, furthermore, that the young person had a daughter who resembled him too closely for coincidence.

Chapter Eleven

It was three o'clock on the day of Anne's ball, and Jeremy was in the kitchen trying to keep Marcel and Jacques from attacking each other with the meat cleavers.

"You will ruin the little Miss Anne's ball with your clumsiness," railed Marcel.

"It was not I," said Jacques loftily, "who allowed the almond tarts to get burned."

Jeremy sighed and called the combatants to order.

He didn't see why it mattered that Jacques had turned a raspberry syllabub onto a plate that was considered part of the second-best, rather than the best, silver. Nor, to his uncritical eye, did the batch of almond tarts at present cooling on the table differ in the slightest from the previous batch.

"I won't have this bickering," said Jeremy sternly. "Miss Willoughby needs your support, not your tantrums. Too much depends upon the two of you."

This shameless appeal to their vanity was not without effect.

Marcel admitted that the tarts didn't look *too* bad, and if they were served last, perhaps no one would notice their imperfections. Jacques admitted that the syllabub concealed most of the design on the dish, anyway, and so the presence of a piece of silver plate that was not up to the usual standard might be acceptable on a board covered with pastries.

Jeremy lingered for a moment to make sure there would not be a relapse of the guarded amiability now reigning in the kitchen and then went up to the parlor in search of Miss Willoughby. He didn't have any business to discuss with her. He just wanted to see her.

Making certain she had no company with her except for her cousin Anne, he entered the parlor and was about to ask her if she had any tasks for him to perform when Sternes walked past him and handed each lady a box of flowers.

"From Mr. Crawford," said Sternes.

"Thank you, Sternes," said Margaret, putting the box aside.

"Oh, Margaret!" exclaimed Anne, who had opened her own flower box at once. "How beautiful! Mr. Crawford has sent me pink roses!"

"How charming," said Margaret, looking at the flowers over Anne's shoulder.

"May I see yours?" asked Anne.

"Of course," said Margaret without enthusiasm as she opened the box. Inside were nestled two white orchids arranged with long white satin ribbons.

"They are beautiful," said Anne. "Margaret, do you think he will offer for you tonight?"

Margaret looked up in surprise.

"Beverly? Now, what would put that notion into

your head?"

"My father will be here," she said simply.

"I do not need your father's consent to marry, love. I've been of full age for over a year."

"How can you be so cruel," said Anne, "when Mr. Crawford is quite devoted to you? Have you forgotten that he saved your life?"

"And I am excessively grateful to him," said Margaret, "but that doesn't mean I am obliged to marry him, after all."

She noticed Jeremy in the doorway.

"Come in, Mr. Watson," she said. "Do you require something?"

"No, ma'am. I wondered if there is anything you want me to do in addition to keeping Marcel and Jacques from murdering one another."

"If you can achieve that," said Margaret, smiling appreciatively, "you will have already accomplished miracles. No, I think everything is done. All we need to do is wait until the proper hour and receive our guests."

"How soon do you think we should go to dress?" asked Anne eagerly.

"My dear," said Margaret kindly. "It is only three o'clock. We needn't go to dress for at least four hours."

"That long?" asked Anne, crestfallen.

"From the look on your face one would never guess that you have spent virtually every night for the past two weeks dancing until dawn," said Margaret.

"This will be different," said Anne, her eyes sparkling.

"Yes, I suppose it will," Margaret said, remembering her own debut ball nostalgically. With what hope had she begun that evening. She soon learned, though, that London beaus were no different from Yorkshire beaus. Not one of them interested her until she met Jeremy Verelst. She sighed a little sadly.

"Miss Willoughby, I was wondering if you would have any objection to my making use of the little sitting room off the blue room tonight," asked Jeremy.

"Of course not, but whatever for?" asked Margaret, surprised.

"Your aunt is especially anxious to hear some new verses which she has borrowed from one of her friends, and I told her that if you had no objection I would be happy to read them to her."

"Have *you* no objection, Mr. Watson?" asked Margaret. "I must say it is extremely good-natured of you. There is no reason for you to stay in the house tonight. Surely you will be bored."

"No, not really," he said. "I must admit that, like your aunt, I am anxious to see these verses. I think that by using the sitting room we can avoid disturbing your guests. I know the library and most of the lower rooms will be open to the company, and the refreshments are being laid out in the green salon—"

"You must do as you please," said Margaret.

"It seems a shame after all your labors that you will not be allowed to attend the ball, Mr. Watson," said Anne. "But I dare say being a man you wouldn't enjoy it as much as we ladies do."

"Perhaps I will peek at the guests from the banisters."

"Oh, Margaret!" exclaimed Anne. "Remember when we used to do that as little girls? Remember the time Sir Leonard became intoxicated and saw us, and came up the steps and tried to kiss you?"

"Yes," said Margaret in distaste.

"And Edward came out of his room and raised a fuss."

"And he got a caning for being rude to your father's guest," said Margaret grimly.

"I didn't know that," said Anne indignantly.

"You were very young."

"Oh, Mr. Watson!" exclaimed Anne. "You did remember to send Mr. Crawford a card for dinner as well as the ball, did you not?"

"Yes, Miss Willoughby," said Jeremy patiently. "It went out with the others."

"Anne, love," said Margaret. "One would think Mr. Crawford is your suitor instead of mine."

Anne's face turned a fiery shade of rose pink.

"I'm not pretty enough," said Anne.

Or rich enough, Margaret added mentally, then chided herself for her bad temper. She could acquit Beverly of dangling after her fortune, at any rate. He only wanted to marry her because she reminded him of her dead friend, and because, like Margaret, he wanted children someday.

"Beverly will be here," said Margaret. "A man does not send a woman two orchids on the day of a ball unless he has been invited to dinner as well. One orchid, perhaps, but not two."

"I suppose you're right," said Anne. "If he asks you, you *will* marry him, will you not?"

"Anne!" exclaimed Margaret, glancing significantly at Jeremy.

252

"If you don't, you will be a great fool," said Anne, her face crumpling. "For he is the kindest, most heroic—"

She burst into tears.

"Forgive me," she said, rising and running from the room.

Margaret and Jeremy watched her departure with astonishment.

"It's the ball," said Margaret excusingly. "It's too much excitement for her poor nerves."

"Then, if you'll pardon my asking, ma'am, why are you going to all of this trouble?"

"She'll be all right once it begins."

"It's not like she has never been to a ball before," said Jeremy.

"No. But this is *her* ball. It's very different."

"If you say so, ma'am," said Jeremy, unconvinced.

Sternes came to the door and caught Margaret's eye.

"Mr. Edward is here to see you, Miss Margaret," he said.

"Very well," said Margaret. "Show him in."

Jeremy excused himself and started to leave the room. He came face to face with Edward, who gave him a curt nod and a glare. Jeremy returned the nod and escaped.

"Good afternoon, Edward," said Margaret after Jeremy had left the room. "Have you come to wish your sister well? How kind of you. She isn't feeling quite the thing right now. Nerves, you know."

"If it isn't like Anne to get vaporish after boring us silly with talk of nothing but her precious debut for the past six months," said Edward, with no

253

particular interest in the welfare of his only sister, "but I've come to talk with *you,* Cousin."

"Indeed? Won't you sit down?"

"Margaret, it's about that fellow Watson," said Edward. "He has a mistress in London."

Margaret stared at him for a full minute.

"That is the most absurd thing I've ever heard," said Margaret.

"I have proof," said Edward. "I saw him leaving her house with my own eyes."

"This is your proof? And when did you see this?"

"Yesterday morning."

"I don't believe you," said Margaret, turning away.

"Her name is Molly Harnish. She is nineteen years old. And she has a three-year-old daughter."

"Stop it!" said Margaret.

"The child has fair hair and blue eyes."

"Half the children in London have fair hair and blue eyes. Does that mean he fathered all of them?" she said tartly. "I don't care for this discussion, Edward. If your only purpose in coming to visit me today is to tell me lies about my steward, you can go away again."

"Margaret, listen to me—"

"No," she said. "I think you'd better go now, or I'll call Sternes."

"And Sternes will throw me out?" he asked with a smile. "My dear, I'd like to see it. Does this mean I needn't return for my sister's ball?"

"Oh, go away!" said Margaret crossly.

He wasn't surprised by her refusal to acknowledge that she had erred in the choice of her precious steward. But he knew Margaret's standards of propriety were high, and he was confident that she would do the right thing and discharge the man. Edward saw nothing incongruous in his condemnation of the steward for keeping a pretty mistress when Edward himself had similar intentions toward the same lady.

Edward was certain that when Margaret was free of the steward's influence he and his family would again be installed in Margaret's good graces. Despite Margaret's protests that she felt nothing for Edward, he didn't seriously think she could remain impervious to his charms forever. Crawford was a serious rival, but he had seen nothing to indicate that Margaret returned his regard. He had only to look in his mirror to be reassured that Margaret would eventually succumb to his own tepid ardor despite her protests.

He had great hopes for the evening. He would be at his most charming and do his best to cut Crawford out. He was not sensitive enough to atmosphere to realize that Margaret was not anticipating the ball with any particular expectation of enjoyment.

When it was time to dress, Margaret reflected that if the ball weren't going to be held in her own house, she would probably send a politely regretful note to her hostess excusing herself. Margaret didn't seem to enjoy dancing very much lately. Although she had accompanied Anne from one glittering entertainment to another during the past week, she found herself strangely impatient on these occasions. Was it because she had gotten tired of balls after all these years? Or was it because she knew that she couldn't expect to meet Frank Watson at any of them?

As Miss Poole smoothed her ravishing blue crystal-beaded gown with reverent fingers, Margaret allowed herself to be dressed like a doll. She vaguely was aware of Miss Poole's precise genius in securing sapphire brilliants in exactly the most effective spots in her gleaming brown tresses. She stared blankly at her reflection in the mirror as Miss Poole fastened a heavy collar of sapphires around her slender throat.

At least, Margaret reflected sourly, she didn't have to fear that she would be run down in the street on this night. But the attempts on her life took second place to a more painful sorrow. She had somehow managed to accept the possibility that one of her closest relatives would try to kill her for the sake of her fortune only to be devastated by Edward's contention that her steward might have a mistress.

Of course, the fact that he was seen leaving the woman's house didn't prove she was actually in keeping. But it did indicate that he had some relationship with the girl, and that was enough to arouse Margaret's jealousy.

She writhed in self-contempt at her own naiveté. Did she think that just because she paid him wages and occupied most of his time that he had no room in his life for anyone else? She was certain she had surprised a particularly warm look in his eye several times when he looked at her, and there was no mistaking his concern about the attempts against her life. But he must know, as she did, that she would never stoop to intimacy with an inferior, so why should he not seek a woman closer to his own station? The thought made her want to throw herself across her bed and weep for hours.

Several times that afternoon she had actually gone in search of him to demand an explanation, but each time she abandoned her quest because she knew if he admitted he had a mistress she wouldn't be able to hide her agitation from him.

She wondered what Molly Harnish looked like. Was she beautiful? And was the child his? She pictured a child like Kate's, all golden hair and eyebrows and eyelashes with sky blue eyes and pale, pink-tinged skin.

After being in Margaret's house all day, did he seek this girl's embraces? Did they lie together in bed and did he discuss his employer with his mistress? Did he describe Margaret as a brown-haired, rather ordinary woman with colorless eyes whom one could pass on the street without noticing except for her bags upon bags of money?

Miss Poole was slightly daunted by Margaret's lack of animation. Usually her mistress made civil conversation with her while she plied her trade. This silence made Miss Poole most uncomfortable.

"Miss Willoughby," the dresser asked hesitantly, "is something wrong? Would you rather wear another gown? Or do you dislike the way I've dressed your hair? Or would you prefer—"

"No, Miss Poole," said Margaret, giving her dresser a forced smile. "I assure you, it looks quite well. I am very pleased. Now, if you'll just fetch my fan and my reticule—"

"At once, miss," said Miss Poole uncertainly.

"It is almost time for dinner," said Margaret

brightly. "My aunt and uncle have already arrived."

"Will that be all, miss?"

"Yes. And don't wait up for me, if you please. I plan to be very late."

"Yes, miss," said Poole submissively, beginning the task of putting all Margaret's brushes and hair-pins away.

"Oh, Margaret!" exclaimed Anne, her amber eyes sparkling as she danced into the hallway from her bedroom. "How beautiful you look!"

"Thank you, love. Let me look at you," said Margaret.

She surveyed her young cousin's pink taffeta gown and dark hair threaded with pearls approvingly. Was I ever this young? she asked herself, without grudging Anne her radiance.

"I wonder if anyone has arrived," said Anne.

"Your parents are here," said Margaret. "Sternes sent me word. Beverly is here because he is always prompt. Your brother will probably be late. He always is."

She took a deep breath, bracing herself for the inevitable exchange with her aunt and uncle. They would, of course, receive guests with their daughter between them, sharing the honors with Anne's aunt, who was her sponsor. Although Margaret, too, would be in the receiving line, Sir Robert would play host and, if Margaret knew him, do his best to hold on to the role when it was time for him to leave.

Margaret didn't look forward to her Aunt Samantha's barbs. Lady Willoughby had always considered the town house her primary social asset, next to her husband's title. Having reigned over

Margaret's town house for so long, she was capable of doing anything in her power to recapture her former position.

"My darling!" said Lady Willoughby, offering Margaret an overly rouged and scented cheek to kiss.

"Good evening, Aunt Samantha," said Margaret, dutifully kissing it. She permitted her uncle to kiss her forehead.

Beverly was in the room and smiled reassuringly at Anne, who, now that she was downstairs, was beginning to look nervous.

"How pretty you look, love," said Samantha to her daughter, fussing with her curls as Anne wriggled impatiently under her fingers, and passing a critical look over Anne's dress. Anne hated it when her mother fussed over her as if she were a baby who couldn't be trusted not to soil her gown or disarrange her hair before company. Lady Willoughby liked to maintain the social fiction that she was a fond mother, and annoyed both her children very much by forcing them to endure her caresses in public.

"What a pretty gown," said Samantha. "It is a little plain, but it is very well, I assure you. It should have been white, of course—"

"I chose it myself," said Anne, who knew her mother and recognized a criticism of Margaret's taste. "And I'm tired of white. Everyone wears white. I wanted something different."

"Nothing becomes a very young girl more than white," persisted Samantha, an edge of steel showing through her determined affability.

Nothing could have been more calculated to raise

259

the bristles of a sixteen-year-old who was determined to present the appearance of a young lady of fashion in front of Margaret and her sophisticated London friends. Even so, Anne's tone was conciliating as she replied.

"You're probably right," said Anne, "but I fell in love with it, and Margaret didn't have the heart to refuse me."

Samantha regarded her daughter with pursed lips. Samantha thought Anne's tendency, manifested in the past week or so, to assert herself in small matters, was most unbecoming, and she had no hesitation in attributing this unwelcome development to Margaret's influence. Samantha was still smarting because Anne recently had defied her mother's wishes and accepted Margaret's invitation for Anne to stay with her at the town house for the rest of the season.

Anne didn't plead or cry or pout. She calmly pointed out there was hardly any room left in her Uncle Gilbert's house now that Sir Robert and his lady had taken up residence with Samantha's kindhearted brother, and she wouldn't dream of inconveniencing her poor aunt with an additional guest.

Samantha, whose thick hide of complacency was usually impervious to hints, detected under Anne's remark a criticism of her parents' determination to remain in London for the rest of the season at someone else's expense no matter how much inconvenience they might inflict upon Samantha's innocent brother and his long-suffering family.

A truly dutiful daughter would more properly use her influence with Margaret to impress upon that spoiled beauty her obligation to Sir Robert

260

and his lady for looking after her affairs all these years, and Samantha was considerably annoyed when the usually obedient Anne told her she would do no such thing.

However, Samantha had come to the town house tonight determined to placate and perhaps effect her return to the town house on a permanent basis. At the very least, Samantha was hopeful that Margaret would settle her more pressing bills, if for no other reason than to save herself embarrassment.

Margaret saw through her aunt's stratagems with little trouble, since the lady's belief in her own cleverness was quite misplaced. Although Margaret disliked her cousin Edward excessively at that moment, she almost wished he would arrive. His parents usually did not behave in too outrageous a fashion in his presence. They learned long ago that he was impervious to their bullying because of his independent means.

"Your flowers are so lovely," said Margaret to Beverly, indicating the orchids pinned to her bodice when she had escaped from her aunt's caresses. "How kind of you to send them."

"It was my pleasure," said Beverly.

"Oh, thank you for mine, too," said Anne, evading her mother's attempt to pat her cheek. "They are precisely the right color!"

"I am glad you like them," said Beverly with an answering smile.

Then the principal dinner guests arrived, people who were strangers to Anne but who would nevertheless assure her acceptance in the eyes of the ton, and conversation became general. Edward was among the last to arrive, and he managed to take

261

his cousin's hand and pull her away from the rest of the company for a brief conversation.

He looked magnificent, and Margaret was impressed despite the fact that he was hardly in her good graces at the moment. Samantha beamed at them with fatuous approval, a sight so repulsive that Edward deliberately took Margaret's shoulders and turned her slightly to shield her from it.

"Please don't be angry with me," Edward said gently, pressing her hand. "Perhaps my jealousy led me to jump to conclusions."

He didn't believe that for a moment, but he was anxious to reestablish himself in Margaret's esteem.

"I don't want to talk about it," said Margaret, forcing a smile to her lips. "This is Anne's night, and I have hundreds of people arriving in the next two hours, and I have no intention of worrying about my steward's, er, domestic arrangements, this evening."

If Margaret implied uncertainty as to the success of the ball, she needn't have.

For the rest of the night, her pretty young cousin was never at a loss for partners, and the ballroom was jammed to capacity. Margaret realized that her labors and her steward's had not been wasted.

Her aunt and uncle were reveling in the triumph of receiving guests in their former home, and Margaret was content to let them enjoy it for the time being. However, she was determined to be firm if they attempted to prolong their residence in the house.

Margaret was, as she expected, quite as much in demand as Anne for every dance, and her suspicions weren't in the least aroused when one of her partners, a young man who had lived near her family in Yorkshire all of his life, asked her to take the air with him in the gardens, which had been opened to the guests because of the balmy weather.

She had no sooner stepped through the archway of the dimly illuminated rose garden where several guests had gone for respite from the heat of the ballroom, when her companion crushed her to his chest and pressed a burning kiss full on her affronted lips.

"How dare you?" she said, wriggling to free herself from his embrace. "Bertram, if you don't let me go this instant I am going to tell your mother!"

"I am inflamed by passion for you! You must let me speak!"

"No," said Margaret, freeing one hand and putting it in front of her mouth to foil his obvious intention of kissing her again.

"I love you!" he said ardently.

"You do not!" Margaret replied crossly, "and if you have dared to tear my dress I'll never speak to you again. Of all the clumsy—"

"My ardor made me too impetuous."

"Ardor, my foot," said Margaret. "As if everyone in the neighborhood didn't know the terms of your late father's will. Your funds are tied up in trust until you are five and twenty or married, and it's just as well if this is any indication of your judgment."

"I was going to ask you to marry me," he said, afraid he had not made his intentions plain.

"I am aware of that," said Margaret, panting a little from her exertions, "and I am sorry if this gives you pain, but I cannot return your regard."

"Oh," he said.

This remark struck Margaret as so inadequate that she started laughing. Bertram, most pardonably affronted, abandoned her and his manners to escape her presence, leaving her alone in the darkened garden. Walking past the couples who were laughing and talking in soft whispers around her only made her more depressed. Her head was beginning to ache, and she longed to pull the jeweled pins out of her hair and run distracted fingers through it to relieve her throbbing temples.

She noticed that Martha was missing from her favorite spot on a sofa in the ballroom and assumed she had gone to the sitting room to listen to her steward read poetry. It was not quite eleven o'clock, and she thought it was too bad of her aunt to leave possession of the ballroom to Samantha, who was doing the rounds, blandly accepting compliments on the quality of the entertainment she had no part in arranging and generally queening it over the assembly as if she were still the lady of the house.

This sight disgusted Margaret so much that she turned away, only to see Bertram's mother, wreathed in insincere smiles, preparing to descend upon her. She turned from her only to see Edward bending upon her with the intention, no doubt, of embarking upon another flirtation with her. She saw that Anne was dancing with Beverly, and knew that she would come to no harm in his unalarming company, so she began making escape plans.

While she was intent upon evading Edward and Bertram's mother, she didn't see another of her suitors bearing down upon her, and the merest civility obliged her to dance the waltz with him. To her disgust, encouraged by her excellent wines and the low neckline of her gown, he mauled her quite shamelessly on the dance floor, which embarrassed her so much that she threatened to have him thrown out if he didn't keep his hands where they belonged for the duration of the dance.

They eyed each other in mutual hostility and both seemed relieved when the waltz was over. She went from this man's arms to another's, and, when he whispered into her ear that he adored her, she couldn't be rid of him soon enough.

She walked to the balcony to cool her reddened cheeks and saw Edward lounging by the archway. He followed her.

"What is wrong, Margaret? You look fit to commit murder."

"Nothing," she said. "I am not in a good mood."

"So I gathered."

"And if you are going to inflict your company on me, just stand there and don't say *anything*."

"What is this?" he asked smiling. "Why is the most beautiful woman at this insipid affair—"

"Enough of that," she said sharply.

To her annoyance, he put his arm around her shoulders and drew her close. He would have kissed her if she had not pushed him away rather violently and stamped her foot in her temper.

"What is *wrong* with men lately?" she demanded.

"Margaret, if I've offended you—"

"Well, you have," she said incorrigibly, "but don't worry about it. Just go back into the ballroom. Or, if you'd prefer, I'll go back to the ballroom and you can stay here."

She stalked away, her eyes sparkling with anger, and more than one guest wondered what had happened to put Margaret in a passion. Margaret saw her Aunt Samantha take a step toward her and dodged her neatly. Beverly, she could see, was approaching. She recalled with some surprise that he had only asked her to dance once, and she assumed he was going to ask her again. She wasn't even in the mood for his pacific company.

It was just past midnight. She fled to the library for refuge, hoping she would be alone, and surprised a pair of embarrassed lovers there. All of the salons were full of people drinking tea or playing cards or gossiping or trysting. In a state akin to panic, her steps guided her to the small sitting room her steward and Martha had used during the evening, but which she now expected would be deserted. Her aunt, she knew, had probably sought her rest an hour ago, and she hardly expected that her steward would still be up.

She went into the room and closed the door behind her, shutting her eyes as she leaned against it.

"Miss Willoughby!" said Jeremy, who had been sitting in an armchair reading by the light of a lamp on the table. "What is wrong?"

He started forward in concern as her eyes flew open.

"I'm sorry, Mr. Watson," she said unsteadily. "I didn't know you were still here. Has my aunt gone to bed?"

"Yes. Has something happened?"

She realized her hasty entrance had alarmed him. He was, in fact, worried about another attempt on

266

her life.

"No. I'm sorry to have disturbed you," she said, biting her lip.

"Something obviously is upsetting you, ma' am. Is there any way in which I may be of assistance?"

His voice was so kind that she was absolutely furious with him.

"No," she said. "I'm just weary of being mauled by people. What is it about champagne that makes otherwise perfectly stable men *paw* one as if—"

"It's not the champagne," he said, smiling. "It's probably that dress. If you *will* insist upon displaying so much of yourself, you surely can't blame certain men if they forget themselves."

"Nonsense," said Margaret, annoyed. "The dress Miss Marsdon is wearing is *much* lower—"

"I don't believe I've met the lady," said Jeremy, with a crooked grin, "but perhaps it isn't quite the same on her."

She eyed him with acute dislike.

"I certainly know better than to expect a *man* to understand."

"Forgive me," he said, contrite. "It is infamous of me to laugh."

"Well, it is," she said. "I was hoping this room was unoccupied, and I was surprised to find you here."

"I see," he said. "Well, I can certainly absent myself if that is your wish. I shall see you tomorrow, I expect, ma' am. If I have your leave, I will probably return to Yorkshire in the afternoon."

"Frank, do you have a mistress in London?" she blurted out.

"Who told you that?" he said, his eyes narrowed.

267

"It is true then," she said in disbelief. "I owe Edward an apology. I told him—"

"If your disgusting cousin Edward has laid one hand on Molly I'll—"

"Yes. That was the name," said Margaret, her eyes bright with unshed tears. "I've been a fool."

"She is not my mistress," said Jeremy, "but a lady who has some right to my protection."

"I don't care who she is," said Margaret, mortified, as she attempted to make good her escape.

He caught her arm and turned her around to face him.

"You don't understand," he said.

She glared up at him.

"On the contrary, Mr. Watson, I'm quite sure I do," she said defiantly. "Under the skin, you're all alike. I hate you all!"

"Margaret, listen to me!"

"I did not give you leave to use my Christian name."

This annoyed him so much that without realizing how it happened, he found his hands around her slender throat, the sapphires cold against his fingers.

Whatever he was going to say died on his lips.

"Are you going to throttle me, Mr. Watson?" she asked in a subdued tone.

"Yes," he said, and kissed her.

It was really, as kisses went, a chaste affair if the attentions of her other suitors were any indication, but it succeeded, somehow, in robbing her of breath, thought, and will. She looked at him dreamily.

He was about to kiss her again when he heard

an intake of breath and looked up to see from the corner of his eye two shocked faces at the doorway. Margaret's reputation would be ruined, and it was all his fault. No gentlewoman could survive the stigma of being caught in a compromising position with one of her own employees.

He had to save her, and so his methods had to be desperate. Hoping that he had not underestimated Margaret's experience in dalliance, he pulled her into his arms and kissed her again, aggressively thrusting his tongue between her parted lips.

Her body stiffened and her eyes threw open in indignation. She hit him. Hard.

The door slammed shut, and she realized immediately what her steward had done.

She had been so startled by his disgusting and insulting act that she had reacted instinctively. Unfortunately, her erratic brain, recalling a bit of instruction from her cousin Edward, guided her aim.

"If you're ever in a desperate situation," Edward had told her at a time when boxing was the passion of his life, "don't hit your enemy with your open hand. Hit him with your fist, preferably in a vulnerable place." When the teen-aged Margaret had asked him *what* vulnerable place, Edward had rather hastily suggested the nose.

"Damn your chivalry," Margaret hissed. "You've sacrificed your reputation for mine, and I won't have it!"

"I'm afraid you have no choice in the matter," said Jeremy, who had put both hands to his sorely afflicted member and was making an extremely unpleasant gurgling sound through it. "It hardly matters, so don't give it a thought. I'm sure I haven't a

269

shred of reputation left with your cousin prattling to anyone who will listen about my supposed mistress."

Margaret deliberately ignored this provocative statement.

"Do you think I've broken it?" she asked, nearly overcome with remorse. She took his handkerchief from his pocket and began dabbing at him in distraction.

He took it from her and moved out of her reach.

"I can manage," he said. "I might bleed on you, and I should hate to be responsible for the destruction of yet another ravishing ball gown. I quite see now why it was necessary for you to bring so many."

"Oh, shut up," she said, nettled. "Does it hurt awfully?"

"No. You had better go back to your guests, and I'll go to an inn by the back entrance. I'll take my leave of you now, and I promise to remove my mother from the brick house as soon as—"

"No," she said, distress written plainly on her face.

"You must see I can't remain in your employ after what I've done," he said. "I most humbly beg your pardon for—"

"What fustian," she said. "It was as much my fault as yours."

"No. The fault was entirely mine."

"But I permitted—"

"Yes, and I shall remember it always," he said, smiling through the wreckage of his face. "Has it stopped bleeding now?"

"Yes."

"You're quite sure?"

"Yes," she said. "Mr. Watson, I'm so terribly sorry—"

"So I'm Mr. Watson again, am I?" he said with a sigh as he advanced on her. She didn't trust the look in his eye and backed away.

"Frank!" she squeaked, startled.

He reached her and pulled her close.

"What are you doing?" she asked, panic in her eyes.

"We have a saying in Yorkshire," he whispered. "It goes, 'You might as well be hanged for a sheep as for a lamb.'"

He kissed her thoroughly but not, to her relief, in the manner that had so offended her sensibilities. She was leaning against him because her knees seemed suddenly turned to wax.

"Frank—"

Tenderly, he placed his forefinger on her lips and released her.

"Don't look so worried, my darling," he said. "I am willing to apologize for the violence I have done to your dignity, but I am unrepentant. I assure you that even if I am horsewhipped through the streets of London for my crime tomorrow, it will have been worth it."

With that, he walked past her and out of her frivolous, quite empty life.

Chapter Twelve

Jeremy took Fanny Watson to London almost as soon as he returned from Yorkshire. The women that Frank Watson had loved took to each other immediately, with the happy result that instead of being compelled to support two women and a child under two separate roofs, Jeremy could now support all three under one.

Therefore Edward found, to his fury, that there was no getting near Molly these days. Instead of her complacent friend Maria, her constant companion lately was a middle-aged female who threatened to call the law on him whenever he tried to importune Molly for a word with him.

"It's a fine state of affairs when a young female can't take the air without being annoyed by *men*," said Fanny, the last word of this statement uttered with such loathing that, in spite of himself, Edward was impressed.

Molly, her nose in the air, followed in the wake of her tiny, but formidable, protector.

Edward stood on the sidewalk, seething impotently, as Becky, looking like the cat that ate the canary, gave him an impudent look of triumph and sidled by him after her mother.

He was about to slink away, the better to hatch other plots to get his quarry alone, when he saw the cavalcade of females stop at the sight of a small, belligerent figure in their path.

Martin, who was desperate to learn Jeremy's whereabouts, had unwisely sought enlightenment of Molly. Like Edward, he was soon sent about his business, menaced by Fanny's umbrella, which she leaned upon when she got tired because she was too stubborn to carry a cane.

Edward grabbed the little man by the collar and shook him, happy to have some outlet for his frustration.

"And what, may I ask, is your business with that young woman, my good man?" he asked threateningly.

"No harm, no harm," said Martin in alarm. "I just wanted to learn the whereabouts of a mutual acquaintance."

"What acquaintance?" asked Edward warily.

"You wouldn't know him," said Martin, vainly attempting to extricate himself.

"Try me," said Edward.

A few hours later, Edward, a light of triumph in his eye, accosted Margaret in her drawing room where she was rather listlessly sketching a vase of flowers on the table before her. It had cost him a bottle of gin to learn his enemy's diabolical plan, and it was well worth it.

"Edward!" exclaimed Margaret.

"Good afternoon, Cousin," he said. "Pardon the intrusion, but I must speak to you without delay."

"Is there some trouble, Edward? You seem very excited about something."

"Yes. Margaret, I have just learned the most

shocking thing about your erstwhile steward."

She rose stiffly to her feet.

"Edward, if you think you can barge in here—"

"Margaret, listen to me. I won't pretend to be sorry that that upstart is out of your house, but what I have learned means he is a threat to the Verelsts as well."

"What do you mean?" asked Margaret, torn between her reluctance to hear her former steward maligned and bewilderment that even in his wildest imagination Edward could think her former employee could harm her friend's family.

"He's been plotting to establish himself with the Verelsts as their long lost heir, if you please, come back from the dead."

"Jeremy," she breathed, wide-eyed.

"See here," said Edward impatiently, "you aren't going to faint, are you?"

"No. Certainly not," said Margaret, getting a grip on herself. "Pray continue—not that I believe a word of this ridiculous story."

"I tell you, I have proof. I talked to his former valet, who says between them, he and your precious Frank Watson are planning to trade on his resemblance to Jeremy Verelst in order to convince Lord and Lady Shallcross that he has survived the fire and exchanged identities with the real Frank Watson, who died in his place."

"He has those burns on his back," she said slowly.

"And under what circumstances, my girl, did you happen to see the fellow's back?" Edward demanded wrathfully.

"When he was wounded—Oh, never mind that," said Margaret impatiently. "He tried to rescue them.

That's how he got burned."

"Running away, more likely, and got singed in the flames," said Edward contemptuously. "The scars would only seem to support his preposterous story, don't you see?"

"No, I don't," said Margaret angrily. "He has made no attempt to establish himself as Jeremy Verelst."

"The valet explained that," said Edward. "He's been waiting for the Verelsts to return from the Continent. He thinks his tender-hearted sister and mother would be more likely to swallow his lies than anyone else. It makes sense. Who was the most upset by his death? He's counting on his bereaved family to accept him with open arms and endow him with Shallcross's worldly goods. If the Verelsts accept him, what will it matter what anyone else thinks?"

"No," said Margaret. "I won't believe it of him. He is incapable of such a cruel deception. I am certain of it."

"Someone should warn—"

"No," said Margaret. "Please go."

Edward knew that look of old. Curtly, he turned on his heel and left her to her misery.

Jeremy was alone now except for the occasional visits of Mathilde, who came to cook and clean for him because he had paid her wages until the end of the quarter.

Jeremy tolerated her ministrations because there was really no polite way to tell her that he preferred sitting in a darkened room, eating nothing and seeing no one, to listening to her gossip.

From his servant, who really had no way of knowing she was giving him pain, he learned that almost as soon as he returned to Yorkshire Margaret had become engaged to Beverly Crawford.

Mathilde could talk of nothing but the reputed sterling qualities of the bridegroom, the number of bride clothes Margaret was said to have ordered, the modest army of bridesmaids that would support her at the altar, the sumptuousness of the wedding feast Marcel and Jacques would create for the nuptials, and the lavish hand with which a celebration in the village was being planned.

Margaret had decreed, Mathilde reported ecstatically, that bonfires would be lighted and that several oxen would be roasted. There would be a dance and kegs upon kegs of beer and wine so that everyone in the village could lift a glass or mug to the happy couple.

It was no wonder Jeremy soon decided that it was time for Frank Watson to return to the sea. He didn't know how he was going to fulfill his promise to the dead man's mother. Would he dare exhume the body and bury it privately with an appropriate headstone in a parish church in another county, the Verelsts none the wiser?

Margaret had paid his wages through the end of the quarter, so he couldn't resist staying in the brick house for just a few more weeks, looking after Margaret's interests by bullying her bailiff into resentful efficiency and gazing at her house in his unguarded moments exactly like, as he reminded himself sternly, a besotted mooncalf. He hoped the threats against her life would stop now that she had a protector. He assumed she would tell Crawford about the "accidents" and he would be able to shield her from whoever wanted to harm her. Perhaps her enemy would give up now.

Jeremy also spent those last few weeks riding near the grounds at Crossley, wishing that just once he could enter the house where he was born. More than that, he would have liked to have seen his sisters, his cousin Mark, his niece and nephew, and, of course, his mother. But how could he reveal himself to them without claiming his inheritance and upsetting their lives? Would they truly prefer to have their scapegrace back if it meant that he could disinherit his sister's husband and their children?

One day he learned that Margaret had returned from London for a short visit. The poor young lady, said the informative Mathilde, had been quite worn out with all the gadding about she had been doing in preparation for her wedding, and so had come to the country for a rest. She also wanted to see that her house was in order, for she would be married from her estate in the fall.

Jeremy resolved to be gone by then. He couldn't bear the thought of seeing her married to Crawford and, perhaps, watching their children grow up in her house.

He had grown gaunt and stern in his agony, the aristocratic bones of his face being thrown into relief, and his blazing eyes seeming to dominate his face. His manner was aloof and his demeanor coldly competent as he dealt with the bailiff.

On a glorious day in June, Margaret's steps led her to the ruined chapel at Crossley, where she found an outlet for her restless energies in arranging flowers on the grave of a perfect stranger.

She thought of her fiancé, and of her altruistic aim of bringing him some happiness to compensate for the loss of his late wife now that Margaret's own happiness was at an end.

Beverly had been a widower for three years, and, if at first he had courted Margaret because of her resemblance to his late wife, his perseverance in being one of Margaret's most loyal and faithful suitors might argue for his transferring of his devotion to Cynthia's memory to Margaret herself.

At any rate, Beverly would be a kind husband who would fit in perfectly with her world and administer her estate with cool competence. She needn't worry that he would game away her fortune or attempt to bully her, and, if he should seek pleasures outside their marriage, she knew he would do so with discretion. After all, he was handsome and charming. Perhaps in time he might even succeed in dislodging Frank Watson from his place in her heart if, that is, he cared to do so.

She was really very fortunate, she told herself determinedly as tears of self-pity threatened to spill from her eyes. She looked at Jeremy's cold marble face for comfort and found none. It looked too much like Frank Watson's.

With a tentative finger, she touched the strong, square jaw, the one feature that saved the marble face from absurdly feminine beauty.

A rustling noise by the darkened nave broke in on her musings, and suddenly a thrill of fear shot through her.

There had been, after all, several clumsy attempts on her life. That was why she had had her groom follow her and wait outside with the horses while she paid her respects to the dead. But did someone, anticipating her movements, hide himself in the chapel, waiting for the moment to find her alone?

"Who is it?" she asked with a tremor in her voice.

Silence answered her.

Then she knew who waited in the gloom, although later, when she tried to recall the incident, she couldn't say why. There were no more sounds, and she saw nothing moving in the dark corner.

"Frank," she said in a steadier voice.

A shadow separated itself from the darkness of the nave and became outlined in the faint light from the window.

"I did not mean to frighten you," he said harshly, as his features became more distinct. There was even a note of amusement in his voice as he continued. "Really, if you must haunt this chamber of gothic horrors—"

"What are you doing here?" she asked.

"Waiting for you," he said, joining her in front of the statue and taking her basket from her hands to put it on a table. "How are you?"

"I am well, I thank you," she said, averting her face from his avid gaze.

"I should think a young lady so recently engaged would have better things to do with her time than decorate graves. I understand I am to felicitate you."

"Frank, why are you doing this to me?" she blurted out. Her voice ended on a distinct sob.

"What is this?" he asked in astonishment, putting a tentative hand out toward her. "I only wanted to see you before I go. I wouldn't even have spoken if—"

"No, don't touch me!" she cried out.

279

"Are you so unhappy?" he asked. "Is it this marriage? If so, you must break it off—"

"I can't. It has gone too far," she said, really weeping now. There was a curious relief in unburdening herself to him. "The announcement has not appeared in the papers, but everyone knows we are engaged. I couldn't behave so shabbily to him."

"Margaret, listen to me," he said, putting his hands on her shoulders. She tried to free herself, but he tightened his hold. "No. Don't try to run away. If you don't feel right about this marriage, you must tell Crawford that you cannot marry him. Or, at the very least, you must tell him that you need more time to consider."

"I can't do that! He doesn't deserve the disgrace of being jilted."

"The gossips will forget it in time, and he will find someone who can return his regard," he said soothingly. "You'll do him no favors by dooming him to a life shackled to a woman who doesn't love him."

"But what about honor—"

"What about it?"

"You don't understand," she said, beginning to cry again.

"No," he said coldly. "I don't. But then a lady of quality like yourself couldn't seriously expect a bastard to understand the scruples of the civilized mind, particularly when it comes to duping an innocent man."

"That's not what I meant," said Margaret, breaking free. "I never think of you that way. And I am not duping Beverly."

"My understanding *is* deficient then, because I can't imagine that he'd have you if he knew you're

280

only marrying him because it is impossible for you to have the man you really want."

"How *dare* you suggest—," she began, horrified that he had put her hopeless longing for him into words.

"I *suggest* nothing. You told me about it yourself. You've made no secret of your infatuation with a dead man," he said angrily. "Tell me, Margaret, is it quite comfortable to have a lasting passion for a corpse? He doesn't talk back, I suppose. That would be one advantage over a real man. Does it satisfy you to visit him here? It gives new meaning to the term 'companionable silence,' does it not?"

Margaret was torn between relief that he apparently didn't know about her agony of longing for him and exasperation that he could be dim-witted enough to think she still cherished her sentimental infatuation for poor dead Jeremy Verelst.

"Mr. Watson," she said coldly, "you forget yourself."

"Just tell me this," he said angrily. "Do you think for one minute Crawford would have asked you to marry him if he knew you were in love with a dead man?"

"Why not, if he is in love with a dead woman?" she snapped. She put both hands over her mouth and stared at him in dismay.

"My God, Margaret," he said, horrified. "That is the most disgusting—"

"Stop it! I won't listen to another word," Margaret said, desperation and pain in her eyes. "It must be wonderful to be you, Frank. You must not have ever lost anyone you loved, or you wouldn't be so callous about the emotions of others."

"You wrong me, Margaret," he said gently.

"I think not. Yet you are the more to be pitied, Frank. I may suffer, but at least I can feel *something*."

"Spoken like a true woman of sensibility," he said sardonically, made reckless by the sheer injustice of her words. He took a hasty step toward her, but she checked him with a look of pure anguish.

"Go, Frank. Get out of my life. Please," she said with a catch in her voice.

Recognizing his defeat in her strained face, he gave her a bow with no mockery in it for once and left.

More than anything she wanted to call him back, to plead, to explain. But her pride held her back.

For the next few days, they avoided each other. Neither went to the chapel again. Margaret's trunks were packed for the return to London, where she was to be honored by a fête at her future mother-in-law's town house. Jeremy's belongings were also packed. He could have left days ago, but something indefinable had chained him to Yorkshire.

Each was determined to relinquish the other.

Margaret's staff was puzzled because their lady's demeanor had nothing in common with that of the happy bride. The more charitably minded attributed her serious expression and tendency to start at small noises to prenuptial nerves.

Mathilde gossiped to her cronies that her young man was a walking ghost of his old self. He rarely smiled, never laughed, hardly ate. Jokes made in his presence were accorded a polite grimace that was meant to pass for a smile, and the choicest gossip was received with utter indifference.

No secret was made of his intention to return to sea. A few tantalizing rumors came from the servants who had accompanied Margaret from the city. There were some who said the steward had presumed upon his privileged position as Miss Willoughby's retainer and dared take liberties. The mistress quite rightly took umbrage, which explained why this formerly trusted employee was about to return to the oblivion from which he had come.

This caused some sighs from impressionable young maidens in the village who had been swept away by the romantic figure Jeremy made as he haunted the countryside like a wraith upon his black horse, but their thoughts were soon turned to what they would wear for the grand celebration of Miss Willoughby's wedding at the village feast, so they did not pine for the loss of one bachelor, however handsome, for very long.

One day the garrulous Mathilde informed him that the family had returned to Crossley. Intent upon the information she had to impart, Mathilde didn't notice the look of anguish that crossed his face, and later in high dudgeon she told one of her cronies that talking to such an uncommunicative gentleman was hardly worth her breath.

While one part of his mind stood back and condemned his action as sheer folly, pointing out that the fat would be in the fire if he got caught, Jeremy furtively watched his unsuspecting family as the group sat outdoors in the rose gardens which, he noted, had been improved remarkably from the days when his mother, who had no taste for the country, had allowed it to fall into benign neglect.

Mark and Kate's young family and Mark's nephews made a pretty tableau as they sat along benches and strolled in the shrubbery. Jeremy's eyes strayed often to the sturdy little boy who was his namesake and the fairylike little girl who was the picture of his sister as a child. The two of them were alternately befriended and bullied by lively twin boys, whose resemblance to Jeremy's dark-haired, mischievous cousin Serena, Mark's sister, was comically evident to his appreciative gaze.

Kate and her husband were having tea in the gardens and their obvious pleasure in one another's company made Jeremy ashamed of his role as spy.

"My love," said Lord Shallcross, playing with an errant chestnut curl upon his wife's serene brow, "you cannot imagine how much I am looking forward to having you all to myself again. When we decided to go on our much-delayed honeymoon, I hadn't bargained for your mother and my sister's family inviting themselves along."

"Poor Mark," she said tenderly, "did you dislike it so very much?"

"On the contrary," he said, "I enjoyed it more than I expected. Even your mother was, for her, quite well behaved. But perhaps I am grown stodgy in my old age. The grandeur of Paris and Venice are nothing to me compared to the comfort of my own home."

"You love it here, don't you?" asked Kate.

"It is as if I've lived here all my life," he said. "To think five years ago I was in despair because I feared that someday I would have to stand by while you married another because of my lack of fortune."

"Silly. As if I wouldn't have married you whatever my parents said."

"I didn't know that then," he said, "but I could hardly have expected you to become a soldier's

284

wife."

"I would have done it."

"I believe you. But I'm sure you will agree that marrying the heir to your father's handsome fortune and estate has been much more comfortable."

"Poor Jeremy," said Kate with a sigh.

"I know," said Mark, patting her hand. "I would not have chosen to inherit the title at such a price, my dear. Even though it means that after we're dead our Jeremy will have all this."

"It's hard for me to believe that I am older than he was when he died," said Kate dreamily.

"Don't, my darling," said Mark. "Let the poor boy rest in peace."

"You are right, of course," said Kate.

His sister's tone was sad, but she looked far from broken-hearted. In fact, she was blooming. Obviously she had come to terms with her brother's "death." Jeremy could leave her to her husband, her children, and her home, knowing that her love for them would more than compensate her for the loss of one rather unsatisfactory brother.

He had been closer to Kate than anyone else in his family, even his mother, who had remarried and was gleefully occupied in spending her second husband's considerable fortune. He could leave them without regret or, if not that, at least without guilt.

Before long the sun began to set and the family party moved inside. Jeremy stole away from his hiding place to brood in the red brick house that had become a prison.

The following afternoon, Margaret burst in on Kate as she took tea with her sister-in-law in the parlor. The four children were seated at a low table in one corner. Jeremy was helping his little sister to

285

cakes, and Serena's boys were throwing gumdrops at each other.

"Margaret!" exclaimed Kate, giving a little squeal of pleasure.

"Wretch!" said Margaret fondly. "How *dare* you sneak into Yorkshire yesterday while I was occupied at Miss Lacey's all day? I just learned you were back. How ravishing you look!"

"Thank you, love," said Kate, noticing that although Margaret was as lovely as ever, there were dark circles under her eyes and she had lost weight. "It is these Paris fashions. My love, you would not believe the shops!"

"I think I would, and I sincerely envy you. Good afternoon, Serena. How delightful to see you," said Margaret, smiling at Kate's sister-in-law.

The noise from the children's corner increased, and Margaret blinked at Serena's calmness in the face of her sons' outrageous behavior. Kate kept stealing helpless little glances toward the children, and Margaret thought that the gumdrops would probably leave sticky patches on the carpet.

"John and I are firm believers in Monsieur Rousseau's theories," Serena said, obviously picking up the thread of the conversation that had been in progress when Margaret arrived.

"How very interesting," said Margaret politely.

"Tea, Margaret?" Kate asked.

"Yes. Please," said Margaret, holding her hand out for the cup Kate was pouring.

"You see," Serena continued for Margaret's benefit, "Monsieur Rousseau believes that children are born into a state of goodness and innocence, and it is adults and civilization that corrupt them. So, if one interferes with their natural tendencies as little

286

as possible, children will grow up with a natural nobility of character."

"I see," said Margaret uncertainly.

A squeal of indignation issued from the corner, and Kate excused herself hastily, returning with her daughter, who looked at Margaret with a shy smile on her tear-stained face. Margaret had seen the boys teasing the child and wondered that Serena could sit calmly and talk about natural innocence while her brats tortured a one year old. Soon Jeremy left his cousins and came to stand beside Margaret, putting his sticky little hand in hers.

At that moment, Sir John Morgan came to claim his wife.

"My dear," said John, "could I interest you in a stroll?"

"Of course," said Serena, her eyes lighting up at the sight of her husband. "I will just go and put on my bonnet."

He greeted Margaret and turned his attention to his sons.

"Boys, come with your mama and me. We are going for a walk in the gardens."

"Yes, Papa," the boys chorused, clattering to their feet and spilling the last of the cakes on the floor, icing side down.

Kate sighed as her in-laws left the room. "Oh, thank goodness," she said in humorous dismay. "You have no idea what it was like traveling all over the Continent with those boys. One managed to throw himself into the Grand Canal in Venice, and what must the other do but jump in after him!"

"I wonder that they are allowed to grow up so wild," said Margaret in astonishment.

"Serena has this bee in her bonnet," said Kate,

"and my mother, who raised us up as strictly as you please, endorses her and encourages their naughtiness."

Kate patted her daughter's head.

"You are going to grow up to be a lady, my precious, natural innocence or no natural innocence," she said, placing a kiss on her child's disheveled curls.

"Darling," she added to little Jeremy, "why don't you go out to the garden and play with your cousins so I can talk with Aunt Margaret?"

"Do I have to, Mama?" he asked pleadingly.

"No, love," said Kate sighing. "Our children are afraid to stir from my presence, because the twins torment them so. What am I to do? I cannot discipline Serena's children if she will not. They will listen to no one but John and sometimes Mark if he is angry enough."

"I have an idea," said Margaret thoughtfully. "Why don't you send Jeremy and Amabel home with me? I would adore having them visit."

"No. It would be too much trouble for you," said Kate.

"Nonsense. I'll take very good care of them, I promise you. You can send one of the nursemaids with them."

"If you would, it would certainly be a blessing," said Kate. "I haven't had a minute's peace. There is all the baggage to be disposed properly, and between us, Nurse and I are absolutely frantic to keep our children safe without offending Serena and John. We cannot be with them every minute."

"How long is Serena's family staying with you?"

"Until tomorrow."

"Well, then, after they leave, you have only to

288

send me a message and I will bring the children back to you."

"Would you do that, Margaret?" asked Kate. "Oh, what a wonderful friend you are! Do you hear that, my precious? You and your little sister are going to stay with Aunt Margaret until tomorrow!"

"Can we go now, Aunt Margaret?" asked little Jeremy, his mischievous smile back on his face.

A little while later, Margaret and the children were just entering the stables where they were going to admire the foal which had just been born to one of Margaret's mares, when she encountered Jeremy, who was leaving the stable with Sulieman. There was no stable attached to the brick house, so it had been arranged for him to board Sulieman with Margaret's horses.

"Mr. Watson," said Margaret with a cool nod.

"Good afternoon, Miss Willoughby," he said guardedly.

"You are the angel," said little Jeremy, smiling up at him. To Jeremy's astonishment, the child walked up to him and held up his arms. Jeremy picked him up and the boy hugged him around the neck. He couldn't resist returning his nephew's soft embrace.

"My friend Kate Verelst's children," Margaret explained in embarrassment. "Your new friend is Jeremy, and this little darling is Amabel."

"I am charmed, ma'am," said Jeremy, "but what is this about an angel?"

In spite of herself, Margaret's lips twitched.

"That's what he calls the statue at his uncle's grave," she said, enjoying the look of revulsion on Jeremy's face.

"I am not an angel, you know," Jeremy explained to the child in his arms.

"Is this your horse, sir?" asked the boy. "What is his name?"

"Sulieman."

"Sool-ee-mon," the child pronounced carefully. "Can I ride him?"

"Certainly," said Jeremy, placing the child on his shoulder. "If I have Miss Willoughby's permission."

"Please, Aunt Margaret?" pleaded the boy.

"All right," said Margaret.

"Amabel too?"

"I don't know," said Margaret. "She's awfully small, and that horse is awfully large."

"I'll take good care of her, ma'am," said Jeremy quietly.

Margaret was surprised by the tender look in his eye and wondered what possible interest he could have in her friend's children. An ugly suspicion crossed her mind, only to be dismissed. Ridiculous, she scolded herself. No one could be so base as to use Kate's children to learn enough about their family to worm his way into their circle.

For a half-hour, she watched Jeremy patiently lead the horse with the two children on it in slow circles around the stable yard. Eventually, both children were tired and ready for their afternoon rest. When he brought the children to where Margaret was standing, Amabel was half-asleep in his arms and her brother's steps were weary.

Margaret reached for the sleeping child and Jeremy shook his head.

"She's too heavy for you, ma'am," he said. "May I carry her to the house for you?"

"If you please," she said with what she hoped was polite indifference as she took little Jeremy's hand and led the small party to her house.

Serena departed with her family the next day, and the dust had no more settled on the road again when a messenger from Crossley came with a note from Kate, asking that Margaret bring her children home.

By then, both children were a little homesick and eager to be reunited with their parents, even though Margaret had indulged them shamelessly.

"Can Mr. Watson come, too?" asked little Jeremy as Margaret's coachman helped him into the back of the carriage.

"No, darling," said Margaret, wondering what sympathy had grown up between her godson and her former steward. "Mr. Watson is busy today."

Jeremy was, in fact, very busy as he prepared to close the red brick house and leave Yorkshire for good. He had already told Mathilde, rather firmly, that she would not be needed. Why are you lingering? he asked himself in contempt. Do you enjoy this torture? The sooner he could get away, the sooner he would get over his heartache, he reasoned. So why was it impossible for him to make the break from this spoiled beauty who despised him? Someday, perhaps when the hurt had healed, he could return to Yorkshire and reveal himself to his family in secret.

Later that day, he learned that Margaret had left for London as soon as she returned from restoring the Verelst children to their mother's arms. Jeremy had just made up his mind to leave the next morning, no matter what, when a groom from Crossley banged on his door.

"What is it?" he asked the man, whose coat was dripping water all over Mathilde's spotless floor.

"It's young Master Jeremy from Crossley, sir," the

291

man said. "The lad is gone. His Lordship has every able-bodied man out lookin' for him. Have you seen him? He's three years old and has yellow hair—"

"I know what the child looks like. No, I haven't seen him," said Jeremy, alarmed. "How long has he been gone?"

"At least an hour, sir, and it's comin' on rain. Her Ladyship is kickin' up a dust."

"I can well imagine," said Jeremy, reaching for his coat, which was on a hook behind the door. "I'll come aid in the search."

"Thank you, sir," said the man, leaving hurriedly.

Crossley was full of hiding places for an imaginative child, but Jeremy could think of only one, a favorite of his own when he was young, that a three year old's tiny legs would find a comfortable distance from the Verelsts' manor house.

"Jeremy!" he shouted, entering the three-sided shelter of the ruined keep where he had stabled Margaret's horse the day she met him at the chapel.

"I'm here!" a small voice answered.

Jeremy found the boy huddled in a corner, trying to keep out of the rain. His face was tear-stained, and he held his arms out to his rescuer with relief. His small sturdy legs managed to take him to his hiding place, but were far too tired to take him home. The man opened his coat and held the boy inside it so he could warm the small chilled body next to his on the ride to the manor.

He saw several other searchers on his way and shouted that he had the child. He rode right up to the front door at Crossley and, when the door was opened by the Verelsts' butler, set the boy down.

"Mama! Mama! Mr. Watson found me," the child

shouted as he clattered into the main house from the hall.

"Wait a minute, sir," said the butler, holding Jeremy's arm to detain him as he turned to go. "His Lordship will want to thank you personally for bringing the boy—"

"That isn't necessary," said Jeremy, desperate to get away before the child's parents discovered him. "I must go—"

At that moment, Kate, her child in her arms, liberally smearing her figured muslin gown with mud, ran into the hall.

"Oh, sir, I can't thank you enough—"

She stopped with a bemused look on her face and cocked her head interrogatively as she gazed at Jeremy. Without taking her eyes from his face, she carefully set her child on his feet.

"The pleasure was mine, ma'am," said Jeremy gravely.

"Jeremy?" she asked wonderingly. "It is you, isn't it?"

"Yes, Kate," he said with a half-smile on his face. He forgot his intention of leaving Yorkshire in the joy of being with her. He held out his arms, and she ran into them with an unladylike shriek of delight.

"Kate?" asked Lord Shallcross, blinking at the spectacle of his devoted wife in the fervent embrace of a wet, muddy stranger.

Jeremy looked up from whispering endearments to his half-laughing, half-crying sister and encountered a cold stare from the lady's husband.

"It can't be," breathed Mark. "Can it?"

"I'm afraid so, Mark," said Jeremy.

"Why is Mama kissing Mr. Watson?" asked little

293

Jeremy plaintively.

"Mr. Watson is your uncle, love," said Kate.

"Wait just a moment," said Mark, refusing to abandon himself to sentiment. "We haven't established that this gentleman is your brother, Kate."

"Don't be ridiculous, love," said Kate. "*Look* at him."

"I know he *looks* like Jeremy, but that doesn't mean he is. Your grandfather's, er, natural son—"

"Mark, darling, I beg of you. *Not* in front of the child!"

Her spouse looked at the butler, who was trying to be impassive but was obviously hanging on every word, and the small crowd of footmen who had gathered around.

"I think," said Mark, taking his wife's arm and nodding for Jeremy to follow, "we had best discuss this most unexpected development in privacy."

Chapter Thirteen

Jeremy Verelst's return from the dead was the proverbial eight-day wonder, and the romantic tale was on everyone's lips.

Jeremy, who had gone to London with Mark and Kate so that Mark could formally hand over the title and property to him, soon was so weary of being stared at that he almost immediately expressed his wish to return to the country, and his sister and brother-in-law wholeheartedly endorsed this excellent scheme.

Waiting only for a tearful, though ecstatic, reunion with his volatile mother, Jeremy was happy to abandon the city in the heat of summer for Yorkshire.

"Well, that is over," said Kate wearily, tossing her excessively becoming straw hat into her maid's waiting arms.

"Now we can be comfortable again," said Mark with a sigh of relief.

"If you say so," said Jeremy soberly.

"Whatever do you mean, dear?" asked Kate, surprised.

"Well, I *hope* that you consider the gain of one brother, rather worse for wear, worth the loss of your title, a handsome property, and an equally handsome fortune," said Jeremy frankly.

"How can you even *mention* such a thing?" she asked in astonishment. "Of *course* we would rather have you back. What a silly thing to say.'"

Jeremy looked skeptically at Mark, who burst into laughter.

"It is perfectly all right, Jeremy," Mark said. "Truly it is. Your sister and I are not paupers, you know."

"Are you not? But—"

"Father left me a very handsome fortune when I came of age," said Kate, "besides a very pretty property not ten miles away from here. It will do very well for us."

"I hesitate to mention this," said Mark ruefully, "but I've been diverting part of your income into that property for years now in the belief that I had a right to do so. Kate and I thought it would make a comfortable legacy for a younger son, if we are fortunate enough to have more children. I suppose the proper thing would be for me to offer to pay you back—"

"Don't you dare," said Jeremy. "I accept that my sister, sentimental darling that she is, would rather have her scrapegrace of a brother than remain a viscountess, but *you* Mark? That's doing it much too brown."

"Your father left me a legacy as well," said Mark. "I won't deny I have enjoyed the title and the estate, but we are very well to pass, after all. Of course I would rather have you back, you stu-

296

pid cawker!"

"Don't be afraid that we mean to impose ourselves on you," said Kate. "We will remove to the other estate as soon as we can get our personal effects and the children's belongings packed."

"No! Oh, no! I wouldn't throw you out of your home," said Jeremy in dismay.

"It is *your* home, now, love," said Kate soothingly. "It is to be expected, after all. You will want to marry and—"

"But not just yet, if you please," said Jeremy. "Really, if you wouldn't mind living with a bachelor, I would rather have you stay. And I would take it kindly, Mark, if you would show me how to go on. I would like to get to know the children better. For the time being, at least, they are my heirs."

"Well, if you wouldn't mind," said Kate hesitantly.

"Of course not," he said. "I've only just found you again. I wish you would not hurry away."

"I must say that's handsome of you, considering I had you put aboard that ship four years ago," said Mark. "It would be natural for you not to be trusting of my intentions. I had some ideas about the estate that I was going to implement, but, of course, it is none of my bread-and-butter now. I would enjoy discussing them with you."

"I would like to hear them."

"We are going to be besieged with curious neighbors," prophesied Kate, amused.

"They probably want to have a look at me for themselves to see if I am an unscrupulous adventurer," said Jeremy, laughing.

Although he had been joking, one of his neighbors didn't just suspect he was an adventurer, she was convinced of it.

Margaret had learned about the sensation at Crossley while she was in the city being feted by her future in-laws, and when she learned that Jeremy, his sister, and brother-in-law had returned to the country, she stayed only for a ball in her honor and immediately followed him to Yorkshire so she could give him a piece of her mind.

Little Jeremy greeted Margaret with acclaim when she alighted from her closed carriage.

"Aunt Marg'ret!" he shouted as he sat on the back of an old cob whose reward, after years of working in His Lordship's fields, was to spend the little time it wasn't eating its head off in transporting Jeremy in slow circles around the yard under the aegis of the child's nursemaid and a groom.

"Hello, darling," said Margaret, walking to the child and reaching up to kiss his cheek. She absently patted the old cob.

"Mr. Watson is here, only he is my uncle now and I am to call him Uncle Jeremy," said the child excitedly.

"How lovely," said Margaret, restraining with great difficulty from gritting her teeth.

"Uncle Jeremy is going to buy me a new pony!"

"Kind of him," said Margaret repressively. Generosity, indeed, to buy the child a pony when he was about to steal his house, his title, his property, and his income, she thought furiously.

"Good-bye, Aunt Marg'ret," said Jeremy, whose groom led him away at nod from the nurse.

The Verelsts' butler was amazed when Miss Willoughby cut him off in the middle of his explanation that Her Ladyship was not yet down to breakfast and declared it was not the mistress, but her brother whom she wished to see. Although she phrased her request with perfect civility, he could see the anger in her fine eyes and knew that someone was in for an uncomfortable morning.

Young ladies of good family did not, as a rule, burst into a residence at an hour far in advance of that considered acceptable for visits and demand to see the gentleman of the house without first inquiring after the lady.

"Miss Willoughby, sir," said the butler uncertainly when Jeremy, entrenched in the library with one of the papers from London, answered his knock.

"Good morning, Miss Willoughby," Jeremy said cordially, rising to greet her. The warmth in his eyes disconcerted her. "In what way may I serve you?"

He looked quite different from the haggard young man who had returned to the bosom of his family only a week ago, and Margaret was slightly mesmerized. He was wearing an extremely well-cut coat of blue superfine, and his golden locks had been cut by an artist of the first stare. She didn't quite recognize her former steward in this magnificent nobleman.

The butler lingered hopefully.

"That will be all," Jeremy said in the uncompromising but perfectly civil tone of one accustomed to obedience. The butler left with a regretful look in his eye.

That broke the spell.

"You are *shameless!*" Margaret declared wrathfully as soon as the door was closed behind the disappointed servant. "Just *look* at you!"

"What is wrong with me?" asked Jeremy, amused. "I had persuaded myself these clothes were all the crack. Don't tell me I have been hoodwinked by my tailor—"

"Don't trifle with me, Frank Watson! When my cousin Edward told me what you were about, I didn't believe him. Fool that I was, I told him that you would *never* stoop to such perfidy."

"Margaret, listen to me—"

"No, you listen to *me*, Frank Watson—"

"I am not Frank Watson," he said quietly.

"If you think I am going to stand by while you practice this cruel deception on my best friend—"

The door opened and Kate entered the room with a smile of greeting on her lips.

"Margaret, love," said Kate cheerfully. "We left cards at your town house, but we left London in rather a hurry. I am so glad you came to see us. What do you think of our wonderful news?"

"Kate, it breaks my heart to see you so deceived," said Margaret. "Can't you see he's an impostor?"

"But Margaret—," began Kate, looking at Jeremy in confusion. "Jeremy, haven't you *told* her?"

Jeremy shrugged.

"I don't think the lady believes me," he said.

"Margaret, this *is* Jeremy. I knew him at a glance. So did my mother, and a mother, you know, could never be mistaken on such a subject."

"Doing it a bit too brown, my dear," said Jeremy, smiling. "Our trusting mother questioned me for three-quarters of an hour before she would accept me, and you know it."

"Margaret, there is no way he *can't* be Jeremy."

"Frank Watson grew up in Yorkshire. He would probably know enough about your family to deceive you," said Margaret.

"Actually, that is not true," said Jeremy. "My father was anxious to rid himself of Frank because he was a constant reminder of my grandfather's folly. Frank and I have always looked too much alike. So Frank was sent away when he was a child to serve one disappointing apprenticeship after another. Unfortunately, the poor boy never did learn a trade or adopt a profession. He had great personal charm, but no ambition whatsoever."

"I don't believe you," said Margaret in a small voice.

"It is true," said Kate. "Maybe this will convince you, Margaret—"

Kate broke off at an unmistakable signal from her brother.

"Don't look so distressed, dear," Kate said kindly, and left the room.

Margaret tried to go after her, but Jeremy caught her wrist.

"Don't go, Margaret," said Jeremy. "Please."

"Don't touch me," she said, fighting tears.

"I won't, if you dislike it," he said, releasing her. "What must I do to convince you?"

"You could start," she said suspiciously, "by telling me about the occasion of our first meeting."

"It was at my sister Melanie's wedding," said Jeremy promptly. "My mother invited you because she hoped we would make a match of it. You were wearing peacock feathers and diamonds in your hair. You informed me that I had little address and no conversation, and that although I was good-looking enough, good-looking suitors are hardly a novelty for a lady with a dowry of twenty thousand pounds besides the income from your father's property."

"I could not have been so rude!" said Margaret, shaken by these revelations.

"Oh, but you were, although I admit you were sorely provoked. I fell in love with you instantly."

"That *proves* you are an impostor," said Margaret sternly.

"All right. Perhaps it wasn't instantly, but soon after. Do you believe me now?"

"No. Kate could have told you that."

"She didn't, however."

"I don't believe you."

"No? Perhaps you'll believe this. The day after the ball, you visited my mother at Shallcross House. She invited you to dine that night. I sulked during dinner because I didn't like the way my mother was trying to force my hand. You drank too much wine, and after dinner I invited you to go for a walk in the rose garden to cool your flushed cheeks."

"No! I don't want to hear anymore," said Margaret, a tear starting down her cheek. "You *can't* be Jeremy."

She looked as if she might run away, but he took both her hands and held her so she couldn't escape.

"Do you remember what we talked about in the garden?" asked Jeremy. "You told me I was an insufferable boor, which was quite true, and I kissed you. You slapped me. I laughed and told you I adored you. You didn't believe me. I protested. You said you would believe me if I would stay in the city instead of going to Hampshire, and although I recognized it then as an attempt to force me into dancing attendance on you like the rest of your suitors, now I wish to God I had. You told me that I could call on you when I returned, if you hadn't tired of the city by that time. I kissed you again, and that time you didn't slap me."

"No," said Margaret, her eyes wide and horrified. His words had the ring of truth. She realized that only the real Jeremy Verelst could have known what passed between them that night. "But the body buried in the chapel—"

"That is Frank Watson. The real one. When I saw the hunting box on fire I ran inside to rescue my father. Frank followed me. He must have carried me outside. I remember the stairway collapsing. The next thing I knew I was in Molly Harnish's home, being nursed by her."

"She's the one Edward said—"

"Yes. She is living under my protection in London with Fanny Watson, incidentally, but she is not, nor has she ever been, my mistress. Her child is Frank's. I owed him my life. I couldn't allow his mother, his woman, and his daughter to live in poverty."

Margaret burst into tears, but pushed Jeremy away when he tried to take her in his arms.

"A pretty fool you have made of me," she said bitterly. "Did it amuse you to watch me arrange flowers on your grave?"

"No, it did not," he said quietly. "I didn't recognize myself in your dead lover, Margaret. I had nothing in common with him. He was young and reckless and he managed to capture your imagination with his tragic death. What would you have done if I had told you the truth?"

"I don't know," she said uncertainly.

"I'll tell you. You would have been extremely disappointed. If common gossip is to be believed, you have been pining away for love of me for four years. Suddenly I appear. Anyone with a grain of sensibility might reasonably expect you to fall into my arms. But I was a total stranger and so, if you will forgive my saying so, were you. I thought about you over the years, but it never occurred to me that you might not have married. Imagine my dismay upon finding out that you had made a regular ritual out of visiting my grave and talking about me as if I were your one great love. I am such a dull fellow, Margaret. How could I compete with the paragon you had made of me?"

"You lived in my house, and you saw me every day," she said, her voice brittle. "I trusted you, and you made a fool of me. How you must have laughed, especially on that last night when — "

"Never, I swear," he said, appalled by the direction of her thoughts.

She broke free and ran from the room. He ran after her. Kate, who was in the hallway, allowed Margaret to run past her, but put out a hand to detain Jeremy.

"Let her go, love," she told him. "She needs time alone now. She's had a terrible shock."

Partially blinded by her tears, Margaret ran outide and into her waiting carriage. Ordinarily it would have gone to the stables and a message would have been sent to her coachman when she was ready to leave. She didn't question the fact that this apparently had not been done, but merely thought it a blessing that she would not have to wait for the carriage to be brought around. As she got inside, she heard her godson's plaintive voice calling her. She looked outside the window to see little Jeremy, still seated on the old cob, waving at her. She waved back and gave the signal to start.

The coachman was driving very fast for such a narrow lane, but Margaret didn't notice. She huddled in the corner of the carriage and wept.

It was sometime later that she realized the coachman had passed the turning to her manor, but when she opened the window and shouted for attention, he ignored her.

Instead of slowing, the carriage had picked up speed. She wondered if the horses were running away with the coach and began to fear that she would be thrown into a ditch.

At last the carriage stopped and Margaret, who had been jostled about until her teeth rattled, was fit for murder by the time the door was opened and the steps let down for her. She sprang into the road and prepared to give her coachman a tongue-lashing, only to find herself regarded with fiendish amusement by a total stranger. There was no groom.

"Who are you?" she asked.

"That don't concern you, miss," the man said, leering at her. "You be a pretty piece. It's a rare shame what's goin' to happen to you."

305

"Shut up, you fool," said the middle-aged man who had just come out of the cottage in front of her.

"Uncle Robert," said Margaret thankfully without realizing the significance of what had happened. "This rascal has—"

She broke off, staring at the look of understanding that passed between the men.

"Uncle Robert, what is the meaning of this? I thought you were in London. Am I being kidnapped?"

"Yes, my dear. It appears you are. Such a pity," he said with relish.

Margaret shrank from the coachman, who had reached out and grabbed her arm, none too gently.

"Uncle Robert!" she shrieked.

"Lamentable, I know, my dear," he said sardonically. "Bring her inside," he added to his accomplice, who compelled her with unnecessary violence to enter the cottage.

"What are you going to do with me?" asked Margaret.

"Kill you, of course," said Sir Robert, "and you have only yourself to blame."

"Why?" she asked.

"In a way because you should never have been born, but certainly because you must not be allowed to marry Beverly Crawford and let my birthright pass to your miserable, puling heirs instead of to my son."

"Uncle Robert, you can *have* the estate—"

"And what about the fortune? It takes wealth to run an estate, as well you know, or you wouldn't have so objected to my taking a little of my own

306

back."

"You were embezzling—"

"Is it embezzling to borrow what should have been mine from an orphaned niece who had reason to be grateful to me?"

"Those accidents. They were your work," she said.

"But, of course. You are extremely difficult to kill, my dear niece. A pity, because I would have liked to have done the deed without a resulting scandal. As it is, your body will be found eventually, and no one will be more broken-hearted than I."

"You won't get away with it," she said hopefully. "The servants will initiate a search when I fail to return home."

"Yes. In fact, Edward and I will probably take part in it."

"You wouldn't—"

"I think I shall offer a reward for the capture of your murderer," he added pensively. "That would be rather a nice touch, don't you think?"

"Is Edward in on this, too?" she asked.

"No. Despite the way you have slighted him, he retains a fondness for you. I'm damned if I see why. If you'd married him like you were supposed to—"

"And Aunt Samantha?"

"My dear, she was the one who first hit upon the notion. You've never liked her, have you? Well, it has been mutual, my dear."

"Uncle, please reconsider. Do you really think you can live with murder on your hands?"

"Quite comfortably, I assure you," he said with

an ugly smirk on his face. "We have wasted enough time."

"Now, guv'ner?" asked his henchman, grabbing Margaret violently and pushing her against the wall. His grubby fingers were closing around her throat, and she started seeing dark patches before her eyes.

"No, you incompetent fool," Sir Robert said quite calmly. "Render her unconscious first. I have no desire to listen to the singularly unpleasant sound she will make in her throat as her body is deprived of breath."

Her assailant's fist hit her jaw, and then she felt nothing.

Chapter Fourteen

Margaret awoke in her own room to find her Aunt Martha sitting by her bed. She sat up with a violent start.

"It's all right, darling," said Martha, gently pressing her down again.

"Aunt Martha," said Margaret, whose voice had a decided croak. "What happened?"

"Don't upset yourself," she said soothingly. "The doctor has been sent for."

"Aunt Martha, where is my uncle?"

Martha looked down, as if embarrassed.

"Don't try to talk, love," was all she would say.

Margaret sat up, but closed her eyes briefly as her head swam.

"Margaret, no! You must rest—"

"I am done with resting," she said. "Oh, Aunt Martha, I am so happy to be alive. He was going to kill me—"

"I know," said Martha sadly. "I would never have believed it of him, even though I think I've always known he was not a good person."

Margaret got up purposefully and regarded her crumpled morning dress with dismay. She looked in the mirror and saw her hair was a tangle. She ruthlessly drew a comb through it, wincing a little. She covered the purple blotches on her throat with a lace scarf and left the room as Martha followed, protesting, in her wake.

"Miss Willoughby," said Sternes when he spotted her. "Mr. Crawford has called. He is in the parlor with Mr. Edward."

Margaret took a deep breath and joined the gentlemen.

"Margaret, my dear," said Beverly, jumping to his feet. "I have never been so shocked—"

"I am all right," she said, wondering how much he had been told. "Edward, I would appreciate it if I could have a few minutes alone with Beverly."

"Certainly," said Edward, biting his lip. He looked terrible, but he left the room without protest. She sincerely pitied him.

"I am happy to see you, Beverly," said Margaret. "How did you know—"

"I didn't," he said, looking uncomfortable. "Perhaps I should return another time."

"Nonsense," she said. "I am quite well."

"Margaret, I don't know exactly how to say this, but I cannot marry you."

Her first reaction should have been surprise, followed by indignation. Instead, she was filled with a profound feeling of relief. She liked Beverly. She admired and respected him. But one of her first conscious thoughts when she awoke in her room and realized she was not to die, after all, was that she must break this engagement. She didn't know how she would do it. She only knew she could not marry a man she did not love. She now realized that life, as Jeremy had once told her, is too precious to waste in an unhappy marriage.

"This is very sudden," she said calmly.

"No, actually, my dear, it is not," said Beverly, obviously laboring under great anxiety. The thought that he was about to do anything so ill-bred as to break off his betrothal horrified him. He could hardly bear to inflict such an insult upon a lady. Moreover, a lady whom he held in considerable affection. However, it had to be done, and in his usual methodical manner, he proceeded to do it. "I wish to make known to you how attached I am to you, and how much I sincerely admire you—"

"Please, Beverly. Do get to the point. Am I to understand you wish to cry off?"

"Yes," he said simply.

Hiding her relief, Margaret sat down on the sofa and indicated that he, too, should be seated.

"Am I to know why?" she asked, prompted more by curiosity than disappointment.

"You have the right, I should think," he said. "I am sorry if you should dislike it, but I wish to marry your cousin."

Margaret stared at him in astonishment for a moment.

"Anne?" she asked, thunderstruck. "She is just a child—"

"No, that she is not," he said quietly. "We wish to marry."

"I see," said Margaret. "Of course, I would not stand in your way. It is an excellent match for her. But I wish you would have said something sooner. How mortified your parents will be to learn they have gone to all this trouble for the wrong lady."

"I was so shocked, you see, when you told me you had decided to accept my suit," he said. "I

had never formally withdrawn it, of course.
hadn't the slightest expectation that you would
have me, and I had quite grown accustomed to
forming one of your court. That last week before
Anne's ball, I had come to admire her and, in
short —"

"You began to escort us to parties without explaining that it was for Anne's sake rather than mine. I quite see," said Margaret thoughtfully. She could have kicked herself for being so stupid.

"I hope you will forgive me," he said, watching her anxiously.

"With all my heart," said Margaret. "I would never stand in the way of your happiness, Beverly, or Anne's. We have been such good friends. should like that to continue."

"You are a woman in a million, Margaret," he said. "I thank you from the bottom of my heart. will tell anyone who asks about the affair that we have decided we shall not suit, but I will make no denial if you wish to put it about that you were the one to cry off."

"Thank you, Beverly," she said soberly, "but think the fewer explanations we make to the curious, the better."

"I'll take my leave of you now," he added, kissing her hand.

He looked so conscience-stricken that she was tempted to tell him the truth. She rigorously suppressed this foolhardy impulse.

"Good-bye, Beverly," she said, managing to hide her elation from him.

When he was gone, she let out a huge sigh of relief, but soon stiffened to attention when Edward reentered the room.

"I saw Crawford leave," he said. "We must talk, Margaret."

"I know, Edward," she said. "You must tell me what happened."

"My father is at his house, recovering from his injuries," he said. "His accomplice has been bribed to leave the country. When my father is fit to be seen again, he and my mother will express the desire to live quietly at a small house in Lincolnshire that was part of my legacy from my maternal uncle. It is rather rundown, but it can be fixed up again. The point is that it is remote. He will never bother you again, my dear, I promise you."

"Edward, I am so sorry this has happened," she said. "So they are to be exiled. A neat solution."

"It seems so," he said rather bitterly. "It was one of the conditions your gallant rescuer insisted upon when he agreed not to turn my father over to the authorities."

"My gallant rescuer? Then it was not you who—"

"No, my dear. It was not I who saved you from your doom, although I was on the scene soon after, having learned the truth from my mother. She had second thoughts about the scheme. I should not be bitter. He has behaved quite decently under the circumstances. My father was fortunate to escape with a broken arm, a black eye, and exile."

"Jeremy," she said.

"Yes, although it is fortunate for him that you were unconscious when he arrived. Your hero had the effrontery to ride to your rescue on the back of some misbegotten job animal that looked like it just had been released from the plow—"

"The cob," Margaret guessed, her eyes lighting with wicked amusement.

"My God," said Edward feelingly. "It was like one of those awful plays Aunt Martha is so fond of. The ones that leave bodies strewn about the stage after Act II. You were unconscious on the floor, and that scoundrel my father hired was bleeding all over the place. Verelst was positively rabid. My father tried to stop him from interfering and ended up in the carnage. I almost did, myself."

"I must see Jeremy," she said.

"He was here. He probably still is, somewhere," said Edward vaguely. "I neither know nor care. I wish you joy of one another."

"Edward—"

"I thought I knew my father, and now I realize I never knew him at all," said Edward bitterly. "Do you know what he said afterward? He said that since there was no harm done, he didn't see why he should have to go to Lincolnshire. He said that was a fine return for his care of you."

"I don't believe it," said Margaret, awed.

"In his mind, *he* is the wronged party. He blamed me again for not succeeding in capturing your affections. And you for being too stubborn to marry me."

"My poor Edward."

"Save your pity for someone who wants it," said Edward with some asperity. "I will not suffer in the eyes of the world, nor will Anne. There will be no scandal. Go find your lover. I am done."

He left without a backward glance.

Margaret found Jeremy in the library. He stood when she entered the room and held out his arms.

314

She walked into them.

Much later, she raised mischievous eyes to his face.

"Tell me, my darling, did you really fly to my rescue on that dilapidated cob of your nephew's? And I missed it!"

"I wondered if your cousin would sully your ears with that tale," he said ruefully. "Scoff if you like, but that cob will end the rest of his days in comfort, I promise you."

"But how did you know I was being kidnapped?"

"I didn't. I only knew I had to stop you and make you listen to me. The dashed cob could only go at a placid trot, however, and by the time I caught up with the carriage it was already past the turning to your manor, so I was suspicious and kept following it. I suppose the villain driving your coach thought his scheme was in no danger from a horseman traveling at such a sedate pace."

"My hero," she said, smiling radiantly. "How can I ever repay you?"

"Well, you *are* going to marry me, are you not, Margaret? It really will be too bad of you if you will not."

She did not respond, and he thought he knew the reason.

"Crawford shall get over you in time," he said quietly, "but I never will."

"You cannot imagine how relieved I am to hear it," she said, smiling, "now that I have been so deceived by my fiancé. He has jilted me to marry my cousin Anne."

"You're bamming me," he said, quite forgetting his company in his astonishment. "Why, when he

315

could have you, would any man want to marry that whey-faced—"

"Anne is not whey-faced," she said, "and I am glad of it, for it saved me from having to cry off myself."

"Should you object, my darling, to a very short engagement?" he asked, bending to kiss her again. "I think we have waited long enough as it is."

"What is *that* doing here?" asked Jeremy in dismay when he and his bride of three months, just arrived from their honeymoon on the Continent, entered the formal gardens of his mother's town house prior to an elegant soiree in the newly married couple's honor.

"Oh, my heavens!" exclaimed Margaret, going off into a peal of laughter. Her bridegroom regarded her levity with great disapproval.

"There you are, my darlings," said Arabella Peevers, putting an arm around both of them. "Doesn't it look *wonderful?* It was just what I needed for the gardens. I have always thought it a remarkable likeness."

"No, it does *not* look wonderful," said Jeremy severely. "It looks excessively silly."

He turned on Kate and Mark when they came outside to see what the excitement was all about.

"Kate, how could you have allowed her to do such a thing?" he asked plaintively.

"I tried to put a stop to it," said Mark sympathetically, although it was obvious that he was highly amused by his brother-in-law's outrage. "I would die of mortification to see *my* half-naked body displayed in such a way—"

316

"It is highly unlikely," Arabella told her son-in-law with relish, "that *anyone* would wish to see such a sight."

"Mama," said Kate, her eyes glittering dangerously, "I won't have you saying cutting things about Mark!"

"Hush, sweetheart," said Mark, putting an arm around his angry tigress. "She's perfectly right, thank God. And if you ever dare to put up such a tribute in my honor when I'm dead, I shall come back and haunt you."

"All of this is beside the point," said Jeremy, shouting to be heard above the friendly din of his relatives, who were arguing the aesthetic merits of the classical rendering of Jeremy's youthful body which had once graced the chapel. It now reposed in a marble niche surrounded by pink and yellow roses. A fountain gurgled impotently at the statue's feet.

"I am sorry if you dislike it, dear," said Arabella soothingly, "but I must say I don't see any harm in it. It was quite shockingly expensive, you know, not that we begrudge a *penny* of it, of course, but there doesn't seem to be any point in leaving it in the chapel since you aren't dead after all. It will hardly be wanted to decorate poor Frank Watson's grave. I don't suppose you want us to put it in storage until you *do* die, dearest, so what else should we do with it?"

"Very true," said Jeremy, beginning to see the humor in the situation.

"Oh, darling," said Arabella contritely. "How *terribly* selfish of me. Of course you will want it for *your* garden—"

"No, Mama," Jeremy said, hugging her affec-

317

tionately, as he grinned at his radiant bride, who smiled back, "that I do not. Lord, it's wonderful to be part of a family again, even if one's nearest and dearest so often put one to the blush!"

REGENCIES BY JANICE BENNETT

TANGLED WEB   (2281, $3.95)

Miss Celia Marcombe's dark eyes flashed with righteous indignation. She was not a commodity to be traded or bartered to a man
as insufferably arrogant as Trevor Ryde, despite what her high-
handed grandfather decreed! If Lord Ryde thought she would let
herself be married for any reason other than true love, he was
sadly mistaken. He'd never get his hands on her fortune—let
alone her person—no matter how disturbingly handsome he
was . . .

MIDNIGHT MASQUE   (2512, $3.95)

It was nothing unusual for Lady Ashton to transport government
documents to her father from the Home Office. But on this particular afternoon a gust of wind scattered the papers, and suddenly an important page was lost. A document desperately
wanted by more than one determined gentleman—one of whom
would murder to get his way . . .

AN INTRIGUING DESIRE   (2579, $3.95)

The British secret agent, Charles Marcombe, had done his bit
against that blasted Bonaparte. Now it was time to nurse his
wounds and come to terms with the fact that that part of his life
was over. He certainly did not need the likes of Mademoiselle
Therese de Bourgerre darkening his door, warning of dire emer-
gencies and dread consequences, forcing him to remember things
best forgotten. She was a delightful minx, to be sure, but it would
take more than a pair of pleading emerald eyes and a woebegone
smile to drag him back into the fray!

*Available wherever paperbacks are sold, or order direct from the
Publisher. Send cover price plus 50¢ per copy for mailing and
handling to Zebra Books, Dept. 3246, 475 Park Avenue South,
New York, N.Y. 10016. Residents of New York, New Jersey and
Pennsylvania must include sales tax. DO NOT SEND CASH.*

FIERY ROMANCE

CALIFORNIA CARESS (2771, $3.75)
by Rebecca Sinclair

Hope Bennett was determined to save her brother's life. And if that meant paying notorious gunslinger Drake Frazier to take his place in a fight, she'd barter her last gold nugget. But Hope soon discovered she'd have to give the handsome rattlesnake more than riches if she wanted his help. His improper demands infuriated her; even as she luxuriated in the tantalizing heat of his embrace, she refused to yield to her desires.

ARIZONA CAPTIVE (2718, $3.75)
by Laree Bryant

Logan Powers had always taken his role as a lady-killer very seriously and no woman was going to change that. Not even the breathtakingly beautiful Callie Nolan with her luxuriant black hair and startling blue eyes. Logan might have considered a lusty romp with her but it was apparent she was a lady, through and through. Hard as he tried, Logan couldn't resist wanting to take her warm slender body in his arms and hold her close to his heart forever.

DECEPTION'S EMBRACE (2720, $3.75)
by Jeanne Hansen

Terrified heiress Katrina Montgomery fled Memphis with what little she could carry and headed west, hiding in a freight car. By the time she reached Kansas City, she was feeling almost safe . . . until the handsomest man she'd ever seen entered the car and swept her into his embrace. She didn't know who he was or why he refused to let her go, but when she gazed into his eyes, she somehow knew she could trust him with her life . . . and her heart.

Available wherever paperbacks are sold, or order direct from the Publisher. Send cover price plus 50¢ per copy for mailing and handling to Zebra Books, Dept. 3246, 475 Park Avenue South, New York, N.Y. 10016. Residents of New York, New Jersey and Pennsylvania must include sales tax. DO NOT SEND CASH.